A letter his
father died when he was born. The ....

David Eric Laine always believed his father had died in Vietnam before his birth. His mother remarried and he was adopted by his stepfather and grew up knowing Graham Laine as his only father. Forty years later, a letter arrives and David finds out everything he thought was a lie.His father, Joel Cameron, is alive and living in Bermuda where he came from back in 1968 to attend college. He met David's mother, at the time a much more rebellious child of the turbulent sixties. Following David's birth his mother fled back to the safety of her familiar, protected world and the lie was born. Rather than face her shame, David was told his father died a hero in Vietnam.

Now the lies unravel and the newly married Chris and David embark on a journey to discover the truth.

MLR Press Authors

Featuring a roll call of some of the best writers of gay erotica and mysteries today!

M. Jules Aedin	Maura Anderson	Victor J. Banis
Jeanne Barrack	Laura Baumbach	Alex Beecroft
Sarah Black	Ally Blue	J.P. Bowie
Michael Breyette	P.A. Brown	Brenda Bryce
Jade Buchanan	James Buchanan	Charlie Cochrane
Jamie Craig	Kirby Crow	Dick D.
Ethan Day	Diana DeRicci	Jason Edding
Angela Fiddler	Dakota Flint	S.J. Frost
Kimberly Gardner	Roland Graeme	Storm Grant
Amber Green	LB Gregg	Drewey Wayne Gunn
David Juhren	Samantha Kane	Kiernan Kelly
M. King	Matthew Lang	J.L. Langley
Josh Lanyon	Clare London	William Maltese
Gary Martine	Z.A. Maxfield	Timothy McGivney
Patric Michael	AKM Miles	Reiko Morgan
Jet Mykles	William Neale	Willa Okati
L. Picaro	Neil S. Plakcy	Jordan Castillo Price
Luisa Prieto	Rick R. Reed	A.M. Riley
George Seaton	Jardonn Smith	Caro Soles
JoAnne Soper-Cook	Richard Stevenson	Marshall Thornton
Lex Valentine	Haley Walsh	Missy Welsh
Stevie Woods	Lance Zarimba	

Check out titles, both available and forthcoming, at
www.mlrpress.com

BERMUDA
HEAT

P.A. BROWN

mlrpress
www.mlrpress.com

Copyright 2011 by P.A. Brown

Published by
MLR Press, LLC
3052 Gaines Waterport Rd.
Albion, NY 14411

Visit ManLoveRomance Press, LLC on the Internet:
www.mlrpress.com

Cover Art by Deana C. Jamroz
Editing by Kris Jacen

ISBN# 978-1-60820-160-0

Issued 2011

In 2005 I accepted a contract position in Bermuda. It was for 3 years, working as a Network Engineer for an offshore law firm. It was a total upheaval – they paid and shipped all my household goods and put me up in Ashwood Cove, a hotel used by businesses to temporarily house new employees while they search for their own place. Before they actually hired me, they brought me down for a weekend. The day after meeting with my future employer and getting a tour of the server rooms – they had 2 buildings, and 2 climate controlled rooms – I bought a 1-day bus pass and from the main terminal I took every single bus all around the islands (there are actually something like 147 islands that make up Bermuda) I had a book and a notepad with me and I wrote down all my impressions of Bermuda. It was a great way to see my new home.

Rents in Bermuda are astronomical. Houses for families would start at $15,000 a month. I found a one bedroom apartment in Southampton that cost $2200 a month. It was a nice place, the whole front wall was glass. From inside I could see Little Sound. It was situated just below one of the highest points in Bermuda, where Gibbs Lighthouse stands. Outside, if I stood on the edge of the property, I could see the Dockyards across Great Sound, one of the places where cruise ships dock. It's also where Chris and David have lunch on their first day.

I lived there for a little over a year. I was there when Florence, the hurricane came through. That was quite a show, which is also featured in Bermuda Heat. In the beginning of 2007 I moved clear to the other side of the island, into St. George's, which is a cute little heritage town with narrow winding streets, a lot of which don't have names. It also has a small dairy farm, which supplies some of Bermuda's milk. Taking a walk through St. Georges was like walking back in time. I've never been to Europe, but I imagine the narrow, curving streets were like that. Bermuda has very strict building codes. Nothing over 7 stories, no billboards, no neon and no fast food restaurants. Except for Kentucky Fried Chicken, which got in before the ban was put in place. It's a joy to walk around Hamilton, the main business area, and not be bombarded with flashing signs and exhortations to buy, buy buy. Buildings are constructed under strict codes, which is why they can withstand any hurricane.

It was a wonderful time in my life and I'm glad I had the chance to experience Bermuda. I've tried to relive that a little bit in my fiction.

A fun website that can give a little glimpse of Bermudian slang is: http://pdos.csail.mit.edu/~decouto/bvurds.html

P.A. Brown

2011

CHAPTER ONE

Saturday, 9:20am, Rigali Avenue, Atwater Village, Los Angeles

The brown Ford squealed when it failed to take the corner at sixty. Instead it threw up streamers of dust and stones as it bounced across a gravel verge into an empty parking lot. Martinez cursed as his partner, LAPD homicide detective David Eric Laine, took the same path, their unmarked Crown Vic blowing out whatever shocks might have been left in the aged vehicle when they screeched onto the lot after the fleeing Ford. Martinez reported their twenty and called for backup, then hung on as David maneuvered ever closer to the other car's rusted out bumper.

David ignored everything but the Ford and the two Pinoy boys they'd been closing in on for days. Since somebody stomped a Temple Street Trese boy to death and put all the Asians on edge, ready to stomp back, it was paramount they be stopped. David and Martinez were working with the local gang cops to try to stop the mess before it got uglier.

They'd spotted Sokun, the leader of the Pinoy's, at a liquor store on Brunswick five minutes ago. The chase had been on. David figured they would try and double back, make a break for Rigali. But then a *whoop* and a new cloud of dust announced that their backup had arrived. A black and white roared in, lights and siren on full code three.

What Sokun did next startled David. Instead of braking and coming around, the brown piece of crap's laboring engine roared, tires spat gravel and the car lunged forward. The fence protecting this section of concrete river was old and worn through years of neglect and abuse. Twisted by the elements and vandals, repaired repeatedly, it inclined at a fifty degree angle, sagging as though tired of trying to keep out the world.

The Ford slammed into it at a good twenty miles per hour and snapped off the single metal pole, puncturing the radiator and killing the engine. There was a tortured shriek of metal on metal; sparks flew from underneath the battered vehicle. The engine rattled to a stop.

Both doors flew open. Sokun and his passenger bailed. The passenger, who David hadn't been able to ID, headed north. Sokun scrambled over the battered remnants of the fence and vanished over the lip of the cement trough.

"Oh, tell me he did not just do that," David muttered.

Martinez growled what might have been a reply before he too was out of the door and hot on the trail of the passenger, along with a young female uni. David bolted after Sokun. The other uni followed.

David always figured he was in shape. He ran nearly every day with Sergeant, the Doberman he and Chris had adopted three years ago. He used the free weights at the station. He was still feeling the effects of the pursuit. Legs pumping, he slowed only long enough to clamber over the chain link and he was off, half skidding, half running down the angled concrete wall, avoiding chunks of broken wall, hot on Sokun's ass.

It was long after the last winter rain. The bed of the river was little more than a few scummy patches of rainbow-hued water and scattered weeds that had broken through the concrete and clung to life amid the detritus of a city. He dodged an abandoned shopping cart with a broken front wheel. A black garbage bag had split open, spilling its reeking contents down the slope. A pair of fat gulls took flight when Sokun raced towards them. They squawked and protested as they flew south toward the distant smog-shrouded basin.

Ahead of him and losing ground fast, Sokun clearly didn't do any recreational running. He stumbled over broken concrete and his leather loafers were not designed for top speed flight. David closed the distance between them. Behind him the uni was gaining ground.

"Stop, asshole!"

Not surprisingly, the asshole in question ignored his orders.

David came up on Sokun's left side. The Cambodian gang leader threw one wild-eyed look over his shoulder and tried to dodge right. David body checked him and the two of them went down. An elbow caught David's chin and he kneed Sokun's kidney, missed and caught him square in the groin. The younger man folded with a groan and rolled onto his side, holding his bruised crotch in both hands. At least until David wrenched them behind him and cuffed him. The uniformed cop arrived seconds later and stood over the downed pair, one hand on his duty weapon, the other on his baton.

David sat on his haunches, his butt resting against Sokun's legs. His rested his arms over his knees, panting as he stared across at the graffiti tagged wall on the other side of the river.

"I'm getting too old for this," he muttered as Martinez appeared at the top of the concrete wall, his own prisoner looking as worse for the wear as David felt.

The uni pulled Sokun to his feet as David rose and dusted his linen pants off. "Get him out of here," he said and climbed up to join Martinez. He watched the two uniformed officers, one who barely looked old enough to be out of middle school, lead their prisoners away and shook his head.

Sokun cursed in Cambodian and English.

"Either they're getting younger or I'm getting old."

Martinez clapped him on the back. "It ain't us, *ese*."

"God, I hope not." David scrubbed his hand through his shaggy hair. Together they trudged back to their Crown. He threw a glance back at the Ford, doors still open, water leaking out from underneath.

Martinez grunted as he eyed the messed up Ford. "Well, look at it this way. At least the asshole didn't try to make a run for it down there in that." He stared balefully down the concrete slope. "That would have been a real circus."

"More like the Indy 500. Better call a tow truck." David shook his head and did his best not to think about it. "Get a warrant for that thing, too."

He put his hand on the still warm hood of their city-owned junk heap. He climbed in behind the wheel. "Might be time to trade this thing in, too. Call the motor pool. See if we can't get this one put out to pasture." He slotted the key in and fired it up. It grunted but fired on the first try. Barely. He met his partner's gaze. "Ever think it might be time to hang it up yourself?"

"What? And give up all the excitement? Not to mention the respect and love we get."

"You left out the fabulous pay check."

"I guess I did kind of forget that. Come on. Let's go down and book these mutts. At least earn some of those big bucks."

A second black and white rolled onto the lot and Sokun was loaded into it. The two shops rolled back out onto Rigali, followed by David and his grinning partner.

"Another fine day on the force."

"Hey," Martinez said. "We'll look back on this someday and remember all the fun we had."

CHAPTER TWO

Saturday, 1:35pm, Cove Avenue, Silverlake, Los Angeles

The doorbell jerked Christopher Bellamere out of an online conversation with a client about a new network setup he wanted. The sound unleashed a volley of barking from Sergeant, their five-year-old Doberman. With a muttered "Damn" he IM'd *hold on* and hurried to the front door. He saw the UPS truck before he even threw the door open to greet the brown-suited delivery woman.

Sergeant tried to dart past him to check out the visitor, earning a wide-eyed "holy shit" look from the startled woman. Chris lunged for the dog's collar.

"Don't worry, he's harmless."

Funny, no one believed him when he said that. "Down, Sergeant," he snapped and the dog dropped to the floor. This only modified the woman's look from one of stark terror to surly distrust. Not a dog lover. "Now," he said to bring her attention back to him. "Can I help you?"

"Package for a David E. Laine."

So it was. The package was a business letter-sized piece that Chris took from the still wary woman. He signed for it, nodded thanks and hauled the dog back inside.

Once there he examined the unexpected delivery. It had been sent locally, from Long Beach, as far as he could tell. Who did David know in Long Beach?

Wishing he could open it, knowing he wouldn't, he returned to his home office and finished up his business, all the while the sealed package burning into his awareness. Once he was able to, he snatched up his BlackBerry and called David.

"You coming home soon?"

"Yeah," David said, using his gruff, I-can't-talk-I'm-with-other-people voice. "Why?"

"Got a UPS package for you."

"From who?"

"You know anyone in Long Beach?"

"No. Just hang onto it. I'll be home soon as I can. I hope you're not working too hard. You know the doctor said you still needed to rest."

"I'm fine," Chris said. It had been over a week since he'd been flat on his back from flu and on his last medical check up the doctor told him he was on his way to full recovery, but he still needed to take it easy. David had taken that advice all too closely to heart and bugged Chris at least half a dozen times every day to make sure he was doing just that.

"Don't spend all day sitting in that damn office. Get outside, relax in the sun. Go out and play with the dog."

"Yes, sir."

"Don't start."

"Yes, sir."

"Chris."

"Then come home soon, and you can make sure I'm resting. You can even put me to bed."

David ignored his playful flirting. Instead he said, "I'll be there as soon as I can get away."

Knowing it was the most he'd get out of his husband at this time, Chris disconnected and went back to taking care of his business of monitoring and protecting a number of computer networks throughout the city.

Finally he heard a car door clink shut and he checked the clock on his laptop. David had managed to get away early; he must be as curious as Chris about what was in the mystery package.

He logged out of his laptop, closing the connection to the client's server he had been working on. He hurried out of his home office and headed toward the front of the house. Soft light poured onto the rag-painted kitchen walls he had done himself in one of his more creative moments, and reflected off the Aegean rose tile floor. The front door opened and David's feet scuffed on the marble foyer floor as he kicked his shoes off.

Chris grabbed the last bottle of Peller Estates Merlot from the wine rack and decanted it. David dumped his keys at the front door and stripped off his LAPD gold shield and his Smith & Wesson .40 handgun, securing them in the hall closet lock box. Chris heard the safe door slam shut. He poured two glasses of Merlot, pausing to run stiff fingers through his spiked blond hair in the reflection of the brushed steel fridge. He set the letter down on the carved Santa Fe table and sat. David kissed him before sitting across from Chris.

David studied Chris's face and Chris knew he was looking for signs of tiredness. He did his best to look spry.

"I really am getting better, you know," he said. "You don't need to mother hen me all the time."

"I know you're getting there. I just don't want a relapse."

"Fine, no relapse. Now aren't you dying to find out what's in there?" He looked at the envelope on the kitchen table. Chris had put the letter opener beside it.

David gingerly picked up the envelope. He studied the front of it, then flipped it over to look at the back. "So this is the big mystery." He waved away the wine. "I have to go back."

"Coffee then?"

David nodded and Chris went to put it on.

Oprah, the little tortoiseshell cat David had rescued the year before, appeared out of nowhere. With the recent death of Sweeney, David's old Siamese, Oprah was now the only cat in the house. She had quickly assumed the position of queen of the house.

The package had been sent from Long Beach. As far as Chris knew David didn't know anyone in the southern beach community. Oprah jumped into David's lap and he stroked the purring cat, an absent look on his swarthy face.

"Well, open it," Chris said.

David sipped his coffee, then opened the shipping package and drew out a thick brown envelope. He used the letter opener to slit open the flap and slid out four sheets of paper. He grunted when he opened the first one. "It's from a Walter Dodson, California P.I."

"What does he want with you?"

David scanned the rest of the first letter. He scowled, the flesh of his normally dark face going a little pale. "He says he's enclosing a letter from my father…"

It was Chris's turn to frown. The only "father" David had was his stepfather, Graham Laine, living back in New Hampshire with David's mother. Chris had heard the story often enough; David's biological father had died in Vietnam before he'd been born. Graham had adopted him right after marrying his mother when David was barely three years old.

"He says my father is still alive."

When David slid the letter across to Chris and focused on the second letter, Chris scanned the contents of the first. Dodson had been hired by a Joel "Joey" Cameron in Bermuda in regards to his son, David Eric Cameron, born of Barbara Willerton in San Francisco on April 18, 1970. David's birthday. The rest matched, too. Except, instead of his father being dead, apparently Joel had been told David had died. Chris felt a chill march across his arms.

David read the second letter, the one purportedly from his father. His face grew more ashen.

"David?"

"She lied," David said. "All this time she lied. She lied to both of us."

Chris had never heard such coldness in his husband's voice before. He wanted to say they both knew what a bitch his mother was, but knew David wouldn't like it if he did. David had always been more tolerant of her than Chris could ever be. Even when she had refused to attend their wedding or even acknowledge it, David hadn't turned away from her.

"What? She told the guy you were dead?" Chris muttered. "That's creepy." Deep down Chris knew that David still loved his mother and hoped to get her approval one day. Like that was ever going to happen in this lifetime, or the next for that matter. "Does he say what made him suspicious?"

"No, he doesn't," David said. "I guess if I want an answer to that, I'll have to meet him."

David glanced at the letter again. Chris could see it was handwritten in small, tight script which filled the whole page. "He says he's sorry and he wants to meet me." David scowled, his mouth pursing and his teeth worrying his lips. "He says to bring you along too, he'd love to meet you. Apparently he knows all about us." He flipped the letter from the P.I. over, then slid it back to Chris. He held up the two other things he had taken from the envelope. Chris saw they were Delta e-tickets.

"He wants us—you—to go there?" he asked.

"Both of us," David said.

"To Bermuda?"

David nodded. He still looked shell-shocked. Chris rose and circled around to his side, crouching down beside him. Oprah meowed forlornly when Chris put her on the floor. The cat wound around their feet. Sergeant sensed the tension and slid his wedge-shaped head against Chris's leg. Chris ignored the dog and took both of David's hands in his, wishing he could erase the worry lines now creasing his husband's face.

"Hey," Chris said. "It's okay. Look on the bright side—your dad's alive. That's good news, right? Let's meet him before you condemn him. Your mother always said he was a loser. But if she told so many lies, maybe that wasn't true, either. Maybe he's not the bad guy, after all. Besides," he added with a teasing smile. "I hear it's beautiful there."

"You think?" David muttered. "In case you hadn't noticed,

we have jobs, bills to pay, plans already made. We can't just go jaunting off to God knows where on a whim."

Chris took the tickets out of his hands. They were from Delta. Economy class. He would change that fast enough if David actually wanted to do this. Suddenly Chris wanted to go. His curiosity was killing him. Surely it must be doing the same to David.

"It's hardly a whim. Think of it as a genealogical study. Haven't you always said you wished you knew about your dad's side of the family? Maybe you've got cousins or uncles." Feeling mischievous, Chris wheedled. "Or maybe even brothers and sisters. Besides, we're due for a holiday. What could be nicer, beaches and little pink houses?"

"John Mellencamp?"

"Nah, I don't think he lives there. Though I hear Michael Douglas does."

"You don't get enough celebrities here?" The faint ghost of a smile lightened David's normally dour, pock-marked face. His green-flecked brown eyes crinkled. Some of his color returned. "You really want to go?"

"Don't you? This is your *father.*"

"The father who abandoned me. The one who apparently couldn't stick around to do the job."

"Not really," Chris said. "If he thought you were dead... So why *did* your mother lie? She didn't want you to know he abandoned you? Knowing your mother, I'll bet you there's a lot more to it than that. You need to hear the story from him and find out for yourself."

"You know, I always worry when you start sounding logical. You're thinking too much."

"What kind of clothes do they wear in Bermuda? God, I hope it's not all Bermuda shorts. Even I'd look geeky in those things."

David toyed with the pepper mill on the table. Suddenly the room filled with the sharp odor of fresh ground pepper. Sergeant sneezed and gave him a malevolent look.

"You don't look geeky in anything," he said, but it was clear his mind wasn't on the banter. He set the pepper mill down on the engraved tabletop and brushed pepper onto the floor. "Maybe we should go. I'll have to set it up at work. I'm due some holidays—"

"Yeah, because you never take them," Chris said. It was a long-standing argument between them. They were both workaholics, except Chris's work was with computer systems and never involved violence, and David's was dealing on a daily basis with Los Angeles' lowest forms of life. Every day he went to work, Chris worried about him. And it didn't do any good to tell David that. He'd patiently explain that it was his job. He also reminded him that detectives were mostly desk jockeys, not front line cops.

At which point Chris always countered with the reminder that David's partner had died and it hadn't been behind a desk.

"First things first," David muttered. He picked up the letter from Joel. "He included a phone number. So let's talk to the guy."

Saturday, 5:45pm, Cove Avenue, Silverlake, Los Angeles

David grabbed his coffee and slipped into the living room, settling on the white leather couch. Chris curled up beside him, legs tucked under him. He rested his hand on David's knee.

David took a deep breath and picked up the handset.

He punched in the 4-4-1 area code and the number. It rang six times and he was going to hang up when a breathless female voice answered.

"Hello?"

David glanced over at Chris, who offered him a tentative smile.

"Hello, is Mr. Joel Cameron there?"

"Sure, Dad's right here—"

"Who is this?" David blurted. He didn't know how to be subtle in circumstances like this.

"Imani," the all too sultry voice said. "Imani Cameron. Who's this?"

"This is David Laine. I—"

"Oh my God, David!" She squealed, all pretense of maturity gone beneath a girlish outburst. David smiled. His little sister. His other little sister. "David! You called. Please tell me you're going to come to Bermuda. You must. Dad is so thrilled—"

A second voice, older and definitely masculine, spoke up in the background. "Imani," the gruff voice said. "I hope you're not talking to that boy again. I've told you I don't think Daryl is appropriate for a young lady—"

"No, no, Daddy. It's not Daryl, it's David! From the mainland."

Even through the phone line David could hear the man's confusion. "David? My David? From Los Angeles?"

The phone was taken away from Imani and the gruff voice broke in. "David? Is this really you? You must have received my letter."

The voice had a slight English accent, brushed with Jamaican *patois*. Normally David could get a pretty clear image of someone from talking to them, but Joel Cameron's picture wouldn't come. He was as enigmatic as he had been when David first learned of his existence. He wanted to ask who are you, but he knew he wouldn't get the answers he needed. Not over the phone.

"Yes, I got it." Again he and Chris traded looks. "Just today in fact."

"You must have a thousand questions. I know I do. I know my daughter Imani can be impetuous, but I agree with her. I'd like you to come and visit us."

Imani. David swallowed in a throat gone dry. His half-sister. Did he have half-brothers, too? A whole, ready-made family. The idea was unnerving.

"Well, I don't know, Mr. Cameron—"

"No, no, you must call me Joel. It's altogether too odd to have you call me Mr. Cameron."

David tried it out. "Joel. Ah, I don't know if we can get away right now—"

Chris punched his arm at the same time Joel protested. "You must come. It's already been too long. I'm sorry if you're angry that I left you, but I thought… I never would have left if I'd known."

Known what? That I was still alive? That my mother lied about so many things I can't keep track of them anymore?

Before he could think of what to say, Chris snatched the phone out of his hand. He pushed David's hand away when he tried to retrieve the handset. "Mr. Cameron, this is Christopher. Chris. We'd love to come out and visit. Yes, sir, we'll let you know—"

Grinning, he handed the phone back to David. "He wants to talk to you."

"You will come then?" Joel sounded a lot more enthusiastic than David would have liked. But what could he do?

"I guess we'll be coming."

"Excellent. I'm looking forward to meeting you."

"Yeah, me too."

David disconnected the phone and turned a cold stare at Chris. "Don't even start," he said.

Chris gave him his patented "who, me?" look. Then his smile faded. "So who were you talking to?"

"Joel—"

"No, before that. When you gave your name."

"Imani," David said.

"Imani?"

"My sister."

CHAPTER THREE

Saturday, 6:20pm, Cove Avenue, Silverlake, Los Angeles

David left to go back to the Northeast Station after saying he'd be back around nine. Chris didn't waste any time, he went online with Delta and upgraded their tickets to BusinessElite. Now at least they'd be comfortable for the long twelve hour flight. He didn't want to be crammed into economy, no matter how much they might save. David, with his long legs, would appreciate it, even if he bellyached about the price.

He hoped he'd convinced David he was well enough for this trip. He never let on that he still got tired easily and sometimes in the afternoon, when he knew David wouldn't be home unexpectedly, he would lie down for an hour or two, always careful to remove all signs of his siesta before David did come home.

This really would be a vacation; a good place to rest and get all his strength back. For the first time in years the two of them would have no work demands pulling them away. How could that not be restful?

Back in his office, he logged online and took care of the business he had abandoned earlier. After he checked his email and attended to the important stuff, he picked up his BlackBerry and speed dialed Becky. She answered on the third ring.

"Hey boss, how do you feel? Better, I hope."

"I feel fine. Really, you're as bad as David. What do you two think? That I'm some invalid on the verge of imminent collapse?"

"Of course not, but David told me how sick you were. He made me promise not to pester you about work for at least a week."

"Oh did he?" Chris felt both irritated and warm at the news. David cared. David was a meddling busybody, but he cared. He shook the feelings off along with the strange lassitude that he'd been feeling ever since his bout with that nasty virus left him on his back for nearly two weeks. He couldn't afford to be sick anymore. No matter what David might want, he had a business to attend to. And now he had this.

"What's your week look like, say…" He pulled out his BlackBerry and checked his calendar entries for around two weeks from today. "Let's say starting the twentieth." That would give him time to play catch up before he left again and put Becky in charge.

"So what's up?" she asked.

"David and I are going to Bermuda. Call it a rest-cure-vacation." It was better than calling it what it was; finding out the truth about David's past. That was David's call to explain if he wanted to in the future.

"Bermuda?" she asked. "I am so jealous."

"I'll send you a postcard."

"Gee, no T-shirt?"

"Okay, I'll splurge. A postcard and a T-shirt." While he talked he opened Google and looked up Joel Cameron, not expecting much. He wasn't surprised to see hits. He was disheartened when he saw there were over four million. Even narrowing it with the addition of Bermuda, there were still too many hits to sift through.

"Lucky me," Becky said, breaking his concentration. Chris frowned at his laptop screen.

"You won't have a problem taking over my clients, right?"

"Just send me what you need. I could use the excitement."

"Well, try not to make it too exciting," Chris said. "My clients are delicate souls."

"Not likely, if they hire you."

He disconnected and went back to reading. It was no good. He could spend all day scrolling through all the names and never know if he had hit the right one. Instead, he Googled the history of the place. All he knew of Bermuda were pink sands and expensive living. It turned out there was a lot more.

First discovered in the early sixteenth century it proved the bane of sailors for centuries. More than five hundred ships lay wrecked on reefs guarding the island's shores more effectively than most navies managed. A fleet of ships on their way to the Virginia colonies were separated in a storm and the *Sea Venture* foundered on the reef. All 150 on board survived. Eventually, two replacement ships were built and the castaways finished their voyage to Virginia.

People kept returning to the islands and a British colony was set up. It was still a part of the British Empire; all efforts to have true independence had been defeated to date.

All very interesting, but it didn't get him or David any closer to understanding what had happened forty-one years ago. He shut down his laptop and reached for his BlackBerry again.

He had one more call to make, to Desmond Hayward, his best friend. He needed someone to look after the cat and dog while they were gone and Des was one of his few friends who tolerated animals. Des wasn't as impressed as Becky had been.

"I've heard about that place. They are not nice to our kind of people."

"Our kind of people? You mean Democrats? Library card holders? Spelunkers?"

"You—" Des stopped, momentarily silenced, "You've never been spelunking in your life."

"Okay, forget spelunking, stamp collectors then—and before you say anything, I did collect stamps," Chris said with a barely suppressed laugh which quickly became a jaw splitting yawn. He blinked, but the tiredness wouldn't go away. "When I was a kid, knee-high to a grasshopper."

Des snorted. "Well, you know what I mean," he sniffed.

"It's a holiday, Des. Let's not make it into something more.

Can you watch the animals for us?"

"Yes, I'll watch them. Trev loves the mangy mutt so he'll be happy to take him out for a run. You have to promise you'll be careful. You know what you're like; you just can't stay out of trouble. And don't forget how sick you were just last week."

"Like anyone will let me forget."

"Hey, we all love your stubborn, self-destructive, pretty little tush. Just don't do anything too strenuous. Really, how hard is that? Miss Trouble."

"I am not—never mind, I can't win with you guys." Chris yawned again. "I'll take care, really I will, hon. I'll send you a postcard."

"Forget that. Bring me a juicy twenty-something beach boy. That would be yummy."

"Trevor ought to love that."

"Sure he would. You don't know bad boy Trevor. You tell Fido not to shed all over my Hugo Boss."

Chris laughed and hung up, after promising to talk to Des before they left. He went upstairs, set the alarm for four-thirty so David wouldn't catch him in bed, and crawled between the covers. A sympathetic Sergeant leaped up beside him.

David was supposed to be off work at five. Today, he actually made it home by five-thirty, giving Chris enough time for a wake-up shower, a change into clean clothes and the table set. When he heard the car door slam shut, he slid two seasoned filets onto the grill beside the foil-wrapped baked potatoes already cooking.

David came into the kitchen and bussed Chris on the cheek, his five o'clock shadow rasping Chris's freshly shaved face. "Something smells good."

"You have time for a shower," Chris said. He pointedly rubbed his own face. "And a shave."

David kissed him again and plodded toward the stairs. He returned twenty minutes later, looking almost human. This time the kiss he gave Chris was a serious one.

"Come on." Chris pulled away, albeit reluctantly. "Let's get some chow in us first."

"Dessert then."

"Promise."

Sunday, 12:00pm, Carlyle Street, Glendale, Los Angeles

Church bells rang someplace. Well, it was Sunday, David thought morosely, while he climbed the cracked, weed-infested steps up to the house where his CI said Bart Trimble could be found.

Trimble was a person of interest in a botched liquor store robbery that left one guy dead and another in Glendale Memorial. Supposedly, Trimble had been present at the robbery. No one could say whether he'd been a part of it or simply a bystander. Either way, he and Martinez needed to find the guy.

No warrant, so they had to find Trimble and persuade him to talk. A curtain swayed in the window beside the front walk. David rapped on the wooden door and a dog barked, deep. He shared a glance with Martinez. Big dog.

He brushed his hand over the butt of his Smith & Wesson. Knocked again.

"LAPD. Open up. We need to talk."

The door opened wide enough to let a girl peer up at them. She looked young and scared. David knew Trimble was thirty-six. So... daughter?

"Your dad home? Bartholomew Trimble? Is he here?"

A dog's head pushed the door opened more. The mastiff's scarred muzzle curled open in a silent snarl. David freed his gun.

"Trimble," he called over the dog's growling. "Call the dog off and get out here."

The girl vanished. So did the dog. Replaced by a hatchet-faced man with unshaved cheeks and a cigarette jammed in his mouth.

"Bartholomew Trimble?"

"Yah. Watcha want?"

"I need you to come out here so we can talk," David said. He'd holstered his weapon, but kept his hand near it. No telling when this could turn hinky. "Now, Mr. Trimble."

"All right, all right." He yanked the door open all the way and stood in the foyer wearing paint-covered gray sweats and a loose wife beater that showed off flabby flesh. He carried a half empty bottle of Old Milwaukee in one hand and held the dog's collar in his other.

The mastiff strained toward the two cops and both David and Martinez kept wary eyes on both it and Trimble.

"We're looking for Tony Sutton," David said. "You know where he might be?"

"Sutton? Never hearda him. He do somethin'?"

The dog snarled and twisted in its efforts to reach the two armed men. David had had enough. "Sir, put the dog away." When Trimble hesitated he snapped. "Now. Don't worry. We'll wait."

Trimble grumbled but huffed his way back into the house. A moment later, an inner door slammed and he shuffled back. He took the cigarette out of his mouth, took a slug of beer and popped the butt back between his lips. His teeth were as yellow as his fingertips.

"We'd like to come in, sir. We'll only take a minute of your time."

Inside, a woman's voice could be heard, "What the fuck they want with us? Get rid of them, Bart."

When Trimble returned Martinez snarled, "You want us to vamoose, dirtwad, you answer our questions."

Trimble seemed torn between listening to his wife or the cops on his doorstep. The cops won. He waved them inside.

In the living room a wide screen TV was blaring out some

frenetic music, and some bizarrely colored animated characters were being ignored by everyone. All eyes were on the intruders.

A copper-headed woman sat on a green and gold sofa between two children; the girl who had opened the door to them and an older teenage boy. Four pairs of eyes watched on intently. From the back room the surly mastiff kept snarling and yowling. The hairs on David's neck stood up. They still needed to do what they came here for.

"I want you to tell me what you saw last Thursday at Mike's Liquor Store on Verdugo."

"Wasn't there."

"We know that's not true," David said. "Don't waste our time."

"And we won't waste yours," Martinez added, taking a step closer to Trimble. In the back room, as though knowing it was needed, the dog howled and threw itself against a door. Neither cop looked toward the outburst. Their focus was on the only real threat in the house, the people in front of them.

"What did you see?"

"Nothin'," Trimble said.

"Bull."

"We ain't leavin' till you give him up," Martinez added.

"Give who up?"

"Whoever it is you're protecting."

"Ain't protectin' no—"

"Then whoever it is you're scared shitless of!"

David stepped closer, crowding the smaller man. "Come on, Mr. Trimble. Talk to—"

The boy, who might have been sixteen, snarled a curse and lunged at David, who adroitly sidestepped him. He avoided the boy, but didn't see Trimble's fist until it connected with his face. The first blow caught him square in the chin, the next got him in the eye.

Before the man could take a third swing Martinez had him splayed out on the floor, his arms in cuffs. David snatched the boy and put him down too, over the woman's protests.

"You want to join the party, keep it up lady," Martinez snapped and both mother and daughter subsided back on the sofa. "Yeah, that's right. You're smarter than your old man."

David called for a couple of shops to transport the two to be booked for assault. When he broke the connection, he lightly touched his face and winced at the throbbing pain. Already his cheek was swelling. He'd have a shiner for sure.

"Better get that looked at, *ese.*" Martinez came up behind him. "Lieutenant will be asking after you when he sees it."

"It's nothing."

"I know. He's still gonna want it official."

David knew he was right. "Fine." He knew he was being grumpy, but between Trimble and the web of lies he'd found out his mother had woven all those years ago, he was in a foul mood that he couldn't put off on anybody's shoulders.

"Come on," he said. "Let's go book these mutts."

By the time they reached Northeast, Trimble had a change of heart. They let the boy go and sat Trimble down in an interrogation room with a coffee and a recorder. After less than an hour, they had a name and a location of their killer. David wrote up an arrest warrant and he and Martinez, along with two shops for backup, went and rounded up one Roosevelt Fischer for armed robbery, aggravated assault and homicide.

A good day's work. At the end of the day, David checked out with the division doctor, who fixed him up and sent him off. He called it quits at six and headed home.

CHAPTER FOUR

Sunday, 4:20pm, Cove Avenue, Silverlake, Los Angeles

David had left for work before Chris got up. Chris spent a couple of hours at one of his client's sites. Once he had cleaned up the mess someone else had created, he generated a preliminary plan for the migration to a new network operating system his client wanted started in two months. He took a late lunch at Blairs. Back home he did some cleaning and threw the sheets into the washer. He had meant to go online and tend to more problems, but when he made up the bed, it looked so inviting he sprawled out on it and didn't wake up until nearly five o'clock. Wanting to make it look like he'd spent the day working, he settled in front of his laptop and opened his VPN to log onto one of his client's systems.

He ran some updates and security patches and was about to close the system down at six when his phone rang.

He scooped it up. It was Martinez, David's LAPD partner off and on for nearly eleven years. Chris's heart immediately plummeted into his stomach. Any call from David's partner couldn't be good news.

"M-Martinez? What is it? What's wrong?"

"Davey's okay, Chris," Martinez said quickly. "He took a hit from a crazy mutt we were trying to hook up but really, he's okay."

"Then what? You didn't just call me to tell me he's okay. What is it, Martinez?" Chris would have reached through the phone and strangled the big Hispanic. "Tell me."

"He's got a nasty shiner and a couple of stitches on his chin. The doc says he's okay. You gotta trust the doc, right?"

Chris gripped the phone so hard his knuckles turned white. In his overactive imagination his recurring nightmare was coming true.

"You don't believe me?" Martinez continued. "He's on his way home. I figured I'd give you a head's up so you won't freak out on him." Before Chris could respond he said, "What's this I hear about you guys going to Bermuda?"

Not sure how much David might have told his partner, he hedged. "Yeah," he said. "We could both use a vacation..."

"You just make sure Davey comes back, you hear. We really need him here right now."

Chris bristled. That was the problem, he wanted to say. They always needed David. So much so, he never thought he could even take time off. But before Chris could say anything, Martinez was gone.

Sunday, 6:10pm, Cove Avenue, Silverlake, Los Angeles

Chris took the last of the Merlot and sat in the IChing chair facing the front door. Ten minutes later he heard the keys in the lock and David stepped through the door. His eyes widened briefly when he saw Chris, but he quickly shuttered the look and ducked his head.

"He was right," Chris growled. "You look like shit."

Self-consciously David touched his face where a large bruise was already purpling the flesh around his eye. Before responding he slipped his gun and holster off and locked them up. He ran his fingers through his thick curly hair, unclipped his tie and stuffed it in his jacket pocket. He turned to face an impatient Chris. "It's nothing."

"And if it had been something," Chris said. "What would you say then?"

"Chris—" David shucked his shoes and crossed the room. He perched on the mahogany arm. "It's really no big deal. I just forgot to duck."

Chris didn't buy it for a minute. He also knew he'd never win this argument with David. "At least put an icepack on it." He didn't protest when David took his wine glass and sipped the oaky contents. Chris ducked into the kitchen and came back with a package of frozen peas. David sat down, propped his bare feet onto a footstool, and gingerly pressed the peas to his eye. His other eye met Chris's.

"What would you say if I told you I was seriously considering leaving the force?"

Chris's feet thumped onto the carpet. Merlot spilled onto the granite coffee table. He ignored it, turning slowly in the chair to face David. His mind raced through a million thoughts but the only one he could latch onto was: "Are you for real? *Quit* LAPD?"

"Quit. Retire. Seriously. It's been on my mind for a couple of months now. I'm getting too old for this shit," David touched his recently stitched chin.

Chris traced the outline of the small wound. "Not old," he whispered. "No way."

"Well, not as young as I used to be. It just seems to get more and more dangerous with less and less return."

"But-but, what would you do?" Chris knew there was no way David was ready to retire for real. "You'd go crazy sitting around the house all day with nothing to do. Even you can't garden all the time. And your car doesn't need any more work. Unless you're going to buy another junk heap to fix up."

"That's where you come in."

"You want me to help you fix up a car? Gee, I don't know. I might be good at picking out seat colors. I'm sure I could make some nice fabric choices."

"Very funny." David shifted his make-do icepack around, dripping water on his wool pants. "No, I want your help if I'm going to set up an agency."

"An agency?" Chris took his wine back and stood up. "I think this conversation calls for another bottle."

He returned minutes later with a Kistler Merlot, the one he'd been saving for a special occasion. If this didn't qualify, nothing would. He decanted the wine and grabbed a cloth to wipe up the spill. He set the fluted carafe onto the black marble coffee table after filling each glass, and handed one to David, setting the other one in front of himself.

Chris settled back in his chair. "Okay, start at the beginning," he said.

David swirled the Merlot around in his glass, the ruby tones catching the late afternoon light. "I know it's something you've wanted for a long time, maybe all along."

"Face it, your job is dangerous. We both know that," Chris said. "I can't help but be afraid for you all the time. I watch the news. I hear what happens to cops."

"Mostly patrol cops." David grimaced. "Those are the guys in the line of fire. But, it was my job. I didn't know how to do anything else."

"I'm tired of hearing 'it's my job'" Chris did his best to keep his voice level, knowing David never responded well to hysterics. "You can do anything you want if you'd stop being so negative."

"Let me finish. At first, I didn't *want* to do anything else. But lately… lately I'm not so sure."

"But what would you do?" Chris couldn't help it. He shuddered. Images of a miserable David lumbering around the house, restless and bored, filled his mind. How long before they got on each other's nerves? How much of that kind of stress could their marriage take? He thought they were solid, but even the strongest marriage could break under the right strain.

"I've been looking into getting my private investigator's license. That's really where you come in."

Chris felt his mouth fall open. It should have been everything he'd ever hoped for, but… Something occurred to him.

"Did you tell Martinez any of this?"

"No, well, not exactly. Why?"

Chris recounted the phone call from David's partner. "You must have said something to make him suspicious."

"Maybe," David conceded. "He's been pretty suspicious lately as it is. Martinez has never been the most trusting of souls."

"And what's any of it got to do with me?"

"I'll need to set up an office, computerized accounting and records keeping, that kind of thing. I figure you know more about what that means. In fact, with your expertise we could take on computer security cases. Those pay pretty good, I hear."

"They do," Chris said cautiously. "But is that really why you want to do this?"

Chris knew there had to be a catch somewhere. He wanted to trust David, so why couldn't he believe him? Had he assumed some of David's skepticism? Or was it simply if it sounded too good to be true there must be something wrong?

"As much as anything." David stood and pulled Chris into a warm embrace, nibbling at the smooth skin on his neck. "We can talk about it later, after we mull it over." David found Chris's open mouth and spent several heartbeats exploring it.

"I don't think you'd find this in Webster's Dictionary under 'mull it over.'" Chris sighed and lost his train of thought.

"Too bad. It might make the dictionary more popular. What do you think?"

Only Chris couldn't think anymore. As David's lips worked down his throat, he found his chest constricting. He knew David was just trying to distract him from asking any more questions but he didn't care. He groaned when David's tongue slipped back between his teeth.

"I've got an idea," David said as though it had just occurred to him. "Why don't we go upstairs?"

"The steaks are on the grill."

"Oh, crap." David let go of him. "Then I guess we better eat.

But I'm not done with you."

That's fair, neither am I. But Chris kept that thought to himself. No sense ruining a perfectly good steak dinner with questions.

Sunday, 8:10pm, Cove Avenue, Silverlake, Los Angeles

Chris untangled himself from the sheets. Late evening sun poured through the bedroom window and he blinked at the red tinged brightness. He was getting way too used to being in bed at this time of day.

Glancing over at David still buried under the bed clothes, he couldn't help but grin. The heat that erupted between them hadn't diminished with the years. Whatever problems they might have, their sex life wasn't one of them.

He thought about David's words. Would he really quit? If Chris had been a praying man, he would have prayed for this moment. But... David loved being a detective. For so long he had defined himself as an LAPD homicide detective. Would he really be happy as a P.I.? Doing what? Chasing cheating wives and husbands? Dragging embezzlers into the light of day?

David rolled over to face him, his eyes sleepy and sated. "Penny for them."

"Thinking about us." Chris played his fingers through the thick mat of black hair on David's chest. "I could get used to this. Lying around in bed all day, noodling."

"Noodling?"

"That's another one you won't find in Webster's." Chris draped himself over David. "Like this."

"All day?"

Chris nuzzled his ear. "Can you think of a reason why not?"

David pretended to think until Chris smacked him. He grunted and rolled over, ending up on top of Chris.

"As enjoyable as that might be, I still have work to do. That doesn't stop even if I do retire."

"I already talked to Becky. She can take over my clients anytime."

"Good. It's not formal, but I shouldn't have any problem getting the time off."

"I'd like to see them try to deny it."

David gave Chris a look that shut him up before he could launch into his usual argument. David grabbed a robe out of the closet and slipped it on. "How about a drink at Abbey's?"

"Fine, I'll check my email and tie up some loose ends at Pharmaden. No sense getting there till after ten."

Ten minutes later David came down and Chris trotted upstairs to take his own shower. After carefully shaving his face and chest, he moussed his hair. He donned his newest jeans and a skin hugging T-shirt. He knew he looked hot. It was always important for him to look good, but tonight called for some extra attention to detail. It wasn't every day your husband talked about retiring.

He linked arms with David. "Don't we make one gorgeous couple?"

"Right, a regular Matt Damon and Ben Affleck."

"Ha, we outdo that pair."

They took David's car. He was finally nearing the end of refurbishing it and he took any chance to show off his handiwork. The yellow and white '56 Chevy coupe had occupied nearly eight years of his life, but everyone agreed it was cherry. Chris was still a little irked that David had insisted on paying for all the repairs himself. But it was David's baby and he wanted to do it on his own, just like he insisted on only using legitimate parts instead of knockoffs, even if he had to wait months to find them.

Chris settled into his regular spot in the middle of the newly refinished bucket seat, resting his hand on David's knee.

At Abbey's, David insisted on sitting in the darkest corner of the club. Even then the waiter stared until Chris gave him a dirty look and he went away to hassle someone else. He probably thought Chris had inflicted David's black eye, which might have been amusing if Chris hadn't known the real reason behind it.

Back home David caught the tail end of a John Wayne movie. Chris grabbed two beers out of the fridge and joined David. During one of the commercials, Chris told David about his unsuccessful web trolling.

"Interesting history," David said, barely taking his eyes off the TV as the commercial ended. "I'm not sure if I know of anyone who actually went there."

"It's pricey."

"People want to go to the Caribbean, they hit the Bahamas."

"It's not in the Caribbean. It's actually on the same latitude as South Carolina."

David took his gaze off the screen. "Last time I looked, Carolina didn't have palm trees. Don't they have them in Bermuda?"

"The Gulf Stream keeps it warm all year round."

"Interesting." He reached over and took Chris's hand. "You're really looking forward to this, aren't you? Why?"

For you, he wanted to say. Instead he shrugged. "I think we could both use a vacation. Since our honeymoon, we haven't gone anywhere. It'll be nice to have some 'us' time."

"As long as you promise to rest."

"Cross my heart."

CHAPTER FIVE

Monday, 7:10am, Cove Avenue, Silverlake, Los Angeles

The next morning they lingered over coffee.

"I want to stop in New Hampshire on our way," David said, not meeting Chris's eyes. "Since we'll be on the east coast we can swing by there. I can add a couple of days to my time off. Before the real vacation starts."

Chris wasn't fooled by David's casual remark. He knew damned well what he meant. David meant to see his parents. To confront his mother about her deception? That was like David. He wasn't one to slink quietly away from a problem, no matter who it would benefit. Or who it might hurt. He was straightforward in his life and honest to a fault, and he expected the same from others. To find out his own mother was involved in such a monstrous lie must have devastated him, although David would die before he ever showed that.

Chris couldn't see any good coming from the side trip.

"You sure that's a good idea?"

"Why not?" David spooned some yogurt into his bowl and topped it with strawberries and granola. "I'd like to see Graham again."

But not his mother? Right. Why not? "Sure," he said, still uneasy. "We can trade the tickets in for new ones. How long do you want to stay at your parents?"

"A couple of days. That ought to be enough, don't you think?"

"David—"

"Don't worry, I'll be civilized."

Chris sincerely hoped so. He knew David was not going to argue about it. They were going to New Hampshire and that was that.

Friday 8:35am, Delta Terminal, LAX, World Way, Los Angeles

The cab pulled up to the Delta terminal. The cabbie helped haul their luggage out of the trunk. David grabbed a cart and loaded everything onto it. Chris kept his laptop case as his carry-on luggage while David kept a small bag with their personal affects and his reading material.

As usual he had packed twice as much as David. He had also been shopping. He wore a new Banana Republic T-shirt and pair of Bruno Pieters jeans. David was afraid to ask how much it had all cost. He knew Chris was getting the reaction he wanted as people were turning to look at him, men and women. His beauty was like a jolt of ice water on a hot day and it always took David's breath away when he least expected it.

They towed everything inside and checked in.

They had barely strapped in when Chris turned to him, the look of determination on his face telling David the time for equivocation was past. He still tried anyway.

"I want to talk about this retirement plan of yours."

"Sure, we'll talk, I promise, but I'd rather do it after this trip."

"Don't I get a say in this?"

"Of course. I'd never do anything this major without consulting you."

"Consulting? That's pretty damned insulting, don't you think? We're supposed to be a couple. Partners. That's a lot more than a *consultation*."

"Okay, bad choice of words." David reached over and captured Chris's hand where it lay knotted in his lap. He squeezed the white knuckles. "But I do need to think about it. Face it, it'll be a big change for both of us. I want to know I feel good about it *before* we talk it over. I want to have a chance to consider the ramifications."

Chris wasn't mollified. "And I'm a part of that life, whether you like it or not. I know you've always tried to shield me from the worst and I appreciate that, but you can't shield me from the reality, which is that every time you walk out the door you're at risk. How do you think that makes me feel? The phone rings and a little part of me dies, thinking this is *the* call. That someone at the other end is going to tell me how sorry they are…"

He dashed unwanted tears off his cheek, took several deep breathes to calm himself. "I don't ever want to get that phone call. I don't ever want to get a visit from your buddies in blue. I don't know what I'd do if I lost you."

"You're not going to lose me," David said. "Not if I can help it."

"Yeah, well, I'll hold you to that."

David forced himself to smile down into Chris's earnest face. He knew he shouldn't make those kinds of promises; who could keep them when that kind of tragedy was out of anyone's control. He could argue that he was always careful, but sometimes that wasn't enough. Just look at Jairo. That was a name he knew Chris would not like him thinking about. It would just upset Chris more to carry on with this conversation.

David opened up his science fiction paperback and was thankful when Chris pulled a computer magazine out of his laptop case.

David drowsed off in the middle of a paragraph, one finger still cocked between pages to mark his place. While he dozed, his mind wandered. What would happen if he really did quit? What would life be like if he no longer had the LAPD? Sure, he'd worked with the odd private investigator and found most of them hard-working stiffs who did their best with the limited resources they had at hand. But a downside was that he'd be giving up all the power the LAPD shield wielded. That kind of power opened doors and got things done.

He finally drifted into a deeper sleep where dreams didn't plague him. He woke up when the plane began its descent. The seatbelt lights came on and the captain's voice came over the intercom, telling them they were approaching Manchester

Municipal Airport.

They drove the rental Saturn north toward Little Squam Lake where David's parents had bought ten acres of land bordering the lake over three decades ago. His stepfather, Graham, was an avid fisherman and his mother attended the local summer auctions, always on the lookout for more antiques. His stepfather often joked that he needed to put up a barn to store her treasures.

Chris stared out of the window and David wondered what he was brooding over. He had accompanied David to meet his parents only once before, after they became a couple but before their wedding. The visit had not gone well. David's mother had seemed incapable of seeing beyond what Chris represented: that their son was a pervert. Chris wasn't very good at forgiving that kind of rebuff. David had cut the visit short and vowed never to return. Now his mother's lies had forced his hand and he had to admit he wanted Chris along to strengthen his resolve not to take any more of his mother's crap.

Chris suddenly seemed to think of something. "Did you tell them we were coming?"

"I talked to…Graham." David shied away from his usual address form. Up until he had learned the truth he'd been happy to call the man Dad, since he was the only one David had known. "Whether he told my mother, I don't know." Left unsaid was "I don't care."

CHAPTER SIX

Friday, 5:15pm Valley Stream Road, Holderness, New Hampshire

The car crunched up the driveway. Flanking the drive like silent sentinels, marched a dozen carefully manicured cedars. Past them, beds of flowers filled the vast front yard with a riot of color. The house itself was two stories of fieldstone and red wood trim. Several mullioned windows caught the late afternoon sun and threw back the shattered light. The front of the house looked out over the lawn and a koi pond nearly covered by pink and white water lilies. Behind the house, Chris could just see the edge of the dock jutting out into a lake so blue it burned into the back of his brain. The screen of cedar bushes that had only been knee-high when he last visited had grown into a towering, carefully trimmed hedge. A small craft was tied up at the end of the pier. A figure wearing a hat crouched over the boat, tinkering with the outboard motor. He straightened and looked up. Waving, he hurried toward them, wiping his hands on faded jeans, already stained with oil and smelling of gasoline. He pulled off his Tilley hat when he drew nearer and wiped his brow with the back of his arm.

Chris recognized Graham Laine, David's stepfather. He'd gotten a little grayer over the intervening years. Like David had once, he sported a neat, gray mustache. He extended his hand to David who shook it. Then Graham turned to Chris.

"Chris, I'm so glad you could come."

"Thanks, Mr. Laine—"

"No, no. Call me Graham." He waved at the house and put his arm around David's shoulder. "You must be tired after that long drive. Come on inside. I've got a few bottles of Pig's Ear." They reached the bottom of the veranda steps. "How long do you plan on staying, David? We still have your room, just like you left it. You're mother's thrilled you're here. Come on, I think she's in the kitchen getting dinner ready. Your favorite, prime rib and Yorkshire pudding."

Chris had always admired the Laine home, even from his brief visit. From the two-story foyer with the graceful stairway that cascaded down from the second floor to the living room, to the crystal chandelier far above, it was a marvel of design and atmosphere. Graham had once jokingly told them that the builder had called it "the great room." It had probably added a few extra thousand to the asking price. Chris especially loved the gas fireplace, though on this hot summer day it wasn't in use.

The odor of roasting meat and caramelized onions overwhelmed Chris's senses. Immediately his stomach growled. David led him into the living room while Graham excused himself to change and clean up. Chris looked around the great room. It had changed since the one and only time he had been here. David's mother had replaced the cool leather and copper furniture with her antiques; the woman might be a bitch, but she was a bitch with impeccable taste. He recognized a couple of Shaker pieces and something that could easily have been used by Jefferson.

Graham returned, carrying three bottles of open beer. Chris took his and studied the label. It had a crude cartoon of a pig with the words Pig's Ear Brown Ale. Despite being a brown ale Chris found it surprisingly mellow. Perfect for a hot summer day.

Chris glanced up to find David's mother standing in the doorway. She wore a lace-fringed apron over a burgundy dress with a string of pearls Chris would bet a week's salary were wild, not cultured. There was another woman with her. She bore a faint resemblance to David's mother, but must have been in her eighties, at least. She wore a helmet of gray hair. A pair of reading glasses hung on a cord around her neck. David's grandmother? Chris knew she existed; David had mentioned her once or twice over the years, but Chris had never met her. She was as impeccably dressed as David's mother. The faint smell of lilies of the valley that he always associated with older women—his mother wore the stuff—wafted through the room, competing with the bowls of chrysanthemums and asters scattered around on several antique end-tables.

Like David's mother, she ignored Chris and greeted David stiffly. "I'm glad you could make it, David. I'm just sorry your sister won't be joining us. She's thinking of joining some God-forsaken international charity and has flown out to Botswana or someplace to meet her team."

She clearly didn't approve of her younger grandchild's goal, but then she hadn't approved of David's choice of careers either. Neither of them had. Only David's stepfather had been in favor of it. Chris wondered what they would say if they knew David was thinking of retiring.

Not that David would ever tell them. At least not until it was a fait accompli.

When the two women left, David turned to his stepfather and asked, "Nanna's staying here now? I thought she lived in Manchester."

Graham nodded. "She had a mild stroke last year and had to give up her place in town. We fixed up the basement so that she had her own apartment. She's doing much better now, but still needs daily care."

"You never told me," David murmured. He had made his dislike of his mother fairly clear to Chris early on, but he had rarely mentioned his grandmother. It was pretty obvious there was little love lost there, either.

"She didn't want anyone making a fuss over her," Graham said.

His mother re-entered the room, alone this time, and looked them both up and down. "Dinner will be formal." She spoke to David directly for the first time. "I do hope you brought something dressier than that." She glanced at Graham, who had come back down wearing new, crisp jeans. "You too, Graham. We're not barbarians here."

She never looked at Chris.

Once they had changed into more formal wear, Graham led them to the table. He sat David beside him and Chris opposite.

Chris was a little surprised to see David's mother bringing in trays of food and setting them on the elaborately laid seventeenth-century oak table. He'd half expected a butler to serve. A gold-rimmed tablecloth was matched with napkins and Wedgwood dishes. When Graham offered to help, she waved him into his seat. There was something about the offer and the refusal that felt ritualistic. David's grandmother led grace before the meal was served. David didn't meet Chris's gaze while the dishes were passed around. He made some small talk with Graham on his right, but Chris could tell his heart wasn't in it.

Chris couldn't fault her for the meal. The prime rib was succulent and barely medium rare. The roasted potatoes and corn were perfect and even the Yorkshire pudding was beyond reproach. Under any other circumstances he would have dove in and stuffed himself. As it was he managed a few mouthfuls along with a glass of passable Cabernet, then set his utensils down when David's mother spoke up.

"So how have you been, David? You look peaked. Are you well?"

"I'm fine, Mother."

"I hope you take care of yourself," she said. "That city isn't fit for a civilized man. You never know what you'll catch from some filthy degenerate junkie. Diseases that would never have existed, except for the moral decline of our world."

Chris nearly choked on his Cabernet. My God, she was talking about AIDS. Did she think David was exposed just because he was gay or because he was a cop? He'd thought that kind of attitude had gone the way of the Bush dynasty.

He could see by the white lines around David's mouth that it was taking all his effort not to speak up. It was Graham who defused the situation.

He raised his wine. "Here's to you, son. May there always be a wind at your back."

Chris hastily grabbed his glass and saluted the table. "To peace," he said, earning a bemused look from David, who reluctantly followed suit.

"Peace," he said, not once looking at his mother. "And smooth sailing." Then he set his untouched wine down and turned toward his stepfather. "Have you been out on the lake much this year? How's the fishing?"

"Excellent. I've brought home a few good trout feasts for your mother. She always did know how to prepare a fish to bring out the best in it. If you and Chris are here long enough maybe we can go out some morning. The fish bite best early—"

"Sorry, Dad," Chris could hear him stumble over the word. "But we have to leave the morning after next."

"Back home so soon? You just got here."

"No, we've booked a flight to Bermuda."

Chris was watching David's mother when David said this. He'd give this to the old broad, she didn't flinch. She paled, but rallied quickly.

"A pleasant place for a vacation. Your grandmother honeymooned there sixty years ago. Of course it was a much more genteel place than it is today."

Chris didn't need to ask who had told her that. David's grandmother oozed upper class snobbery so thick the table stewed in it. Chris swore if she wasn't such a blue-blood, her lip would have curled in derision at her daughter's comment. He imagined not much could measure up to this pair's expectations. He tried to think of what it must have been like for David to grow up in this cold house and felt a surge of pride that he had come out of it so honorable and strong. Not to mention with his balls intact. He nearly giggled at the thought of saying that out loud. He had no doubt he could wipe that smugness off the bitch's face. Not that anyone, least of all David, would appreciate it.

Both of them were happy to follow Graham outside to the deck overlooking the lake while the two women insisted on clearing the table. Chris noticed that this time no one, including Graham, volunteered to help. Out on the broad expanse of water a fifty-foot sailboat caught the stiff evening breeze. Somewhere on the far side of the lake a loon called. A second one answered. Chris and David dragged a pair of Adirondack chairs side by side, facing the tiny shingle beach at the foot of the hill that ran down to the water.

The sun slid behind a bank of clouds. Shadow infused the deck. The temperature dropped a degree or two. Chris had stripped off his tie the minute they were outside. David did the same. After a few minutes he took off his jacket too.

"Coffee?" Graham asked. "Or another beer?"

They both took the beer. David's mother was conspicuous by her absence. Graham fussed with a clay chiminea until he had a brisk fire going. Chris could feel the heat envelope the deck and he stretched out his legs to capture the warmth. Beside him, David did the same.

Dusk deepened and with it came the mosquitoes. Graham passed around insect spray, and tossed some pinion wood in the chiminea. "Natural bug repellent," he said, stirring up the fire with a stick of pinion wood. Soon the whole deck smelled like a fresh-cut Christmas tree. All along the opposite shore lights were springing up. The blinking lights of a plane drifted by overhead, too far up to hear. The quiet seemed almost eerie after the continuous noise of L.A. No sirens, no barking dogs or random gunshots. Silence.

Graham seemed determined to ignore the awkwardness that had settled over them.

"Bermuda, eh? Any particular reason, or is it really just a vacation?" Graham asked quietly.

"Can't really say right now." David shifted uneasily. He ran his fingers through his thick hair. "Maybe later we can talk…"

"David," Graham said, then changed his mind. He sighed. "Your mother really does love you, you know. She's just never been able to show it and I know that bothers her."

From what he could see nothing bothered David's mother, but Chris kept his thoughts to himself. This was David's fight, not his.

"Like I said, we'll talk later."

Graham nodded, clearly unhappy. "You know I'm always here for you, don't you, son?"

"Yeah, I do, Dad. And thanks. That means a lot."

Graham's half-smile was bittersweet. "So tell me, how's the job going? You still working out of Northeast?"

David nodded. Chris threw him a sharp look. No mention of quitting.

"What about you, Chris? What are you up to these days?"

"Business is good." He toyed with the label of his beer. "I've picked up a few new clients and may have a line on a couple more. There's always the heavy learning curve to keep up with new technologies. Sometimes I think I spend more time in classes than I do on the job. Thank God it's a business expense."

"Building a business takes time, no matter what kind it is. And it never pays to fall behind in industry knowledge, especially in such a fast changing one." Chris knew Graham had started out with a single pharmacy in Manchester and over time expanded it until now he owned a chain throughout New England. Chris would have loved to talk to him about growing his own business, but he knew David would have a kitten if he got too friendly.

But over the evening things grew more relaxed. David started laughing at Graham's gentle jabs. The rustle of water on the distant beach, the monotonous calls of the crickets and even the odd owl cry broke the night. Along the edges of the nearby forest, fireflies danced through the humid air.

Before he knew it, it was eleven. As though on cue, David's mother appeared in the door.

"I've made up Christopher's bed. There are fresh towels in both of your rooms. David can show you where the shower is."

Chris could feel the tension pour through David. Trying

to forestall a blowup, he laid his hand on David's arm, feeling his rigidity and whispered for his ears only. "It's all right." He glanced at Graham. "I think I'd like to turn in. It was a wonderful evening. Thank you for dinner and the beer."

He shot David a warning look. David subsided, though Chris could still feel his rage.

Graham stood with them and after saying goodnight set about damping the fire.

Chris followed David up the curved stairs, his jacket dangling over his shoulder. The first room was David's. He paused in the doorway and took hold of Chris's arm. Chris stepped into his embrace. "Let's not make a big deal out of it," he pleaded. "We aren't going to be here more than a couple of days."

"Sure," David said. His whole body was stiff now, his anger still vibrant. He ran his hands up Chris's arms, gripping his shoulders through his silk shirt. "Now you know why I don't come here. She's impossible."

Chris stroked his lover's rough face, lightly touching his mouth. "Where's my room?"

David pointed right. "Shower's between our rooms, and there's a shared dressing room."

"See you in the morning," Chris said. He tilted his head up and felt David's lips brush his.

"'Night." David's voice was husky.

It was the first night they'd spent apart since their wedding, outside of the times Chris had needed to travel for business. It felt weird knowing David was just through the bathroom and he couldn't go to him.

The sheets had been changed, but the room still had the faint, musty smell of unused space.

He decided a shower could wait until morning. He stripped and folded his clothes, putting them back in his suitcase. Then he dug out his red silk pajamas and pulled them on. He usually slept nude, but that idea creeped him out, knowing that David's family was somewhere in the big house. Sliding between the combed cotton sheets he burrowed under the down comforter. The room was cool, despite the day's heat. Tired from their long journey, he quickly found himself dozing.

He barely heard the bathroom door open. Before he could roll over a weight settled on the bed beside him and a hand came up to rest on his shoulder. David was in the velour kimono robe Chris had bought for him just because he knew the color, a deep jade, would look sensational on him.

"Did I startle you?"

"David?"

"Yeah, I couldn't sleep. Doesn't look like you had any problem."

Chris sat up and rubbed the sleep out of his eyes. "What time is it?"

"Just after twelve-thirty."

"Your parents—?"

"Are in bed. Neither one of them stays up past the news." David's voice hardened. "I have no idea when Nanna goes to bed."

Chris didn't comment. He figured it wasn't his place and the last thing he wanted was to start an argument.

Instead he asked, "What are you doing here?"

David ran his hand under the sheet, stroking Chris's chest through the silk, squeezing a nipple. "You have to ask?"

Chris was all too aware of David's erection under the robe. He was instantly hard.

"Are you sure? Your parents—"

"Have no business telling me who to sleep with." David leaned down to tease Chris's mouth with his lips. "Or who to love. I missed you. I'm not used to sleeping alone."

"Me neither," Chris whispered and threw aside the blankets. It didn't take either of them more than five seconds to strip. He pulled David down. "Fuck me, David."

"Mmm, I was hoping you'd ask."

CHAPTER SEVEN

Saturday, 6:15am Valley Stream Road, Holderness, New Hampshire

David slipped out of bed just as the eastern sky showed the first blush of dawn. There was no sense embarrassing Chris with the discovery that they had spent the night together. He grabbed a shower and dressed in fresh jeans and an LAPD T-shirt and headed down to the kitchen. Like every day he had known him, Graham was already there, a pot of coffee in a carafe on the kitchen bar, the thick hazelnut cream he favored beside his mug.

David nodded a greeting and grabbed a mug out of the cupboard. He slid onto a bar stool beside his stepfather. He poured the coffee, tasting the hot brew. As usual it was excellent.

"Sleep good?"

David suppressed a grin, knowing what else they'd been doing. "Very well, thanks."

Graham spooned some sugar into another mug of coffee. "What are your plans for today? Going to do some sightseeing? The offer's still open to take in some fishing."

Somehow the idea of three of them sitting in a small motor boat under the beating sun, waiting for some fish to strike, wasn't appealing. He could only imagine what Chris would think about it. His husband's idea of roughing it was a third-class hotel in Mazatlan. "Maybe. Depends on what Chris wants to do." David sipped his coffee and took the plunge. "First I need to talk to Mom. We have a few things to discuss."

Graham's eyebrow rose and David wasn't surprised when he said, "Can I ask what?"

"Sorry, it's between Mom and me. Nothing personal."

Graham nodded, though David could tell he wasn't happy. "Well, I'll leave that to you. I've got to go into town and do some work in the office. Then your mother and I might put in a round of golf. She's got quite a handicap now." He smiled fondly. "Will you be back for supper?"

"Maybe. I don't know what we'll be doing. I'll let you know." David knew damn well after his talk with his mother, they wouldn't be hanging around for supper. The fallout would likely spoil all their appetites, not to mention their golf game.

He wasn't looking forward to this, but his mother had gone too far this time. David could have handled the truth, but he'd never been given the chance. He knew damn well his mother hadn't operated alone, he suspected his grandmother had been involved up to her blue-blooded neck. Anything to avoid a scandal attached to the precious Willerton name.

Chris entered the kitchen and immediately headed for the coffee. He used some of Graham's flavored cream and his usual half spoonful of sugar. He stood behind David, not bothering to sit.

Graham greeted him and after glancing at his watch, said, "Well, I have to run. Enjoy your day." He rinsed his coffee cup out and slipped out of the room. For David the temperature rose several degrees.

"What did he say to you?" Chris asked.

"Nothing. Why?"

"You're upset."

"No, I'm not… Okay, maybe I am a bit. This whole thing just pisses me off."

Chris set his empty mug on the table, settled his hands on David's shoulders and began massaging him. David could feel his tension slip away. Chris's fingers dug into the tendons around his spine. He rolled his head back and sighed. "Oh yeah, that feels good…"

A sound broke them apart. David's grandmother stood in the kitchen doorway, A look of disgust on her face. David stood up, brushing Chris's hands off his shoulders.

"Looking for something, Nanna?"

Without a word she drew herself up to her full five-four height and crossed the room to the cupboard. She took two mugs and the carafe of coffee from the table, set them on a lacquered tray, and left the room. David stopped her.

"Before you get too busy, I'd like to see you and my mother this morning, if it's not too much trouble."

"Young man—"

"We can meet in here," David said and turned his back on her. He met Chris's alarmed looked. "You want to go antiquing later? Once my business here is…taken care of?"

"Ah, sure. That would be nice." Chris bit his lip. "David—"

David reached up to clasp his hand. "It'll be okay. Don't worry about it."

Chris's grin was shaky. "I know it will be."

David's grandmother re-entered the kitchen moments later. His mother had joined her and looked thunderous. She wasn't used to being summoned by anyone in her own home. She threw a poisonous look at their entwined hands.

David ignored them while he turned to Chris. "Why don't you go outside, hon. Take a walk down by the beach. There's even a tree fort in the woods I built when I was a kid."

"Your father built that," his mother snapped.

David turned cold eyes on her. "Only he's not my father, is he, Mother?"

Chris slipped out of the house and David watched him briefly while he made his way down toward the waterfront.

"We never hid the fact you were adopted by Graham. He loved you like a son."

"And my real father? Oh that's right, he died. Vietnam, wasn't it? The great war hero. Gee, if he'd been younger he could have been a Gulf War veteran. I'm sure there's a lot more cachet in that. Vietnam always left such a bad taste in everyone's mouth."

His mother's face grew pale, but she didn't back down.

"I'm not sure what you mean."

"For God's sake Mother, stop lying. My father hired a private investigator to find me. Of course this was only after he found out your stories about my death were convenient lies. He's in Bermuda, but then you knew that, didn't you? You must have been in a panic when I said we were booked to go there. You knew then, didn't you?"

"Anything I did, I did for your own good. He was a horrible man."

"A gold digger," his grandmother added. "He tried to trap your mother into a marriage that would have ruined her. He was a hippy, a wastrel and a drug abuser. Is that what you want in a father? Graham was the kind of man who was there for you—"

"Even though I wasn't his? How noble."

"David Eric Laine. You know very well your father loves you."

He ignored her protests. "Where did you meet this hippy, mother? Somehow I can't imagine one of them would dare to show his face around here." David studied his grandmother's face. He narrowed his eyes and swung back to face his mother. "It must have been one hell of a mistake."

"What do you mean? You can't possibly know anything—"

"I know you. You're an uptight bitch who never gave in to a physical impulse in your life."

"You can't talk to me like that!"

His grandmother snipped, "Just because you rule your life with animal lust doesn't mean civilized people do."

"Well I'm not the product of Immaculate Conception, even you can't claim that," David said.

"Don't blaspheme," his mother said, but it sounded more like rote. She averted her eyes.

The awkward silence was broken by a chilly voice that David

almost didn't recognize. "Well, are you finally going to tell him, Barbara?"

They all turned at Graham's entrance. The easygoing man David had always known was gone.

David's mother didn't seem happy at the interruption. Her mouth thinned and she didn't look at anyone in the room. "Graham, I thought we'd agreed to let me talk to him."

"Except you won't, will you?" Graham's eyes flicked over his mother-in-law. "If the both of you had been honest from the beginning, none of this would have happened."

"We did it to protect—"

"Who, Barbara? The way I see it, the only one you protected was yourself, and your mother."

"That's hardly fair, Graham," David's grandmother said, drawing herself up in outrage.

"How about we stop talking like I'm not in the room." David felt his blood pressure rise. He clamped his mouth shut to keep from saying the words he wanted to let loose.

Husband and wife stared at each other across the tiled floor. Finally Barbara spoke to David, "If you must know, I made a mistake when I was young and foolish and…and impetuous. I let my head be turned by a charming, but empty, man."

"Where'd you meet this 'empty man'? At university? You're a Willerton, of course you went. Some East Coast debutante college no less, I'm sure." He glanced at his stepfather, then looked away. He didn't want to see the distress in his eyes.

"No." His mother took great pains not to look at anyone. "I didn't meet him at Bryn Mawr." Graham looked at his mother-in-law. The look on both their faces said, "Don't go there." For the first time since he'd known her, David's mother ignored her own mother.

"Woodstock," she finally said.

David wasn't sure he had heard her right. "Woodstock. *You* were at Woodstock?"

"She ran away from home," his grandmother said icily. "In a moment of pique she nearly threw away a lifetime of promise."

David swore under his breath. His stepfather sighed and sank into a chair at the kitchen table. He gestured for David to join him but David ignored the invitation.

"There's no need for that kind of language," his grandmother snapped. "Whatever you have become, you are still a Willerton."

"Is that what you told my mother when she came back, knocked up? That she was still a Willerton?"

"Barbara knew her place."

"I'm sure," he said. "Under your thumb." David turned his back on her and spoke to his mother. "You met this man, this Joel Cameron, at Woodstock. What was he doing there?"

"Joey, he called himself Joey. He was attending school. Apparently it's common for Bermudians to travel overseas to get an education. He took time off school to go to Woodstock. It was the biggest thing of the time."

"So I've heard," David said. Try as he might he could not see his mother as a flower child dancing through Max Yasgur's muddy pasture, long hair full of flowers, barefoot and...sexually free? Doing it with total strangers. His mother?

"Sex, drugs and rock n' roll," he muttered. "What happened to him? Did he abandon you once he found out you had a little Joel Cameron in the oven?"

His mother winced at the crude words. "No," she whispered. "It wasn't like that. We finally got out of the festival and I followed him..."

"Followed him where?" Although David already knew. His birth certificate said it all; the birth certificate that didn't list a father's name.

"Were you planning from the beginning to lie to us both? Is that why you wrote my father out of my existence before I was even born?"

"N-no." For the first time in his life David saw his mother

confused.

"Son," Graham said. "Is this really necessary—"

"You tell me. You try finding out everything you believed in was a lie. So Mother." He swung back to face her. "How did you manage to forget to include my father's name on my birth certificate?"

"I can't—"

"Tell him, Barbara," Graham said. "I think the time for lies has past."

"You weren't born in a hospital. We had no money... a woman we met was a mid-wife, but it wasn't legal to use them back then, so I said it was a premature home birth." She ducked her head, a line of sweat on her upper lip. "Afterward, I never added your father's name. It was an oversight—"

"Bullshit."

"Don't talk to her that way!" his grandmother snapped.

"Nanna, stay out of this," Graham said. "Maybe if you had minded your own business back then, it wouldn't have come to this."

"He has no right to speak to his mother that way."

"Why? Only you can?" David studied his mother's face, noting how pale it was. Any pity he might have felt was dispelled by the knowledge of how thoroughly she had messed with his life, as well as his real father's. "So, you followed your new boy toy to San Francisco and dumped me in a pot pad like a litter of unwanted kittens. Don't tell me, Haight-Ashbury, right?"

His mother darted a quick glance at his grandmother and raised her chin. "Yes, but you were never 'dumped.'"

"Despite your lousy mothering skills, you've actually managed to impress me. You had the balls to leave this." He pointedly looked around the modern and very expensive kitchen, then looked at his grandmother. "To leave her. Too bad you didn't have the guts to stay away. Instead, you let her suck you back in."

"I was there for her when your deadbeat father grew feathers and flew the coop." His grandmother stiffened. "Would you rather have grown up on the filthy streets of that disgusting city?"

"A cage is always preferable to the streets. Isn't that what being a Willerton is all about? A gilded cage?"

"You were never in a cage! You were protected and I might even say cosseted."

He noticed she never used the word love. He suspected that word wasn't part of her vocabulary. "I gave up trying to make you happy when I was ten," he said. "It took me nearly another decade before I managed to escape with my balls intact."

"Is that why you chose such a loathsome job? Associating with the lowest dregs of society, murderers and rapists?" Her gaze scanned his face, which he knew still bore the remnants of the bruises from his latest altercation. "It's no wonder you became a degenerate, living with that androgynous faggot. You could have been a lawyer. You could have been anything!"

David had never felt more like hitting a woman in his life. He clenched his hands into fists, digging his fingernails into his palms to drive the urge away. He could feel the blood pumping through his forehead. His jaws tightened. "I'm going to ignore that remark. But hear this, you will never mention Chris again, or I won't be responsible for what I do."

"You dare threaten me?" His grandmother roared. "You disgusting pervert—"

David turned away from her. Standing up, he stared through the screened-in porch's windows toward the lake. He spotted Chris standing on the shore, tossing stones into the unruffled surface. Even from this distance his heart ached with love at the sight of Chris's trim body. How dare this woman try to sully that.

"David, please," his mother wheedled. God she never gave up.

He spun around and shouted, "I'm tired of your lies. You had the gall to tell my own father that I was dead! You told me he was dead. How dare you!"

"We dared because we cared. How can I make you understand that?"

"I've seen how much you cared. I disgust you, isn't that what you've told me I don't know how many times? Trust me, the feeling is mutual."

"David!"

"Shut up!"

Both women recoiled. His grandmother put her hand on his mother's arm. Graham stood up.

"I think you two should leave," Graham said softly to the two women. "This has gone far enough."

David could tell his grandmother wanted to argue, but his mother's grip on her arm tightened. Finally they both turned away. "You're right. This conservation is a waste of time. Leave him, if that's what he wants."

"Yes, Nanna," his mother said meekly, once again giving up the argument without a whimper of protest. He wondered how long it had taken his grandmother to whip the fight out of her. She never looked back as she followed her mother out of the kitchen. The room seemed larger without them.

Wearily David met Graham's troubled gaze. Neither one of them spoke for nearly a minute. Then Graham sighed and massaged the back of his neck. "What will you do now?"

"Go to Bermuda. Meet my father. After that… I don't know."

"Maybe once your business is taken care of you could stop back here. I'll talk to your mother. We can make this okay."

"I don't know, Dad."

"We're family, David. No matter how badly your mother's behaved, she never meant to hurt you. That might be hard to believe right now, but it's true."

David knew his stepfather meant well, but it was all too much to swallow just now. Bitter bile filled the back of his throat. "We'll talk later, okay?"

He left, making his way out to the deck. He took a deep breath, filling his lungs with clean air and washing away the poisonous fatigue in his blood. Chris was still down by the waterfront. David picked his way downhill and came up behind his husband. He leaned over and planted his mouth on Chris's neck, warm from the sun. He pressed his hips against his favorite playground.

Chris jumped. He spun around and grabbed David's arms. "Jesus, you scared me."

"You've got bad nerves." David still held him close.

Chris took one look at his face and tightened his hold on David's arms. "What happened?"

"Let's talk about it later."

"No, I want to know. What happened?"

"I finally realized how much time I've wasted hiding from everyone, pretending I was something I'm not."

He could tell Chris wasn't entirely convinced. He wrapped his arms around Chris, who melted into him.

"You want to see my tree house?" David asked.

"Is that anything like 'come up to see my etchings'? That's a horrible pick-up line."

David's hands roamed over Chris's back, feeling the muscles flex and shiver under his touch. He needed to get away from the toxic atmosphere of his parents' house. He wasn't going to let Chris be poisoned by it, too.

"Later we can take a ride. I've got candy."

"Now that's better." Chris licked his lips. "Will you be bad?"

David kissed him then set him away. "As bad as you want."

Chris grabbed his hand. "Come on; show me your tree house. I'm still trying to imagine you as a little boy all covered in scratches and mud, playing cowboys and Indians in the woods. Did you have a dog?"

"Of course. What self-respecting American kid didn't have one? His name was Butch."

Chris and David exchanged glances then they both burst out laughing.

"Now if that isn't prophetic, I don't know what is. Now, where is this place? You can tell me how it all went down with your mother."

"I don't know, Chris—"

"Don't you dare," Chris dropped his bantering and swung around to face David. "Don't you dare cut me out again. I won't stand for it. What did your mother say?"

"That she only did it to protect me. They were convinced my father was only after my mother's money. But you'll never guess where they met."

Chris studied David's face as though he might see the answer there. "I give up. Where?"

"Woodstock."

"You mean *the* Woodstock? Flower power and all that shit?"

"All that shit. It was as close as my mother ever got to rebelling, I guess. She escaped long enough to get knocked up and wound up in Haight-Ashbury with my father."

Chris plucked a stick off the forest floor. All around them the quiet gloom of the old forest pressed in on them. David heard the whine of nearby cicadas.

"I never would have seen that coming," Chris said. "She got messed up with some hippy?"

"I get the feeling *she* was a hippy for a while."

"So what happened?"

"My grandmother, what do you think?"

"That must have steamed her puritanical ass."

David forced a smile. "I dare say."

"You get the feeling there's more going on here than anyone's admitting?" Chris stripped the buds off the small twig, littering the forest floor. A blue jay screamed at them from overhead.

The rich loamy smell under David's feet brought back sharp memories of a carefree childhood before the discovery came of just how different he was. A freak. Worse, a degenerate. He had fought the feelings for years, until he couldn't fight them anymore. And with the surrender came the shame. What was wrong with him? How could he make it right? Only to realize that it would never be right.

Chris planted himself in front of him. "So talk to me. Was it as bad as you thought it would be?"

David sighed. "Yes," he said. "And no. I never expected the whole rebellion thing. I still can't imagine my mother ever doing anything my grandmother didn't approve of. I can't help but wonder what things would have been like if she'd told Nanna to go to hell."

"Fireworks, I'm sure."

"You don't cross Nanna and come out unscathed. She leaves claw marks. A lesson we all learned years ago."

"Jesus, now I'm feeling sorry for your mother."

"Don't. She was a coward. It was easier to give in than defy her own mother. That was her choice. No one else's. She's damn lucky the woman approved of Graham as suitable. He's probably the only good thing she ever did."

They entered a small clearing in the woodlot. David could hear the whisper of nearby flowing water. A dragonfly zipped through the air past him and a gnarled willow tree dwarfed everything around it.

David pointed up into the tangled strands of whip-like branches. "There."

Chris peered up. "Where? I don't—oh there it is." He studied the sturdy-looking planks that formed a platform nearly ten feet off the ground. Several rungs had been nailed into the tree trunk as a ladder. Where once there had been pristine wood, moss now grew on the warped boards.

Chris reached up to touch one. "Think you could still climb it?"

"I'm not feeling all that suicidal."

"Oh, come on, where's your spirit of adventure?" Chris turned dancing eyes on his husband. "We could play pirate treasure. You can be the dashing sea captain who sweeps his cabin boy off his feet."

"Like you've ever been anybody's boy."

Chris got closer, his breath warm on David's cheek. "I could be yours."

Then before David could stop him, Chris had scrambled up to the platform. He leaned over the edge and peered down at David. His grin was infectious. "Coming?"

"You're crazy," David said, once he had pulled himself up after Chris.

"And you love every minute of it."

Chris lay back on the platform, one knee bent, his hands behind his head. All he needed was a stalk of grass between his teeth to complete the picture of a golden hayseed. A hayseed who was altogether too sexy. David slid down beside him.

"So what do we do now?" Chris asked, rolling over onto his side to face David. He traced David's inner thigh with his fingers, feathering lightly over David's swelling basket.

David tried to ignore his growing erection. He stared up at the treetops. Sunlight danced through swaying branches, concealing then revealing the cloud-flecked deep blue sky. Lengthening shadows threw the tree house into shadow. "We try to get down from here without breaking anything."

"I meant now that we know the whole story."

"But do we?" David finally turned his lantern gaze on Chris. "We have one side of a pretty complicated story. That's not everything."

"Then we go get the other half." Chris began stroking him in earnest. Before David could object he slid the zipper of his jeans down, bent over and tasted him. David completely lost his train of thought.

After, Chris sat up, a smug smile on his lips. "Oh, Captain. My captain."

"You are so full of it," David said, but he was laughing when he said it.

"Yes, I am."

They lazed on the platform for the rest of the afternoon, half dozing at one point, only to wake and make love again. When they finally exited the woodlot onto Valley Stream Road the sun was setting over the lake. They walked down the road to his parents' place holding hands, not caring who might see them. Only when they drew near the house did David drop his hand and make it clear there would be no more touching.

Graham's car was in the driveway. They found him on the deck, drinking a Pig's Ear. He waved them over and pointed at a cooler beside his Adirondack chair. "Help yourselves. And if you're hungry, there's some roast beef left and some fresh bread I picked up in town."

They both cracked a beer open.

"What did you do today?"

"Went for a walk around the property," David said. He traded a warm glance with Chris. "Did you know that old tree fort is still there?"

"Hmph, haven't thought of that thing in years. I remember when you practically lived in it one summer."

David remembered that too. That was the summer he had realized he was attracted to the other boys at school, and not the girls, like all his buddies. It had scared him spitless.

"You should have told me." David reached over and took Chris's hand in his, taking comfort in the familiar touch.

Graham ducked his head. "It seemed easier than the fuss that would surely have followed. I'm sorry, son. That's a pretty poor excuse for years of lies…"

David didn't want to, but he understood. His mother and grandmother were like the force of an ocean riptide, inexorable.

Unstoppable. Graham could no more stand in their way than he himself could have all those years ago. He'd had the option of leaving, something he knew Graham would never do.

"I have to go find out for myself. I hope you understand that."

Graham sighed. "Then I wish you luck. But don't turn your back on your family here. Your mother may not know how to show it, but she does love you. So do I."

David nodded, even if he didn't believe him. Not about his mother, at least. He had never doubted Graham's love. He raised his beer to his mouth. "Thanks. I appreciate that."

All three fell into a companionable silence. They watched the sun slide past the distant canopy of trees and the sky go from crimson to purple, to velvety black. The first stars came out. Soon the sky was ablaze with more stars than David had seen in years. In L.A. celestial stars were a rare event.

Beside him Chris yawned. David finished his beer and stood.

"I'm hungry. I'll make us some sandwiches." He reached for Chris's hand again. Together they said goodnight and went into the kitchen. Chris sat at the marble island while David prepared two sourdough sandwiches, slathering on the Dijon mustard he knew Chris adored. They ate standing up. Then they climbed the stairs to David's room. David shut the door and turned to face Chris.

Chris made a step toward the bathroom. "I need to get my pajamas."

David caught him and pulled him into an embrace, nuzzling his throat. "Why? It's not like I'm going to let you wear them. Come on, your captain needs you."

CHAPTER EIGHT

Sunday, 4:10am Valley Stream Road, Holderness, New Hampshire

Chris grabbed both suitcases off his unused bed. He set them on the floor and smoothed his hand over the down comforter. He'd never expected this leg of their trip to yield so many surprises. David was proving to have layers Chris had never experienced.

When Chris had first met and fallen in love with his big bear he had known that not only had David hidden his orientation from his fellow police officers, he hadn't been comfortable with public shows of affection, even within the gay community. Now that all seemed to be changing. He wasn't sure what had happened between David and his mother—he suspected it was a lot more than David would admit—but he knew it had been incandescent. And now David seemed to have decided he didn't have to hide his feelings.

It was still tentative, there was no guarantee that David wouldn't slam the closet door shut again, but for now Chris was overjoyed. He loved David and it wasn't always easy withholding his desire to show his feelings to the man he loved. He began to think that even if David left the LAPD, it would be okay. They would make it, no matter what.

David entered the room. He looked spiffy in a Madras shirt and stonewashed cargo shorts. Chris admired his muscular legs covered with thick black hair.

"Ready?"

Chris hefted both bags. "All set."

"You want to grab breakfast?"

"Let's wait till we're on the road," Chris said, not admitting how eager he was to leave. "Maybe we can get a bite on the way."

"Suits me."

David popped the trunk open and they piled their luggage inside. Then he closed it with a loud thunk. They both turned to find Graham on the front veranda. He trotted down the steps and held out his hand.

"I'm glad you came, no matter what happened. As far as I'm concerned you're always welcome here. Both of you."

They shook hands all around. David made no comment on his mother's conspicuous absence.

"Let me know how it goes in Bermuda."

"Sure, I'll give you a call."

David slid behind the wheel of the rental car. Chris met Graham's gaze.

"Thank you," he said. "It means a lot to him."

"Well you two take care. Especially you. Take care of him, Chris."

"I will."

David patted his knee when Chris climbed into the passenger seat.

"You ready for this?"

"Yeah, I think so. You?"

"Nervous."

Chris popped a Red Hot Chili Peppers CD into the player. Soon the voice of Anthony Kiedis singing *Californication* filled the small space.

They stopped at a roadside greasy-spoon where Chris loaded up on carbs in the form of a massive pile of Belgian waffles, whipped cream and strawberries. David selected a more modest breakfast of a cheddar cheese omelet and buttered toast. They both indulged in several cups of coffee.

They arrived at the airport a good two hours before their flight. It was still dark outside, though the first faint blush of dawn painted the eastern horizon pink. They checked their baggage and got their boarding passes. Chris bought a gossip magazine while David picked up a new Robert Sawyer science fiction novel he'd heard about. Finally they boarded.

The gossip rag forgotten in his lap, Chris dozed off shortly after takeoff. David shook him awake when the pilot announced they were descending into the Bermuda International Airport. Through the tiny window they watched the island grow and evolve into a series of bays and runways. Grabbing their carry-ons, they waited in line to deplane.

The humidity smacked them like a wet towel the minute they hit the stairs leading to a shimmering tarmac. As one, the passengers hurried through the arrivals door. Once inside, cool air washed over them. A steel drum band greeted them in the corridor playing some sprightly island music. It was a vast improvement over the elevator muzak most public airports played. They collected their bags and went through customs quickly. Outside they found a line of taxis, mostly small vans, waiting by the curb. A thickset black man approached them. "Taxi, mon?"

The man had a slight accent, not musical like Jamaican, but with a touch of British formality, much like David's father had sounded on the phone. David gave their destination, a guest house called Aunt Nea's in St. George's. The cabbie loaded their luggage in the back of the van and David and Chris climbed into the vehicle.

The cab wasn't air-conditioned. Instead, most of the windows were open, letting a scented breeze in. They left the airport and took a roundabout north-east onto a roadway that followed a curving azure inlet.

The road was hemmed in by dense tropical plants on one side and open field on the other. Jewel-colored stucco houses appeared on both sides. Palms, banana plants, an explosion of hibiscus and carpets of climbing morning glories caught the early morning sun. As they entered St. George's they saw a cruise ship, the *Norwegian Majesty*, at dock. On the road in front of it, at a bus stop, a crowd of tourists clustered together, waiting. Traffic increased as they neared the center of town.

Chris was unnerved by the narrowness of the roads. The cab careened down pavement close enough to touch the buildings and dense greenery that crowded in on either side. Scooters by the dozen raced in and out of traffic, braving life and limb. Chris heard the cabbie mutter "kids" when one particularly daring soul nearly plowed into them as it passed a pink and blue bus coming in the other direction. It didn't help that there appeared to be no sidewalks or even curbs. Pedestrians seemed to be unwilling participants in a Death Race 2000 video.

"They always drive like maniacs here?" David asked.

The cabbie glanced back at them.

"They are always crazy. Nothing seems to teach them to slow down, not even the many accidents they have."

"How can you get around besides cabs?" Chris asked. "Can we rent our own car?"

"No, no car rentals. Only scooters."

Chris was intrigued. It might be fun to motor around the island on one of the noisy machines. David clearly didn't share his enthusiasm.

"What are gas prices like?" David asked.

The cabbie told him. Chris did the math in his head. Convert liters to gallons...Chris winced, over eight dollars a gallon. "Good thing we won't be driving." It had to be three times what it was in California. "And we thought we were being gouged."

Ship masts appeared ahead of them. Further down, another massive, white cruise ship lay at dock.

"Lot of cruise ships come in?" David asked.

"All summer long. They come in here, out at the Dockyards and in Hamilton. Ah, we are here."

The cabbie pulled off the main road, eventually turning into a narrow alley, through a gate, passing a white stucco wall. The driveway was lined with palmettos, tall, elegant cypress and hibiscus. The cabbie collected his fare and helped them unload their luggage. David grabbed the two largest, leaving Chris to pick up the smallest of the three. He slung his laptop over his shoulder. They passed through an odd structure that looked like a hobbit hole and rapped on the wooden door with a warm *Welcome* sign. A middle-aged woman checked them in and directed them upstairs to their room.

"This is our Jasmine room." There was a queen-size sleigh bed with a flowered duvet; the kitchen was fully equipped, right down to the coffee maker. Just through the French doors Chris could see a veranda overlooking St. George's harbor. There was black wicker deck furniture and a glass table. "We're not exactly facing west," she said. "But you'll get a spectacular view of the sunset. If you prefer to make your own meals, you can pick up groceries just down at the market on Duke of York Street. There's a ferry dock near King's Square, on Ordnance Island. It's about a forty minute trip into Hamilton. That's where you'll find the bulk of better restaurants. I have a few brochures from some of them. I'm afraid we don't serve food on the premises."

"What about liquor?" Chris asked. "Beer?"

"You can buy it at the market, over on York, or there's a liquor store across from our place. You can't buy on Sunday. Almost everything's closed Sunday. Do you attend church?"

Chris stammered, "No."

"You'd be welcomed at ours, or there's a lovely Anglican church in Hamilton. It's very beautiful. An historical landmark."

They paused in the kitchen. It held a round tiled table and four comfortable looking chairs.

"I've got several brochures and maps of the island in the office." She continued on, clearly proud of her hotel and eager to share its history. She offered them a genuine smile. "They'll let you know what's available this time of year. It's our busy season, so you might want to call for availability. But there's lots to see— St. George's is a UNESCO heritage site. Let me know if there's anything I can do to make your stay an enjoyable one."

They thanked her and she handed over the keys. Chris closed and locked the door. He found David in the bedroom. They unpacked their clothes and put everything away. Chris bounced on the queen mattress under David's amused eyes. He grinned. "It'll do."

"Glad you approve. What do you want to do first?"

"Well, first things first." He pulled his laptop out of the case and set it up on the kitchen table. "They said this place was wired. Let's see how true that is."

It took him several seconds but soon he was online and pulled up his webmail program. It didn't take him long to figure out there wasn't anything he needed to do. Becky was taking care of business. He sent a quick "we're here" email to both Becky and Des before shutting down the laptop.

They changed out of their traveling clothes and walked down the road to the wharf. Chris had brought along his digital camera and started shooting the minute they left their room.

"You putting together a photo journal?"

"No sense going on a tropical vacation if you can't make everyone at home jealous."

Once on Duke of York Street they strolled east, stopping at Sushi Tei where they got a box order for some octopus, ahi and mushroom rolls. They carried the food out to King Square. Sitting at a wrought iron bench they watched the other tourists. A horse-drawn carriage plodded by carrying six sightseers. A ferry came in to the dock on Ordnance Island, disgorging a small crowd and taking on a new one.

They ended the meal with a mug of ale in the White Horse Tavern, overlooking the harbor where gulls and sparrows fought for scraps tossed by tourists.

Back on the street they made their way to the market, where they loaded up on staples, including two steaks. David also picked up a six pack of Bud and Chris chose a couple of bottles of South

African varietals.

Back at Aunt Nea's they put the groceries away, got drinks and headed out to the veranda. The sun was sinking behind a bank of clouds, staining them pink and purple. The color deepened and lights began to come on across the water, where their hostess said St. David's lay. The *Norwegian Majesty* lit up like a giant floating Christmas decoration.

Chris flipped through a couple of brochures he had picked up from the front desk.

"They're called moon gates," he said out of the blue. At David's puzzled look he added, "Those weird round hobbit holey things. They're Chinese. Supposed to be good luck for newlyweds to pass through them. Think we've been married too long to take advantage?"

"What? We need good luck?"

Chris grinned. "Nah, how could it get any better?" He kept browsing the brochures. "Says there's something called Harbor Nights every Wednesday over in Hamilton."

They were supposed to meet Joel Cameron tomorrow afternoon somewhere in a parish called Devonshire. Joel worked until noon. Bermuda was divided into nine parishes. They were in St. George's, David's father lived in Devonshire.

"How long do you think it will take us to get there?" Chris asked.

David consulted his map. "Depends on traffic, I guess. We should call a taxi to be here by noon."

David grilled the steaks and Chris dished up the salad. Before supper he checked for any urgent emails, knowing Becky would handle anything that came up, but reluctant to keep clear of business entirely. They ate on the deck watching the final remnants of the sunset.

As though by mutual agreement they ignored the gorilla in the room and neither one of them spoke of the impending meeting tomorrow. They were still too wound up over their visit with

David's mother, and both wanted a break from the tension. David went to work on a crossword puzzle, since there were no American sports on TV, and Chris did some more surfing.

Afterward they moved back inside. The local news mentioned a growing tropical storm that was showing up on the radar off the coast of Africa. By eleven they were both yawning. Piling the dishes into the sink they crawled into bed. Both were asleep within minutes.

For breakfast they had picked up the fixings for omelets. While Chris chopped up the onion, David mixed the eggs and grated New Zealand cheddar. Again they ate on the veranda and studied the *Norwegian Majesty* as it left the dock. Chris watched it go with a dreamy expression.

"Why have we never taken a cruise?"

"Don't know," David said. "The subject never came up? We're already on a vacation, let's enjoy this one before we start planning another."

After breakfast they both showered and dressed with care. Even David went through a couple of changes of clothes before he selected a conservative gray suit complete with hand-painted silk tie. He kept checking himself out in the bathroom mirror until Chris planted himself in front of him.

"Enough already," Chris said. "You look great. You're worse than I am."

Two minutes before nine, David grabbed the phone and called for a cab. David locked the door behind them and they waited in the garden. Chris sat down on a wrought iron bench and went through his BlackBerry, checking out his email. David couldn't sit, instead he nervously paced the length of the sidewalk and back. Chris almost told him to sit down, but he knew the words would be wasted. David wouldn't relax until this was over.

It was a relief when the cab turned into the lane. David gave the driver their destination and they drove through the gates onto Nea's Alley then onto the Duke of York Street and back toward the airport.

Between St. George's, the airport island, and the main island was a low stone bridge that the cabbie called the Causeway. Chris stared out of the van window at the shallow, reef covered shoals. Water seemed to lap right at the base of the road, while gulls dipped and cavorted in a cloudless blue sky.

Chris spotted a market on North Shore Road and asked the cabbie to stop. He hurried in to grab a bottle of wine for David's father. For all he knew, the guy didn't drink wine, but he felt safer giving it as a gift than anything else. Even if rum was the national drink, he wouldn't know good rum from swill.

Nearer to Hamilton they turned off North Shore Road and onto Middle Road, passing a sign that said Devonshire Parish. Chris reached between them and gripped David's hand. He saw David glance toward the cabbie, but once he saw the man wasn't paying any attention he half smiled.

"It's going to be okay," he said when David glanced over at him.

David squeezed his hand back, but said nothing.

CHAPTER NINE

College Hill Road was a short cul-de-sac hemmed in by towering ficus, palmettos and hibiscus. The house the cab pulled up to was set back on a spacious, sloping lawn behind a low stone fence. A small, graven plaque outside on the lawn said Rose Grotto. Chris had noticed similar signs along the roads in front of stately mansions and tiny cottages. This particular house was a two-story butter-yellow house made of the ubiquitous plastered walls with hunter green shutters and a wooden door set into a stone lintel. The windows were simple mullioned stone under a fake portcullis. Like all the roofs Chris had seen so far, the roof was made of sloping white tile. An open terrace ran along the front of the house, partially screened from the street by several burgeoning plant hangers in varying states of bloom. A half a dozen chairs and an ancient barbecue filled the small space. Cracked pavement led to a shaded lean-to just big enough to store a dusty Toyota pickup. The truck was full of gardening equipment: a lawn mower, tiller and several obviously well-used hand implements.

A pair of bluebird houses were set amid a cluster of hibiscus bushes. A pale gray cat strolled across the lawn, ignoring them completely. David paid the driver and they climbed out. The yard was full of carefully tended flower beds that were in full bloom. Scents of a dozen flowers, fresh earth and some unique smell under it all. Chris didn't recognize most of the plants, though he did spot some roses along the west side of the house. He thought he saw some nearly ripe bananas and a knobby gray-barked tree covered with large white and yellow blossoms.

The front door opened and a tall, light-skinned black man stepped out onto the terrace. Chris and David traded glances, then David stepped forward. "I'm David Laine, I'm supposed to meet Joel, ah, Joey Cameron—"

"David!" The man hurried down the stone step and held out both hands. "I'm so glad you came. My goodness, son, don't you look handsome."

"Mr. Cameron?"

"Please, son, that's too formal."

There was an awkward silence. What did Joel expect David to call him? Certainly not 'Dad.' David chose to ignore the issue. Instead he said, "I'm, ah, pleased to meet you."

"No, no, the pleasure's mine. You have no idea how happy I am that you accepted my invitation." He glanced at Chris. "Christopher?"

"Yes, this is Chris."

Chris held out his hand. "We talked on the phone." He was good at schmoozing with people he didn't know. Being a freelance IT consultant required it. "Pleased to meet you, sir. Beautiful house you have. And I love Bermuda."

"Joey, both of you, call me Joey."

"I stopped in to see Mother," David said.

Joel seemed taken back. "Is she well?"

"I guess." Chris knew David was being reticent. He didn't believe in airing dirty laundry.

"Come, you and Chris must be tired from all that traveling." Joel led them up to the terrace. "Let me make you a rum swizzle. It be the Bermudian national drink."

He pronounced it Bermujan.

Unsure of what to do, David climbed the steps to the veranda and took one of the chairs. Chris slid into one beside him and handed over the bottle of wine. Joel thanked him and disappeared into the house. Chris leaned toward David. "My God he looks just like you. Except he's… er…"

"What? Black?" David said "It explains a lot."

"How's that?"

"My grandmother's hostility." He frowned and ran nervous fingers through his thick hair. "She would have hated that. I'm kind of surprised at my mother, too."

"She wanted to take a walk on the wild side," Chris said. "When your mother rebels, she doesn't do anything half measure. Kind of reminds me of someone I know."

"Come on," David protested. "When have I ever done something that crazy?"

Chris just gave him a look and David thought it over for a minute. "Oh, right. I guess some people might think falling in love with you was over the top."

"Yeah, just ask Martinez."

"Thanks, I'd rather not re-open that can of worms." He shrugged. David had to admit that had been awkward. For a while, when he had first come out, he had thought he was going to lose his partner. "He came around in the end."

Joel returned with three highball glasses, handing them to Chris and David. "Rum swizzles."

Chris sipped the drink. It was cool and sweet, tasting of pineapple and lime juice. Beside him David still seemed tense.

"Please," Joel said when he returned. "You must tell me all about yourself. What have you been doing all these years?"

"Believing you were dead."

"What? I don't understand—"

"My mother told me you died in Vietnam. She never even mentioned you weren't American." Or black, but he kept that thought to himself. "She was ashamed of both of us."

"I can't believe she was ashamed of you—" Joel stared down at his drink. "Your mother was very confused, but she was a good woman at heart. I do not believe she was ever ashamed of you. When you were born I have never seen a happier woman. I had hoped to marry her… Then when she told me you had died,

I was devastated. I'm sorry she thought it was necessary to lie to you."

Talk of marriage must have gone over good with David's grandmother. No wonder she had put the kibosh on it and sent Joel packing. "And what about you, she lied to you, too."

Joel leaned forward in his chair, the metal frame creaking. "Please, David. I know these last few days have been terrible for you. All you thought was true has been turned upside down. But don't blame your mother. She was only trying to do right by you—"

David abruptly stood, nearly sending his chair tumbling. "If I hear one more time that everything was done for my own good..." David let it trail off. He stood over his father. "Tell me how you found me, since you thought I was dead."

Joel grimaced at the coolness in David's voice, but he remained calm as he replied, "It was purely an accident. The son of a friend of mine was attending Stanford University as a medical student last year."

Chris perked up at that. Last year David had investigated a human trafficking ring and killed the man who ran it. He had also very nearly had an affair with another cop. Chris had a sinking feeling he knew where Joel was going with this. He had always hoped those days could be left behind them.

"The boy apparently was following a story in Los Angeles and he came across a *Los Angeles Times* story on it. He couldn't believe it. He called his father up and said one of the officers involved looked exactly like me."

David grunted. White lines around his mouth revealed his tension.

"He forgot about it until he returned to Bermuda and found the article in his school baggage. He showed the article to his father, who brought it over one day, laughing over how much this detective looked like me. He joked about you being my love child." Joel twisted a plain gold band on his finger. "When I saw you, I wasn't laughing. I knew then. I knew you were alive."

More repercussions of that terrible time. Chris couldn't help but wonder whether this one would be good or bad.

"I had to find you then," Joel said. "Even if you were angry and would never forgive me, I had to see you face to face. You have no idea—"

A tall, chunky black man, several years younger than David, stepped out of the house chewing on a carrot stick. He bore enough of a resemblance to David to send a shudder through Chris. He stared. The other man noticed the stare and glared back.

"Who are you?" he asked.

"Jay, these are the ones I told you about," Joel said. His voice was firm and strong. There was no shame in him.

Chris couldn't help but admire the man. Not many could go through the onerous job of explaining a bastard son to his legitimate children. Chris wondered if there was a Mrs. Cameron in the picture and what she thought of her husband's youthful peccadilloes. Even under the glare of his son Joel remained unruffled. David showed more agitation.

"This is David," Joel went on. "Your half-brother from the mainland. And this is Jayvyn, my eldest son. Well, after you, of course."

"You actually came." Jay glowered at David then turned his hostile gaze to Chris, raking his slender form with a sweeping glance. "Who is this?"

"This is Chris," David said, moving closer in a protective stance. Chris half expected him to put his arm around his shoulder. He was definitely staking his claim. Totally unlike the David of old. "My partner."

Chris noticed he didn't say husband. He lowered his gaze and stared at the drink in his hand.

Jay's mouth dropped open. "My God," he said. "My brother be backin' up? That's fat."

"Jay! Weren't you supposed to be doing some work out at the

Pearman place?"

"They out. I come to get some greeze." Suddenly Jay glared at his father. "Why'd you call him? Why he be here? I told you I don't need any help from you or anyone!"

"Jay!"

Jay threw one last dirty look at Chris and David then stomped into the house. They could hear him banging around in what was presumably the kitchen.

"I'm sorry about that," Joel said. "He's angry because I told him I wanted to get in touch with you. I couldn't believe it when I found out you were alive. I'm afraid he's not used to coming second in anything."

Chris wanted to say that Jay wasn't angry over any perceived slight, he was flat out homophobic.

"If you loved my mother so much and you knew she was pregnant, why did you leave us?" David asked, the anguish in his voice only apparent to Chris.

"It wasn't like that—" Joel sighed. "I didn't leave until after you were born and it was never my idea."

"My mother's?"

Joel ducked his head. Chris could have sworn he was embarrassed. "Not your mother. We were living in San Francisco, in a place called Haight-Ashbury—did you know that?"

"Yes, she told me."

"You got sick and I finally convinced her to take you to the free clinic. While you were gone, the police, ah, broke the door down." Joel wouldn't meet David's eyes. "You have to understand, it was the sixties, there were a lot of…drugs around the place. And anti-war memorabilia."

"You got busted," David said.

Chris knew David was not amused, but he couldn't help it, he thought it was funny. David's mother and this man smoking dope, dropping acid or speed, whatever it was they did in those days, chanting "Make love, not war" to gun-toting National Guardsmen.

"You got busted and they deported you?"

Joel nodded. "She refused to follow me, not that I blame her."

"You called her?"

Again he nodded. "Many times. At first she took the calls, but she refused to come and bring you. I told her a family should be together. Then her mother started taking my calls and refused to let me speak to Barbara again. The last time I telephoned, her mother told me Barbara was getting married and that you had contracted some childhood disease and passed. At the time I thought it strange that she would go ahead with a wedding in the face of such tragedy, but it never occurred to me that there had been no tragedy. She wouldn't tell me what illness either; now I know why. I was told never to call again. I never did. I thought you were gone… Now I am sorry for that."

"It just keeps getting better and better," David muttered. "God, they buried themselves deeper and deeper in a shitload of lies. Sorry…"

A high-pitched, metallic whine broke the stilted silence. They all looked up, startled when a small blue scooter roared out from behind the house and skidded onto College Hill Road in a cloud of dust and sand. Nearby a raucous yellow and brown bird raised its voice in protest from the flowering tree. It sounded like *qu'est-que-ce, qu'est-que-ce*. Joel saw him watching the colorful bird.

"Our kiskadee. Very noisy. Bad for the other birds."

David dismissed the ornithology lesson. "You still think my mother was only doing what was best for me? I could have had a father; you could have had a son."

"I tried to find out when the funeral would be, but your mother refused to talk to me. And once I feared you dead… It seemed pointless. But then I started wondering. I was ashamed at first, thinking I had been lied to, but I'm afraid I became a bit obsessed with the idea. Finally I had to know. I tried to call your mother again, but they had changed the number and I never knew her married name." Joel toyed with his half-empty high-ball glass. "When my friend showed me the picture of you in the *L.A. Times*, I still wasn't sure. Perhaps she had told you the truth and you didn't want to contact me. And I wasn't sure about hiring someone to find you. It was so expensive, and while I knew he'd have no trouble finding you, there was still no guarantee you would be glad to be found. But then I realized I had to know. I had to see you for myself."

Joel's bright eyes met David's. "How long have you been a detective in the Los Angeles Police Department?"

"Nineteen years on the job. Eleven as a detective."

"I confess I never would have expected Barbara's son to become a police officer."

"Don't tell me," David said. "You think I should have been a lawyer, too."

"What? No, police work is honorable. What is the motto of the Los Angeles police? To protect and serve? There is no more noble calling."

David blinked and a look came over his face that Chris had never seen before. Pride. An affirmation that what he did was something good.

Chris suddenly felt bad for the times he had all but nagged David to give his job up, to quit. Chris still lived in terror of David's job. He couldn't help it, every moment David was out of his sight, Chris imagined the worst. He knew why so many cops got divorced; their wives couldn't take it anymore.

"Are you a good policeman?" Joel asked.

"I like to think so," David muttered. He glanced at Chris and the pride was still there, along with something so simple it almost broke his heart. David was happy.

The door opened and a young girl stepped out. She was beautiful, with skin the color of sea-darkened sand. Waist-length black hair was tied back with a bright yellow scrunchy. She wore a matching yellow blouse and a knee length skirt. Gold earrings dangled from her earlobes. Her shrewd look took in the three men on the terrace. Chris could see her evaluating them, building niches to store them in. A knowing look dawned on her face.

Joel stood and put his arm around her shoulder. "My daughter, Imani. She's getting ready to go to Western University in Canada this fall. Honey, this is David, your half-brother and his partner, Chris."

She nodded. Chris was sure she had them pegged at once. Unlike her volatile brother, it didn't seem to faze her.

"Daddy's been so excited since he found you," her voice was liquid and far too sultry for a young woman. "I'm so glad you came to visit us."

"Sit, join us," Joel said. She obliged by taking a chair beside him. Her gaze never left David.

"You really do exist. We would sometimes tease dad that you were a figment of his imagination. That he only wished you to be. We thought he was wasting his money hiring that private detective."

Chris couldn't help but like her. Her laughter was a rich contralto and her voice was amazingly seductive, it even sent a few neurons firing along his synapses, though he hadn't looked at a woman in that way in years. She must be beating men off with sticks.

David seemed restless. He stood up, then sat down and drained his drink. Before Joel could offer to get him another one he bounced back to his feet. "Mind if I take a look at your garden?"

"Certainly." Joel puffed up in pride. His daughter laughed.

"Oh, now you've said the magic words. He'll bend your ear for hours. It's all Dad thinks about."

"David, too," Chris said. They were both grinning. Chris waved David off. "You go look at your flowers. I'm going to stay here in the shade and have another national cocktail. Or maybe two. I'm sure your little sister will be a good hostess." He winked at Imani.

As they walked away, Chris heard David ask about the roses that proliferated everywhere. "I wouldn't have thought they'd do so well here, no winter and so hot in the summer."

Chris watched the two of them round the corner of the house. He marveled at how much alike they were, not only in appearance, though that was strong, but in mannerisms.

He desperately hoped this would be good for David. After the fiasco of his mother the last thing he needed was more disappointment in his life.

"How long have you known David?" Imani asked.

"Nearly seven years," Chris said.

"You live together?"

"Over five years. We're married," he blurted out. Chris didn't get into the whole "how he met David" tale. It was too bizarre for someone not familiar with it through the intense media coverage they had endured at the time. "We were married a little over a year ago."

He watched her face for the inevitable disgust. He figured it was enough of a shock just to hear the word marry.

He could tell she was skirting the whole gay aspect of their relationship, while at the same time she was dying of curiosity. He'd run into that a lot with some straights. They were too liberal to admit they were secretly uneasy around gays, and were usually vocal in their support of live and let live, but underneath there was always a tinge of revulsion or fear.

Imani seemed to be missing that.

So he asked her, "Does that bother you?"

"No," she said softly. "Though I confess I don't understand. I know it's not popular on the islands."

"Sometimes it's not popular back home."

They watched David and his father reappear on the east side of the house. The pair crouched over another mass of roses growing up beside the house. Joel dug his hand into the black soil and showed it to David, talking all the time. Behind them was a tree bearing a crown of brilliant scarlet flowers.

Imani saw him looking. "A royal poinciana. My favorite tree."

Chris didn't recognize half the plants that filled flower beds and planters around the carefully manicured lawn. He had no doubt David would be able to rattle off every name and whether or not he could grow it back home.

"What's with the white roofs?" he asked. "All the houses have them. Heat reflection?"

"No, they're limestone. They act as water collectors. All the houses are built with cisterns underneath instead of… what do you call them…?"

"Basements? They don't have them much in L.A. either—earthquakes."

"Here drinkable water is rare. There is no fresh water outlets anywhere. All our water comes from the cisterns."

"What about the name, Rose Grotto? Is that Bermudian?"

"Actually it's British. They often name their homes and estates."

"Nice idea," Chris said, wondering what he would call his home if he had the chance to do that. The Haven? Or The Bowery, since it was such a nest for him and David?

He was dragged out of his romantic fantasy when another scooter, much like the one Jay had fled on, blasted up the driveway, stopping beside the terrace. David straightened when the rider undid the snap of his helmet and stood, still straddling the scooter. The young man, clearly Joel's son and David's half-brother, sneered at him.

"So you're the faggot pretending to be my father's son."

Monday, 11:15 am Rose Grotto, College Hill Road, Devonshire Parish, Bermuda

David stepped toward Chris. Joel put his hand on his arm, but David shook it off.

"Baker," Joel said. "This is David, your half-brother." Baker took off his helmet, shaking loose a thick mat of densely curled hair hanging down nearly to his shoulders. His eyes were dark and feral. They studied David then turned to rake over Chris's slender form.

"You even have the nerve to bring this pervert with you?" He spun around to glare at his father. "How could you welcome him here? Bad enough you invite him, but then you make him family. My family! You're as sick as he is."

"Baker! You will not talk that way. Where are your manners?"

"You're insane if you think I'll accept this…freak of nature as family."

"Why not," Imani rose to her full five-six height. "He's our father's son. Just like you and Jay. Just as I am his daughter. He was born into this family whether you like it or not!"

"You are too young to understand any of this, sistah. Stay out of it." Baker's voice was low and deadly. "Do you want to be labeled a pervert, too?"

"I don't care what anyone calls me. This is my brother and yours too, even if you can't see it."

Baker stepped off his scooter and balanced the helmet on the worn vinyl seat. He advanced on his father, while ignoring Chris and David.

"I need to borrow the truck. Got some greeze to bring home."

They were all silent while Joel pulled a set of car keys out of his pocket and handed them over. Without another word Baker climbed into the aging Toyota and skidded out of the driveway.

"I am sorry, David—"

"Don't." David held up his hand. "I'm used to it."

He glanced at Chris when he spoke and Chris knew he was lying. You never got used to it.

"I don't believe it," Imani snapped. "How could you get used to that?"

"You don't," Chris said softly, ignoring the quelling look David shot him. "Well, it's true."

"You're young," Joel said. "Only the young can be so innocent."

"Oh, Daddy, I'm not a child."

"But you are, sweetheart. Young and good."

Imani rolled her eyes. "I swear you still think I'm five years old."

Joel's return smile was lopsided. "It's the price of being a father. Your children never really grow up." His gaze met David's and he sighed. "I am so sorry I was not there when you grew up. I can't help but see you must have been a wonderful boy."

Chris couldn't believe it. David actually blushed.

Joel gestured toward the door. "It's getting hot. We'll be more comfortable inside."

He was right. The dimly lit living room was cool and smelled faintly of coffee and lemon verbena. A large crystal vase of anthuriums took center place on a large, exotically grained dining room table. Chris was immediately drawn to the elegant furniture.

Joel saw his interest. "My great-grandfather fashioned that out of Bermuda cedar, before the blight nearly wiped them out."

"It's beautiful," Chris said. He ran his hand over the smooth surface, marveling at the burls and whorls that were practically alive. The piece had obviously been well cared for if it was as old as Joel implied. It would have taken days, if not weeks, to hone to perfection. He immediately wanted to know where he could get one.

"I know a fine local artist who works in cedar," Joel said. "But I warn you, he is expensive."

David visibly winced; Chris smiled, but didn't back down. He didn't bother hiding his excitement. "Oh, I'd love to meet him."

To a bemused Joel, David muttered, "Can you set up something?"

"I'll call him at once." He left the room and they could hear him on the phone.

David sighed. He met Chris's gaze. "This is going to be an expensive trip, isn't it?"

Chris shrugged.

"Well, it's your money," David said.

Chris knew it was a sore point with David. But between his grandmother's indulgence in leaving nearly everything she owned—including her Silverlake home—to him, and his own growing business, Chris had a tidy nest egg. None of which David could compete with. It had been the source of a lot of tension early in their relationship. Chris was stubborn; he wouldn't accept David's advice on money matters, or alter what David saw as his profligate habits, though he had no problem letting David run the household finances. He happily handed over his half of income and never asked about the details. They compromised: Chris spent what he wanted and David ground his teeth.

Joel came back into the living room. "If you want we can go see him this afternoon. He said he has some new pieces he hasn't put up for sale yet. If you'd like we could have lunch first, then I'll take you to see Mr. Trotter."

"Do you have someplace in mind?" David asked. "Where is this sculptor?"

"On the west end, in Sandy's North."

"Oh, then we can go to the Frog and Onion," Imani said. "They make the best hamburgers in the world."

"Frog and Onion," Chris said. Sounded like an English pub. "That mean something?"

"The Frog is a Frenchman." Imani laughed. "The Onion is what we call ourselves. After the Bermuda onion."

"If we go to the Dockyard you can see some sculptures done in Bermuda cedar. Some of them might be more agreeable to your wallet."

They took a cab, since Baker hadn't come back with Joel's truck. Joel wanted them to wait, as he was loath to pay what he thought were exorbitant cab prices. But Imani was impatient and Chris agreed with her.

"We can split the fare."

During the half hour drive, Joel and Imani gave a running commentary on the island sights. He pointed out the Southampton Fairmont hotel, a sprawling pink monstrosity perched atop a hill, overlooking Great Sound, Gibbs Lighthouse, one of the highest points in Bermuda, and over Somerset Bridge, the world's smallest working drawbridge. Chris couldn't help notice that no one mentioned either of David's half-brothers or their vitriolic reaction to their long lost sibling.

Chris was surprised and a little unnerved at first by how readily Bermudians used their car horns. He kept looking around, expecting to see angry faces or one-fingered salutes, instead being met by waves and smiles. Bermudians, it seemed, honked to greet everyone they knew, which seemed to be just about everybody on the road. But then if only locals owned cars, it made sense that on such a tiny island everyone would have at least a nodding acquaintance with everyone else. Joel waved at nearly every pedestrian and a broad grin sheathed his face. On Middle Road, traffic got backed up behind a duo of pacing ponies whose drivers sat in small racing carts. Joel said they were from a local stable. They raced at the Vesey Street track. He and his deceased wife used to go there every weekend the ponies ran.

"How long has your wife been gone?" Chris asked, knowing David never would, but knowing he would want to know.

"Ten years now," Joel said. "In some ways she reminded me of your mother."

Chris almost expressed his sympathy then realized Joel didn't mean anything negative by the comment. He still had a rose-tinted view of Barbara Willerton, lover and mother of his child. Faded memories of a willful flower child. Or maybe his memories weren't so faded. Maybe he remembered every second of the short time they spent together.

The Frog and Onion was at the Dockyards in what, at one time, had been a cooperage, where they turned out barrels for the British navy. The cabbie dropped them off and Chris and David followed Imani and Joel through an old fortress. Chris pulled his digital camera out and took shots of everything, very much to Imani's amusement.

He caught her look. "Hey," he said with a weak grin. "I'm a tourist. I'm allowed."

David shook his head and grimaced.

Joel ignored them and continued his running commentary, "This used to supply the royal navy with victuals. The British were well established here by the time of the Civil War. Upper class Bermudians tended to be pro-Confederacy—the Yanks came in during World War II. In fact, a lot of warring countries have used Bermuda to detain prisoners over the centuries. It is hard to get to and hard to get out of. The reefs are always treacherous." It was clear Joel knew Bermudian history, and it was equally clear he was proud of his country.

He led them into the cooperage itself, a vintage 1700's stone room with a massive fireplace. A waiter brought menus and suggested they might try the beer sampler tray—six local microbrews. Imani did just that. Chris looked at her questioningly.

"Don't worry, I'm legal," she said. "The drinking age in Bermuda is eighteen." She rolled her eyes at her father this time. "Like he'd let me drink before that."

Chris held up his hands. "Not my place."

After studying the menu and wondering aloud what a Snooty Fox was, or a Tumble Down Dick, both Chris and David chose to stick with rum swizzles, while Joel picked the Somer's Amber Ale. With Imani raving about the hamburgers, both David and Chris ordered the Frog and Onion Burger.

The burgers were everything Imani claimed. Chris emptied his plate and looked longingly at David's unfinished meal. Since that wasn't going to happen, he ordered banana and strawberry crepes with a black rum sauce for desert.

Finally it was as though Imani couldn't hold it in any longer. She looked up from her plate and met Chris's gaze. "I hope you don't believe everyone here thinks like my brothers do."

"I'm sure neither David or Chris want to talk about that." Joel began.

David held up his hand. "No, it's okay—"

"No, it's not," Chris was tired of playing diplomat. "I'm sick to death of being despised because of what we are. I'm sorry, but I'm a gay man and I always have and always will be. That's not going to change no matter how much you or anyone disapproves."

"I understand—" Imani said.

"No, I'm sorry, you don't. You can't. It's being lower than a second class citizen. Every day we're assaulted by hate, hate because we love someone the great religions of the world say we shouldn't. We're bombarded with the message that even God hates us. So no, you don't understand."

"I'm sorry," Imani said so softly Chris almost couldn't hear her. "If I could change it, I would."

Just as suddenly the anger went out of Chris. He looked from David, who looked pissed, to Imani, who looked like she really was apologizing for the whole world, and he flushed. "No, I'm sorry. I had no right to blow off like that. I'll climb down off my soapbox now."

"Imani," Joel said. "Let us talk about something else—"

"I wish that were so," Imani said. "I would change the world if I could."

"Listen," Chris said earnestly. "You're a good kid. I didn't mean to lay that kind of heavy sh—stuff on you."

"Kid again," Imani said with a rueful laugh. "I gotta wonder if I'll ever grow out of that."

"Sure you will," Chris said, trying to lighten the mood now. He was all too aware that diners at nearby tables were turning to watch them. "When you're old and gray and your grandkids come to visit. Trust me, they'll think you're plenty old enough."

"Gee, thanks. I think."

"Hey, I'm always good for it." He met David's gaze and sighed. "It's funny, I've never been a political animal. My friend Des would tell you he's been trying to get me to care about his causes for years now, but I never got involved. But there's been so much negative stuff lately that it's hard not to."

"I'm going to confess I never really thought about it before." Imani said.

"S'okay," Chris murmured. "Most people don't. They have their own worries to occupy themselves. They find it easier to believe what they're told by misguided church leaders."

David snagged the bill as soon as it was presented and insisted on paying for the meal, over Joel's protests. He guided Chris out of the pub, his hand firmly in the middle of Chris's back. Chris didn't need to be a mind reader to know David was still angry. Joel didn't seem very happy about the way things had gone, either.

Chris squared his shoulders, for once not ready to back down. Tough if they didn't like it.

In silence, they left the cooperage through the sunlit atrium. Across from the pub was a craft market. Joel led them inside. The market was a treasure trove of maps, old and new, glass sculptures, the typical shells and beach knickknacks, fresh Bermuda honey and something called Outerbridge's Sherry Peppers. David picked up a bottle. "Hot?" he asked Joel.

"Burn your tongue," Joel said cheerfully.

"Try that one out on Martinez," Chris said to David, still trying to ease the mood. He hated it when David was unhappy with him.

"Who is Martinez?" Imani asked.

"My partner," David said. "My LAPD partner. He's always

challenging everyone to serve him something so hot he can't eat it. No one's succeeded yet."

Chris wandered off in search of cedar. He came back with a couple of small pieces that he proudly showed David. One was a sinuous carving of a Bermudian woman, her hair piled high, limbs raised in dance. "Des will love this." The second sculpture was a pair of leaping dolphins. He got that for Becky, along with a T-shirt that proudly proclaimed its wearer was a Bermuda Onion.

The sculptor's house was a single-story lavender building surrounded by verdant green. The man who answered the door made David think wrestler instead of sculptor. He was huge, bald-headed, with his arms and thighs as big around as telephone poles. He hugged Joel, dwarfing the large man, slapping his back. Imani was swept into his arms.

"Girl, you get prettier every day."

When Joel introduced Chris and David, Trotter held out his hand and gripped David's.

"You the one who wants to see my tables?"

David shook his head. He jerked a thumb back at Chris. "Him."

Trotter held out his hand. Chris took it gingerly. He felt the calluses against his soft, white-collar skin. "Come, I'll show you my studio," Trotter said.

Skylights and a broad bay window flooded the room with natural light. Raw blocks of curing cedar were stacked in one corner; the rich smell of cut wood filled the room. Lying against the far wall were several planed boards, stacked and ready to be turned into art. David took a deep breath and tried not to watch Chris go into a rapture over one piece after another. Then he spotted the biggest table, hidden away in the far corner, under the bay window. Light danced over the burnished surface. There was nothing ornate about the piece. The legs had been shaped slightly into graceful curves. The tabletop itself was sanded and buffed with obvious love and attention to detail.

"Oh, this is exquisite," Chris cried. "How much?"

Trotter had kept up with Chris, giving him the history of each item. The table, he said, had been started two years ago from a choice piece of Bermudian cedar. "It called out for something special."

"It is special," Chris said. David wasn't surprised when his next question was, "How much are you asking?"

He really wasn't trying to listen, but the silence in the room was so complete he could hear faint traffic sounds coming from Middle Road, and a nearby kiskadee calling out its question.

"Normally I ask thirty thousand for a piece this size."

David almost bit his tongue. He tried to catch Chris's eye but it was obvious Chris was avoiding him.

All Chris's attention was on Trotter, and even from this distance David recognized the gleam in his eye. He was in bargaining mode. Sometimes David thought Chris loved the challenge of bargaining as much as the resultant purchase.

"Twenty."

"It took nearly two years to make this piece."

"And it shows," Chris said. "Twenty-five."

"Twenty-eight and not a penny less."

They finally agreed on twenty-six and a half, which still made David's teeth ache.

They talked about having it shipped and what kind of duty Chris could expect to pay. Chris signed over a VISA check with all his personal information. Imani touched David's arm.

"Is he always this way?"

"What way?" David said through clenched teeth.

"This impulsive? That's a lot of money—"

"Don't tell me what I already know."

"You must love him very much."

"Why, because I don't kill him when he spends that kind of money on a table?"

Imani grinned. "Well, yeah."

David sighed. "Yeah, I do."

"You're lucky. Not many people find that kind of love."

"Not many people could afford it."

"There's that, too." She laughed. "I wonder if he knows how special you are."

"Let's hope so."

Chris bounced over to them. "Ready to go? I'm all done here."

"That's good to know," David said.

Trotter called them a cab, and it arrived soon after.

David took Chris's arm and followed Joel and Imani out to the cab. Chris couldn't help but grin at him. "Making sure I get out with a few checks still in my wallet?"

"You'll thank me one day," David growled, but he couldn't hide his amusement. He knew damn well Chris was never going to change.

Out in the driveway he was still holding Chris's arm. A car flew by and through the open windows they heard a rough male voice shout, "Take it home, faggots. Your kind ain't welcome here."

CHAPTER TEN

Monday, 4:25pm Rose Grotto, College Hill Road, Devonshire Parish, Bermuda

They pulled into Joel's driveway to find two scooters and the pickup truck present. No one came out to greet them. Imani raced up the steps and threw open the front door, but instead of entering, she spun around and stormed to the edge of the veranda.

"Did you hear those ass—those jerks? God, do they ever stop?" She was almost in tears. She clenched her hands into fists. "It makes me ashamed to be Bermudian."

"Now, honey," Joel said. "You don't mean that. You know as many good people as I do. It's not fair to paint everyone with the same brush."

As though to challenge his words, Imani's brothers came out of the house. Baker was a lithe, dark man barely out of his teens; Jay favored his father in height and build. Neither of them looked any too pleased to see Chris or David.

"It's not enough you drag them all over dis rock," Jay said. "Giving all our friends a chance to stare and laugh, shaming us all, but you have to bring them back here when we said they wasn't welcome."

"You're a nasty piece of work, aren't you?" Imani jammed her fists against her side, glaring at each brother in turn. "I'm ashamed to be related to you."

"You don't know what you're talking about," Baker snapped. "It ain't natural. No real man sleeps with other men."

Chris nearly looked heavenward as though for help. Next they were going to start quoting Leviticus. He felt David's body tense and he waited for the outburst, but it came from Joel rather than his son.

"You're all my sons, but you overstep yourselves. You are being rude to my guests. I thought I had raised you better. Apologize."

"But poppa, he's—"

"He's my son, and Chris is the friend of my son. You will respect that or you will leave."

Instead of cooling them off, Joel's words only served to fuel their fury.

"I'll leave all right." Jay stalked down the steps to the lawn, brushing past Chris and nearing knocking him over. "And I'll stay gone until you come to your senses and send this sick fuck out of here."

"Jay! That kind of language is unacceptable. I insist you apologize—"

"Screw that." Jay straddled his bike and jammed his helmet down on his head. "I'll be back once this pervert leaves. I can't believe you thought he could help me. Really, Dad, I thought you knew better."

He threw the bike into gear and popped a wheelie on the way out onto College Hill Road, spewing gravel as he slid onto the pavement.

Imani looked stricken. Joel merely looked grim. "Fool," he muttered. He shook his grizzled head and turned to face David.

Before he could speak, David took Chris's arm and drew him toward him. "I think we've done enough damage for one day," he said. "Thank you for inviting us. I hope we can see each other again before we head home."

"No!" Imani said. She looked at her father. "You can't just let them walk away like that. Not because of Jay or the other island bigots. That's so unfair."

David tried again. "I think it's better for all of us—"

She did everything but stamp her feet. "No, it's not better.

How can you say that? I'm your sister, this is your dad. Maybe you're still pissed that he ignored you for all those years, but that wasn't his fault. Don't you see, he wouldn't have stayed away if he'd known."

"Let them go." Baker sneered, clearly enjoying the show from his vantage point on the veranda. He stuffed a sweet roll into his mouth and chewed noisily.

When the door popped open again everyone turned to look at the young man who stepped out onto the veranda. He was followed by two others who, in sharp contrast to the first man, looked like street thugs. One bore an armful of tattoos and the other had a thick mat of Rastafarian hair that looked like small animals might nest in it. The first man was a real beauty, rich bronze skin with startling gray eyes. His hair hung nearly to his shoulders, but on him it looked right. His gaze swept around the frozen tableau.

"I'm interrupting. Sorry." A lazy smile said he really wasn't.

Chris was startled to see Imani blush and duck her head. "Daryl. I didn't know you were here. I didn't even know you were back."

Joel stiffened and Chris could have sworn a flash of dislike crossed the older man's face before he suppressed it. The smile he gave the younger man was clearly forced. "Daryl," he said. "I had no idea you were home. What happened to your school year in Florida?"

"Nothing," Daryl said quickly. He never looked away from Imani. "I'm just back."

Chris looked away from the trio quickly when they looked at him. He was no coward, but he knew better than to get in the face of hostile straights. Guys with a chip on their shoulders usually weren't open to reason. But his eyes were drawn back again to Daryl. He didn't seem as unfriendly as the others. In fact he seemed more relaxed than anyone else in the fractured tableau, including Joel and David.

Imani certainly seemed thrilled to see the newcomer.

Chris watched their interaction with curiosity. Joel strode up, interrupting the two.

"But I don't understand, Daryl," Joel said. "Your father sent you to Florida. Am I right?"

Daryl smiled. "Miami. Mom got sick so I had to come back."

Joel spun around to face Baker and Jay. "You should have told me your friend was back. At the very least you should have told me Mary was ill."

"Pop, he asked us not to. He didn't want to make a fuss—"

"He's right, sir," Daryl said. "Mom wasn't really that sick and she didn't want it blown out of proportion by well-meaning friends. No offense, sir."

"I'll still speak to your father about this. This isn't right, you throwing away your schooling. I'm sure your father will agree."

"Please don't do that, sir," Daryl said. "We've already talked about it. He understands."

It was clear to Chris that Joel didn't agree. Probably just unhappy Daryl was back in Imani's life.

"But please, enough, join us for a drink, Daryl. I'll call your father tomorrow." He looked at Chris and David. "You don't mind, do you?"

Chris answered first. "No, not at all."

"Excuse me," Joel said. "I should introduce you. This is Thomas and Emmanuel Cray, and this young man is Daryl Billings. His father and I are cousins. We worked together many years ago on one of his deep-sea fishing boats until I decided I'd rather dig in dirt than water."

Chris held out his hand. "Hi, Daryl, I'm Chris, this is David."

Daryl's easy smile sent Chris's pulse thundering. He barely noticed Imani slip in beside Daryl, laying her hand possessively on his arm. If Chris had been a better family friend, he would have hooted with amusement. David's little sister had a big time crush.

Joel still didn't look happy, but then having a good-looking man courting his young daughter was bound to tie any man's shorts in a knot.

"I thought we were heading out to St. David's," Baker whined.

"You go on ahead," Daryl said. "I'll catch up with you later. Pa's expecting you. Just tell him I got delayed. I'll catch a bus later." The look he flashed Imani's way was not the least bit coy. "Maybe I can't get someone to drop me off in Hamilton."

Reluctantly the three of them climbed onto two scooters and raced out of the driveway in the same direction as Jay.

Imani made a rude noise. Her look was apologetic. "My brother can be such a stubborn fool sometimes."

Daryl patted her arm. "Don't let him get to you. He's just a kid."

"He's older than you." But Imani was laughing now. "But you're right, he acts like a little brat sometimes."

"He's always been that way," Joel said. "I'm sorry."

"Don't." David held up his hand when Joel started to speak again. "Don't apologize."

"We run into that all the time," Chris said.

Chris and David sat back down while Joel got drinks for everyone. Daryl pulled up a lawn chair beside David.

"You're from L.A.? That must be cool. I watch all the TV cop shows." He grinned, displaying beautiful, white teeth. "You have the right to remain silent." He laughed. "You really say that? Bet it'd be easier if you could just bust a few heads open."

"Start doing that and the wrong people end up in jail," David said. Daryl shrugged, unperturbed by David's unspoken censure.

Joel returned with their drinks.

"We really can't stay long," David said.

Joel swirled his rum swizzle and looked down at the clinking ice. "I'm sorry I didn't try to find you sooner, David," he said. "I let my pride keep me from my son. What kind of man does that?"

"You shouldn't be too hard on yourself," Daryl said. "I'm sure David understands."

You don't know David, Chris almost said. But David wasn't talking, so he kept his own mouth shut. Chris thought of David's mother. Wondering what she would think of this little gathering. Probably be horrified. The thought cheered him.

"My biggest regret—" Joel started. When Daryl opened his mouth to speak, Joel held up his hand. "No, let me speak. My biggest regret is leaving your mother alone when I should have been there for her. And for you."

"My mother wanted it that way," David said. "And I know my mother. When she wants something she tends to get it."

"You should not disparage her."

"I know, I know," David said. "She tried."

Bull was Chris's only thought. But he kept the sentiment to himself. No reason to keep stirring that pot.

"Do you really have to go?" Imani asked when they had finished their drinks and refused another one. "I could make supper, cassava pie, Portuguese red bean soup and codfish with bananas. I'll bet you don't get anything like that in Los Angeles. Daryl, you could stay, too."

Was it his imagination, or did Joel frown over Imani's invitation? Chris studied Daryl. He could see why a father might be uneasy about his young daughter's obvious interest in a good-looking, but older man. Men always seemed to have a hard time dealing with potential lovers for their daughters.

The moment passed. It wasn't exactly something Chris could ask about.

David shook his head. "Tempting, but we really have to leave."

Joel called a cab and they waited outside for it, sipping a beer that Imani brought out for them. Daryl stood close to Imani and it was obvious to Chris that Joel really wasn't impressed.

The kiskadee, or one like it, screamed at them from the

scented plumeria tree. A small green gecko ran up one of the butter yellow walls while several bees hummed around various blossoms.

The taxi van pulled into the drive. Chris glanced at his watch as they climbed into the backseat. "You sure you don't want to stay here? It's early."

"I think I need some time to take in everything that's happened."

Chris nodded. "Fair enough. You want to go into town then? Do some sightseeing? Since we're at this end of the island anyway."

David raised an eyebrow. "Not done spending?"

"I only want to look."

"Yeah, right." David sighed. "Why not? Let's play tourist."

He gave the cabbie their new destination. A radio played in the background. "Tropical storm Fay has shifted position in the Atlantic and predictions are that it may hit Bermuda sometime late Friday afternoon, Saturday at the latest. We'll keep you posted with up-to-date storm tracking throughout the rest of the week."

"Hurricane?" Chris met the cabbie's gaze in the mirror. "You get a lot of hurricanes?"

"Not many, man." The cabbie shrugged. "Florence came through in '06, it busted up some power lines. In 2003 Fabian hit us hard. Lot of damage that time."

"Not like Katrina though, right?"

"Nothing like Katrina, but our homes be built tough. Not much can tear down a Bermuda house. Break the windows, yeah, and bring all the fine palm trees down, but no Katrina. But that one, in '03, that was bad. Two police officers swept off the Causeway. Terrible thing."

"What happens during a hurricane?"

"Now they shut the Causeway and the airport, no getting on or off island. Buses don't run. Most businesses close, too.

Sometimes we lose power. Most power lines be above ground since the whole rock's built on limestone. The buildings be safe, but you don't want to catch it outside. Winds like crazy. Blow you away like you a scrap of paper."

Having never been in a hurricane, Chris could only imagine.

The cab dropped them off on Front Street, across from the cruise ships' dock. Two hulking cruise ships were in port, their massive white super structures looming over a street that thronged with tourists. Chris spotted a rock climbing wall on the back of the *Norwegian Spirit*. A muscular black man in shorts and a muscle shirt pulled himself up the wall. Chris poked David and they both watched the sweat-slicked man as he reached the top, before sliding back down on the line. When he disappeared behind the upper deck railing Chris sighed.

David laughed. "Come on, stud muffin," he said softly, so no one would overhear. "Show's over."

Chris realized they were being stared at. It was as though everyone on the street could read their thoughts and were disgusted with them. Chris dug his fists into his hip pockets, ignoring the urge to take David's hand. He could just imagine the horrified reaction such a simple, harmless act would generate.

They strolled along Front Street, peering in at Versace and Louis Vuitton bags, Rolex watches and Hermes scarves. Chris made a concerted effort to refrain from his usual exuberance. And he hated it. He wasn't used to hiding who he was, he hadn't in years, but he knew David would be mortified if they were exposed and people started staring at them like zoo animals.

Chris wouldn't do anything to embarrass David, so he squelched the desire to stand up and shout at the knowing looks that yes, they were gay, yes they were married. It wouldn't impress anybody, least of all David.

Instead he concentrated on people watching. There was an unending variety. Staid businessmen looking a bit less serious than their American counterparts in their Bermuda shorts and dark knee socks. American tourists loaded down with cameras and tote bags stuffed with useless trinkets to prove they'd actually been somewhere. Even a few teens who seemed to Chris to be a lot less rowdy than their Stateside cousins roamed the sidewalks in packs. But not packs looking for trouble, it seemed.

They walked down Front Street. Night descended; the cruise ships lit up like over-decorated Vegas Christmas trees.

They stopped in a place called Flanagan's where David had a Guinness Stout, while Chris sampled what the server promised was the world's best White Russian.

Once the waiter had delivered their drinks, they settled back in their seats. Chris swirled the white Russian around, hearing the soft clink of ice cubes.

"It's hard, isn't it?"

"What is?" David asked. "Finding out the man I thought was dead is very much alive? I still can't wrap my head around it. I thought my life was pretty straightforward. I had a family when I was growing up, not the best family; there were no Beaver Cleaver moments, but Da—Graham was good to me. Now I find out it's all a lie."

"Not all," Chris said. "Graham was still a good father. At least he tried."

"Unlike my mother, who must have thought she had a doppelganger on her hands. All her lies couldn't make me the son she wanted. I wonder if she blamed my father for the way I turned out. She'd like to blame someone, that much I know."

David was looking over the railing at the scene below, and Chris could see how hard he was working to affect a calm demeanor.

"I don't like this place," Chris blurted. "I thought it would be a lark, but we were doing so good, now it's like we're being forced back in the closet."

Chris could tell David wanted to offer assurances, but the fact that he wouldn't touch Chris said it all. He sighed. Some things never changed.

It was late when they caught a cab and returned to Aunt Nea's. Chris put on his silk pajamas and headed for the deck overlooking Ordnance Island. He carried his laptop with him.

David followed him outside and handed him a glass of wine. He stood next to Chris, their hips touching. Chris set the laptop down on a glass-topped table and leaned on the railing, looking sideways at David.

David reached for Chris's hand and twined their fingers together. "Maybe I can't always show it, but I do love you. That's never going to change."

"No?" Chris whispered. "Sometimes I think you're ashamed to be seen with me. Without me around no one would know, and I can't hide what I am—"

"Don't ever say that." David grabbed Chris's shoulders and pulled him around, staring down into his upturned face. "I could never be ashamed of you. I love you."

He brushed his lips over Chris's. "This is all just temporary. Remember, it's only a holiday. We won't be here forever."

The phone rang. David broke away and headed inside. Chris sat down and opened his laptop. He quickly downloaded his email and began scanning the headers. There were a couple from Becky, detailing what she had done to date. He emailed her back telling her what they had experienced so far. He even told her about the table, though he didn't say how much he paid for it. Like David, she thought he was too profligate.

Chris heard David greet the caller.

"Joel. No, I wasn't sleeping. What's up?"

Chris finished with his email and shut down the laptop. He took his wine and laptop and passed David on the way to the bedroom. Fifteen minutes later David entered the room. But instead of getting ready for bed he leaned over and kissed Chris. "I have to go out for a bit. I'll be back soon."

"Where are you going?"

David shrugged. "Joel wants to meet with me."

CHAPTER ELEVEN

David slipped out of the cottage after seeing Chris to bed. He had been tempted to put Joel off and tell him he'd meet him tomorrow, but in the end he decided to acquiesce and do it tonight. There were still too many questions he had that only Joel could answer. He felt entitled to a few answers. He had the feeling Joel felt the same, but he wouldn't know until he could talk to him face to face, without the rest of his family and Chris around.

He made his way up the path to King's Square. Lights from all around the square and Ordnance Island danced on the undulating surface of the harbor. He found Joel standing in front of the historical stocks used to beguile tourists with morbid thoughts of past punishments.

All around him the voices of reveling tourists rose and fell. He could even hear the clink of glassware from the patios of the nearby restaurants and pubs.

"Let's walk," Joel said, and led them away from the square and out of town. David could tell Joel was still upset by his sons' outbursts and was ignoring David's reassurances. David was having his own problems with assimilating everything that had happened in the last week. He wasn't up to handling someone else's issues.

They strolled off the main road onto what Joel said was called Convict Bay Lane. At least a dozen fishing boats were docked at a small wharf. David went out to stand on the edge of the wooden pier. The hiss of moving water whispered along the pylons below his feet. He heard a bike, the lightweight sewing-machine engine sound, coming down nearby Cut Road, fading away as it passed.

Somewhere a night bird called and tree frogs sang. Across the bay the lights of another town glowed softly. Blinking red lights in the water marked a path of buoys.

He glanced at the glowing dial of his watch. Almost ten-thirty.

"Thank you for meeting me," Joel said.

David nodded. Under the nearby lights Joel looked pale and haggard. He turned to face Convict Bay.

"I'm sorry I dragged you into this," he said. "Perhaps I should have left well enough alone. If you had gone on thinking me dead, you would never have wondered what might have been."

It was too much like an echo of what Chris had said earlier. He hadn't like it then, and he didn't like it now. "Don't, Joel—"

Joel ignored him. "I was unfair to your mother, and I've been unfair to you. That is something I will never forgive myself for."

"I don't regret any of it," David said, hoping he could convince the man. "I used to fantasize that you were alive—what adopted kid doesn't, right? That it was all an accident that I was left alone."

David leaned on the dock railing and watched the restless water lap at the base of the wharf. Several of the docked boats rocked in the gentle waves. Light from the nearby King's Square danced on the restless water. Joel came to stand beside him.

"I wanted you to be somewhere," David said. "That it wasn't true I was fatherless. I know you still love my mother, and I'll be honest, I don't understand why, but I think I know you're a good man. I'm not sorry you found me. You have to believe me."

"Does Christopher know you're here?"

"Sure, I don't keep secrets from him."

"He's a fine man and I know he loves you very much. I know it's hard for both of you, with the way other people look on you as breaking God's laws, but I've seen you together and no God I know would condemn love like that."

David was at a loss as to what to say to that, so he kept silent.

Joel wasn't done.

"I know Imani is very upset by all this. For her sake I hope you won't refuse our offer of hospitality. Please don't hurt her over the actions of her brothers."

"Neither Chris nor I want to be the cause of dissension in your family. It's pretty clear Jay, at least, isn't open to any kind of dialogue…"

"Yes, well, my sons aren't very worldly," Joel said. "I've tried to encourage them to broaden their horizons, but they've always resisted, saying they're happy to be Bermudians and don't see why they need to involve themselves in a chaotic world. That was Jay's excuse for not pursuing school offshore. Sadly, I think his decision is based on fear as much as anything. It's moments like this that I dearly wish my wife was still alive. Dorothy would never have been satisfied with anything but the best effort from any of our children."

But what would she have thought of a bastard child showing up after forty plus years? David left the thought unspoken, knowing Joel probably carried his own guilt over that. Then he realized that he had to know.

"Did you ever tell your wife about, ah, Barbara, or me?"

"No." Joel's voice held a wealth of pain. "God forgive me, I never did. I never told any of my children that, either. Not until I thought you might be alive. I knew their mother would understand, she was a good-hearted woman, but I didn't want to weight her down with the knowledge. I figured I carried enough of a burden for both of us."

"What did Jay mean about being here to help him? Does it have something to do with my being a police officer?"

"He should not have spoken to you…"

"Did you bring me here because I'm a cop? Tonight? Is that what this is about?"

Joel averted his eyes. "I had hoped he might allow himself to be influenced by you. That he could see there was strength there, and goodness."

"And why did you want that?"

"Besides you, Jay is my oldest. He was always a good boy when he was younger, he attended church with all of us, he did well in school…"

"When did he change?" It was an old story. A lot of cops David knew had the same problems with their own kids. One day they were angels, the next they took a train to the dark side. It made him glad it would never be a problem for him and Chris. Bad enough to see the children of cops he knew spiral into drugs or crime.

"In high school. He—"

"Got in with a bad crowd?"

Joel sighed. "You've heard this before, haven't you? But that's right, you're a police officer. You probably see this sort of thing all the time. It must be hard for you, always seeing the worst side of people."

David shrugged. It was the negative side to policing. The dangerous tendency some cops adopted of thinking the people on the lower rungs of society were NHI, no humans involved. It was a soul eating attitude he never wanted to take up.

"What did you think I could do?" he asked gently. "If Jay doesn't want my help, there's not much I can accomplish."

"I know that. But…" Joel swung around to face David. His face was creased with worry. "He used to respect people. He used to respect me. Now…"

"I'm sorry," David said gently. "I don't think I can do anything for him. I can't pull an intervention on a total stranger. You must know that."

"Yes, I do. I guess I just hoped you could talk to him."

David knew he should have just said no, but instead said, "Listen, give Chris and I a couple of days to let things settle down. Then I promise you, we'll visit again. Maybe we can have lunch again someplace, the five of us. Six, if Baker wants to come along. And at that time I'll talk to Jay, if he'll listen." Maybe if the "talk" happened in a neutral place, devoid of the markings of territory and all the baggage that entailed, Jay might listen to his older brother.

"I'd like that," Joel said. "In fact, the Thursday after this one is Emancipation Day. It's a big island holiday when St. George's and Somerset compete in an annual cup match. Cricket. Very competitive, but mostly good-natured, sort of like your Super Bowl. Or the World Cup. The first match game is here in St. George's. Jay never misses them. Neither does Imani or Baker, for that matter."

"Chris would like it, too." A lie, since Chris hated sports, though he pretended to be excited for David's sake. "We're here for two weeks, so we can do that."

"Then it's a date." They shook hands. "You look tired, David. Go home to Chris. We will sort this out." Joel put his arm around David's broad shoulder and they walked back to the square. If anything, the revelry had grown more raucous. "Take care, David. And know this, that no matter what comes of this, I am very glad I met you. And Chris."

David left him then and made his way back to Aunt Nea's. He let himself into the Jasmine room and found Chris dozing in the canopy bed, the gossip magazine he had purchased at the airport in his lap, open to a picture of some anorexic star and her peripatetic boy toy. He woke when David shut the bedroom door and began stripping off his shirt.

He blinked up at David. "You're back." He rubbed the sleep from his eyes. "How did it go?"

David wanted to tell him to go back to sleep, but he knew Chris would ignore the request. Instead he took the magazine off Chris's lap and set it on the bedside table. He perched on the side of the bed and took off his shoes.

"He's upset by the whole thing," David said, folding his socks and yanking his shirt over his head. "He doesn't want us to leave without saying goodbye. I told him we wouldn't. I suggested we could go out for lunch, rather than go back to the house. That way if Jay and his brother don't feel like showing up they don't have to. He suggested some big cricket match a week from Thursday, here in St. George's. I said we'd think about it." He took a breath and let it out slowly. "He wants me to talk to Jay, seems to think I can straighten the guy out."

"Straighten him out how?"

"Wrong crowd kind of thing. Joel thinks having a cop as a big brother might make an impression."

"You sure that's a good idea?"

"No, the kid's not going to listen. What do you think? Should I try?"

"We came all this way," Chris said. "It hardly seems fair to anyone to hightail it home at the first spat."

David scooped up Chris's hand from on top of the comforter. "Hardly a spat."

"Maybe not, but it's hardly an earth-shattering row either." Chris tugged David down so their faces were inches apart. He ran his hands over David's broad back, stopping at the base of his spine where his pants started. He slid his fingers under the belted material. "I know something we could make earth-shattering."

"And what might that be?" David's voice was husky.

Chris fumbled with the belt buckle. "Just come here, and I'll show you."

CHAPTER TWELVE

Tuesday, 6:25am Aunt Nea's, Nea's Alley, St. George's Parish, Bermuda

Chris woke to find the bed beside him empty. He threw aside the covers and padded into the other room. He found David in the kitchen, nursing a cup of black coffee.

"What time did you get up?"

"Bit before six." David smiled. "You were totally out of it."

"When does Joel want to do this cricket match?"

"We didn't work out the details. Next Thursday. Though he did say the first game was here in town someplace. Said it was like the Super Bowl."

"Cricket?"

David shrugged, bemused. "I gather it's big here."

Chris grabbed himself a coffee and straddled a chair. "At least we can see Imani again."

"You like her, don't you?"

"You don't?"

"Of course I do. She's a sweet kid."

"Baby sister, remember. That makes you her older brother." Chris laughed. "Really older, older brother."

"Ha-ha." David sipped his coffee. "I think I proved I'm not so old last night."

Chris's smile was smug. They took their coffee out to the veranda. Chris slid into a deck chair and put his feet up on the railing. An odd looking bird with a long white tail drifted overhead. The cruise ship, or perhaps another one, was still in the harbor, a white behemoth among the jeweled buildings lining the shore. The sun was just high enough in the sky to bring everything alive with rich color. It looked like a manufactured postcard of paradise.

"Assuming you don't want to call Joel just yet, what do you want to do today?"

"I'd rather leave that for a day or two." David finished his coffee and set the mug down on the terracotta tile table. "I was looking over the brochures you picked up. We can take a couple of sea kayaks out to one of the reefs to go snorkeling. Or we could check out the Crystal Caves. Mostly, I think I'd just like to get out of here."

"I can go for that. Let's go swimming first. We should check with the manager about where the closest beach is—"

The morning was interrupted by the ululating wail of sirens. Close sirens. It sounded like it went right by the guest house, though Chris couldn't see anything. David and Chris exchanged alarmed looks.

The sirens abruptly cut off. Chris stood.

"It's close. Maybe we should go see what it is."

David pulled him back. "The last thing any emergency responders needs is a couple of rubbernecking tourists interfering."

"But what is it?"

"I don't know. Could be fire, ambulance or even the police. I don't recognize the siren. I'm sure we'll hear about it soon enough."

As though on cue, the manager appeared at the foot of the stairs. She saw them on the veranda and waved.

Chris and David met her at the front door.

"It's the police," she whispered, as though afraid she'd be overheard. "They're down by Convict Bay."

"Do you know why?" David asked.

"No, I don't. But it can't be good."

Chris reminded himself that this wasn't L.A. People here

weren't used to hearing sirens day and night. Back home you got used to the constant wail. As long as it wasn't for you, most Angelenos ignored them.

Looking toward King's Square, where he assumed Convict Bay was, judging by the sirens, Chris couldn't see anything. The urge to find out what was going on intensified. David must have sensed his uneasiness, because he waved Chris back toward their room.

"Come on," he said. "Let's go into town, there's nothing we can do here."

Chris almost refused, but made no protest when David pushed him inside.

"Get changed. We'll find something to do in Hamilton." Chris changed into a pair of jeans and an Izod shirt. David dressed much the same way.

On their way down Duke of York Street they altered their course and strolled through King's Square instead, but even though they looked, they couldn't see any sign of the police anywhere. Chris had David pose in front of the life-size replica of *Deliverance* that had been used by shipwrecked mariners to return to Virginia, after their original ship had been wrecked on the treacherous reefs as they were trying to get from England to the new colony in Virginia. He marveled at the idea of spending weeks at sea on such a tiny, fragile ship.

Suddenly Chris laughed. "Things must have been very cozy for those sailors."

"Somehow I doubt you'd find any mention of that in their Captain's log."

"Old salty dogs."

"You have a one track mind," David said, but Chris could hear the laughter in his voice.

"Like you're complaining."

They stopped for coffee at Cafe Gio, where they sat at glass tables in the courtyard watching the same gulls and sparrows vie for thrown scraps of food. Afterward, back in King's Square, they mingled with the other tourists, watching people put their heads in the stocks, and staring at the dunking stool where hapless scolders would get dunked and encouraged to mend their ways.

Chris had no luck getting David to pose with his head in the stocks, but he cajoled him into taking a picture of Chris in one, head and hands dangling out of the wooden enclosure. Several amused tourists looked on. Chris was grinning when he took the camera back. "That could be an interesting addition to our place, don't you think?"

David pursed his lips and squinted while he considered Chris's words, then his face cleared and he laughed. "Oh, you are wicked."

After lunch at St. George & The Dragon, overlooking the Square, they decided to change again before they headed into Hamilton for a day of playing tourist.

"I don't want to get turned away because I'm not wearing the right thing," Chris sniffed. "Like they could fault me for my fashion sense."

"You tell them, Miss Thang."

They both laughed. They were still laughing when they turned into the driveway and found a navy blue and white checkered police car with a young black officer, incongruously dressed in black Bermuda shorts with dark knee socks, standing outside the vehicle. He watched them approach with the same emotionless face that David wore when he was on a case. The face Chris had always hated, because never was David more remote than when he was in "cop mode."

Apprehension sent a jolt of fear through Chris's nerve endings. He looked at David, who couldn't stop staring at the officer. Chris noticed the man didn't carry a gun, instead his belt held a small baton, a set of handcuffs and the ubiquitous two-way radio.

"Mr. David Laine? I'm Constable Darrel Lindstrom."

"Constable," David said. "How can I help you?"

"Are you familiar with a Bermudian man named Joel Cameron?"

"Y-yes. I am. Why?"

"May I ask how are you acquainted?"

"He's my father."

Chris could see David was getting scared. He didn't think he'd ever seen David fear anything.

"I'm sorry, sir," Constable Lindstrom said with that same hateful calmness, like they didn't feel; like they weren't fully human. "But Joel Cameron has met with foul play."

"Foul—you mean he's dead?" David's normally strong voice broke. He glanced at Chris with confusion and mounting fear. "I don't understand, I just saw him yesterday…"

"When did you see him, sir?"

Chris wasn't surprised when the constable pulled out a notebook and began jotting things down. It was such a cop thing.

"Yesterday Chris and I went to meet him at his house in Devonshire Parish. We just flew in the day before—"

"Flew in from where?"

"The States, my parent's place in New Hampshire, to be exact."

"But I thought Mr. Cameron was your father."

"My stepfather and my mother live in New Hampshire." He glanced at Chris again. The skin around his mouth wrinkled and worry lines deepened around his eyes. "We live in Los Angeles."

"He's an LAPD homicide detective," Chris interjected, wanting to put this island bobby in his place. The constable seemed duly unimpressed.

"Are you here on business, sir?

"No." David grew more and more uneasy. "I—we came to meet my father."

The constable wrote something. "You hadn't met him before

this?"

"I didn't know he existed," David muttered. This perked the constable right up. Chris wished David had kept silent. Something he didn't like was running through the cop's head, but then cops always thought the worst of everyone. He'd learned that lesson the hard way.

"I'm going to have to ask you to come to the station with me, sir."

"The station? I don't understand…"

"I'm afraid, Mr. Cameron, your father, was murdered last night around eleven o'clock, just east of here, near Convict Bay. There are some questions we need to ask you." The constable looked at Chris, dismissing him just as quickly. He indicated the patrol car. "Please, sir."

CHAPTER THIRTEEN

Tuesday, 5:45pm Aunt Nea's, Nea's Alley, St. George's Parish, Bermuda

David didn't know how many times he had done this during the course of an investigation. Whether the person being investigated was a suspect or just someone who might have information, there was always the awkward request which rarely went over well. No one wanted to be questioned by the police in the cop's own territory. It left the civilian at a distinct disadvantage, which was the idea, of course. Confused, unstable people often gave things away that could be used later to contradict them when they tried to change their story.

David now understood that reluctance all too well. Stiffly, he nodded and advanced on the small cruiser. He glanced back once at Chris, who couldn't hide his fear, and murmured, "It's okay, Chris. Let me take care of this, and I'll be right back."

Chris didn't look convinced, but he nodded anyway. What else could he do? The last thing David wanted was for Chris to do something harebrained and end up joining David at the police station.

Great way to start a vacation.

To David's surprise, Lindstrom didn't take him to the St. George's substation. Instead they made the long trip into Hamilton and parked in front of a large white building on Parliament Street. Lindstrom led David inside. Familiar smells and sounds: the constant ring of telephones, the smell of stale sweat and testosterone lingered in the heavy air. Somewhere an air conditioner labored and a tepid breeze washed the stink across David's face. He realized he was sweating. That never looked good to a cop. He wished he could wipe his face.

"This way," Lindstrom said. David followed and found

himself in a small room with a table and two scarred chairs that wasn't made any bigger by the presence of a two-way window. "You are not obliged to say anything unless you wish to do so," Lindstrom said. "Anything you do say will be taken down in writing and may be used in evidence."

That sounded suspiciously like Lindstrom was reading him his rights. The guy was clearly a rookie. No seasoned cop would read anyone their rights until they were arrested. His heart jolted.

"Am I being formally charged?" David demanded even before the door closed on them. He didn't wait for an answer. "What happened to my father?"

Lindstrom indicated one of the chairs. He sat in the other, across from him. Knowing he wouldn't get any answers unless he followed directions, David took the offered chair across the table. He leaned over the table, hands clasped in front of him.

"What happened?"

"Let's start with your full name, address and occupation," Lindstrom said, pen poised over a large yellow legal pad.

David looked around. No recording device he could see, but it didn't mean the conversation wasn't being taped. He'd always claimed that honesty was the best way to deal with officials, but he found it easier and easier to understand why suspects lied. But he wasn't a suspect, right? He would never have harmed his own father. So David told him.

"David Eric Laine, that's Laine with an 'e.'" He gave the address he shared with Chris, leaving that tidbit out. No telling what the Bermudian police would think of a gay cop. Probably not much more than the LAPD thought of them. "I'm a homicide detective, level two, for the LAPD, deployed out of the Northeast Community Police Station."

Lindstrom scribbled away. Without looking up, he asked, "Exactly what time did you arrive on the island?"

"Sunday morning—"

"And where are you staying?"

"Aunt Nea's, on Nea's Alley, in St. George's. Where you picked me up." A little bit of a dig.

"How long do you intend your stay to last?"

"We're booked for two weeks."

"At which point you would return where? To New Hampshire or Los Angeles?"

"Uh, L.A. is my home. We'd be flying back there."

"Who is 'we'?"

David had deliberately avoided mentioning Chris. He didn't want his husband dragged into this, though he knew it was unlikely the police would overlook their relationship. Everything became relevant in a police investigation.

His only thought was to minimize the impact. He knew Lindstrom wasn't going to make it easy for him.

And he still didn't know what this was all about. Just what did they think had happened?

"Who were you traveling with, Mr. Laine?"

"My partner, Christopher Bellamere."

"Your partner? You mean your LAPD partner?"

"No." David met Lindstrom's gaze and said, "My domestic partner."

He'd give the guy credit. He didn't flinch. He just wrote it all down in his notepad. "And exactly what brought you to Bermuda?"

"I came to meet my father." David knew better than to give out too much information. Too many suspects hung themselves with their own motor mouth. But with no charges being bandied about David figured it was too early to bring in a lawyer. It didn't help that he didn't have a clue how the Bermudian legal system worked.

"You mentioned that before. Can you elaborate?" Lindstrom asked. "What do you mean 'meet him'? Was this your first meeting? You said something about not even knowing about your father. Could you explain that, please?"

David knew he had to tell the whole story. It would come out anyway, if the local police were determined enough. He folded his arms over his chest and leaned back in the chair, squarely meeting Lindstrom's gaze.

"Up until about two weeks ago, I thought my father was dead. It's what my mother told me, years ago. I was raised by my stepfather, who adopted me when I was only a few years old."

"Who told you your father was dead?"

"My mother," David ground out. "With my grandmother's help." Reluctantly he added, "And my stepfather. They were all involved with the lie."

Lindstrom leaned forward, his pen hovering over his pad. "Did anyone ever tell you why this subterfuge occurred?"

"Their excuse was they were protecting me."

"But you don't believe that?"

All David wanted to do was leave. He hated answering such personal questions for this total stranger. He knew Lindstrom was forming his own impressions of him, and he doubted they were positive. Cops tended to look on humanity with a jaundiced eye.

"How long have you been a police officer?"

"Nineteen years."

"A very long time. Do you enjoy it?"

"I have…" David said edgily. Enjoy wasn't exactly the right word, not when you were dealing with the ugliest side of human nature. But there was a definite satisfaction in solving a puzzle and delivering justice to the ones who couldn't seek it for themselves. He had to wonder what this young constable knew about that aspect. He looked green enough to be a wet-behind-the-ears rookie. And how much real crime did a place like Bermuda even get? Clueless. "It's a decent job." Then he blurted, "What happened to my father?"

Lindstrom studied his notes again, as though he hadn't already memorized every word. "Tell me again what happened yesterday when you met your father."

He should be used to this. Cops never answered questions, they only asked them. He recounted the previous day, the initial meeting, the trip out to the Dockyards and their arrival back at Joel's. He left out Chris's extravagant purchase or the jeering youths in the car. He did recount how Joel's other sons had shown up, but not the ugly words that were exchanged.

Like most cops, Lindstrom had a strong instinct for lies and mistruths and things left out. From the skeptical look on his face, he knew David wasn't being completely honest, but before he could challenge David, there was a knock at the door. Lindstrom opened it to reveal an older, white police officer, whose gaze quickly scanned the room, skimming over David, then returning to Lindstrom. He had three bars on his black jacket, unlike Lindstrom, who had none.

"Thank you, constable. I'll take over from here. Leave your notes."

The new man took the seat Lindstrom vacated and scanned the notepad in front of him.

"Mr. Laine? My name is Detective Sergeant Stewart MacClellan. I understand you're an LAPD detective."

"That's true."

MacClellan then asked David all the questions he had already answered. Another standard operating procedure. Always ask the questions again and again, word the questions a different way, put them in a different order, all geared to try and trip the guilty up. A good interviewer could wring confessions out of even the most recalcitrant suspect just by twisting them around so they contradicted their first set of lies. Sometimes they even wrung them out of the innocent.

David repeated his answers, refusing to show the impatience boiling through him, wishing they'd get to the point.

"Did you see your father after yesterday afternoon?"

David hesitated. He knew eventually they would talk to Chris and if he said anything that contradicted David's statement, the shit would really fly. It might even get Chris into trouble.

"Yes," he said. "He called me last night and wanted to meet."

"And did you?"

David nodded and braced for the next question.

"What time did you meet?"

"It was just after ten when I left Aunt Nea's," David said. "Joel wanted to meet down in King's Square, since he knew I wasn't driving. Instead of picking me up, he said. It was simpler. I got the impression he didn't tell his family where he was going... But once we met up he wanted to walk—I assumed it was to get more privacy."

"Why would that be, detective?"

Good question. "I think some of his family was giving him a hard time."

"About what? About you?"

"Yes."

"What time did you leave him?" MacClellan scratched more notes. "What did you talk about?"

"Nothing much. Cricket," David allowed.

"Kind of late to be out talking about nothing but cricket, especially if he was doing it behind his family's back. He called you, you say, there must have been something he thought was important."

"I guess he changed his mind."

Easy to tell MacClellan didn't believe him. But David was damned if he was going to air his family's dirty laundry to this officious prick. "What time did you leave Mr. Cameron?"

"I don't recall, about an hour later, I guess."

"Be more specific, Mr. Laine," MacClellan asked. "What time did you leave your father?"

"Are you accusing me of something, Sergeant?"

MacClellan studied a second piece of paper. This one was a computer printout. He raised cool blue eyes to stare at David. "Should I be, Detective?"

"No," David said. "When I left my father, he was fine. And no, I didn't see anyone else around the area at the time. What exactly happened to my father?"

"He was attacked and badly beaten. It appears he tried to drag himself away from the wharf, perhaps to his vehicle, which we found this morning, the door still unlocked. Someone returned later and when they discovered him still alive, took a knife to him. Our initial tests confirm it was probably a fish-gutting knife. Whoever it was, moved him into the brush beside the road. He wasn't found until well after sunrise."

David felt sick. "And you think I had something to do with this?"

"Did you?"

"No!" David squeezed his hands into fists. Sweat popped out on his forehead; he hoped MacClellan didn't notice but knew he had. It was the first thing he would have looked for in an interrogation. Stress signs that indicated your interrogation was drawing blood. "Where's your DNA evidence? Your trace—" David stopped. He wasn't helping himself with this outburst. He took several deep breaths which MacClellan watched with an impassive eye. Finally, he collected himself as best he could and met the other man's cold gaze. "I think it's time I talked to a lawyer."

CHAPTER FOURTEEN

Tuesday 10:50pm Parliament Street, Hamilton, Bermuda

They left him alone then. The air grew stuffy in the closed-up interrogation room. David stared at his reflection in the window, wondering who was on the other side. Studying his face no doubt. He tried to school it into the flat facade Chris hated. His cop face, the one that gave nothing away. He knew they wouldn't leave him alone long. Soon it would be time for round two. If they really believed he had something to do with Joel's death, they'd be sure to take the gloves off. He fiddled with the tie he'd stuffed into his pocket earlier that day, a little surprised they hadn't taken it away from him. But then he hadn't actually been charged with anything, had he? He'd be searched only if they arrested him.

Finding a lawyer was going to be fun. Short of searching through the local yellow pages, he didn't know anyone. That was a lousy way of finding a lawyer. Nearly two decades of experience in law enforcement counted for diddly this far from home. If he was allowed a phone call he was going to have to call Chris. Chris was good at ferreting stuff out. So good sometimes he made David nervous, but hopefully he'd be able to find someone who would take the case. Would he get bail, and if he did, how much would they want? He knew Chris was good for just about any amount, but he hated like hell having to ask that of his husband. What choice did he have? He wasn't going to find any answers in here, and if Bermuda cops were like any others, they'd find it easier to stick to the bird they had rather than root around in the bush for anyone else.

Face it, he was screwed.

Tuesday, 5:40pm Aunt Nea's, Nea's Alley, St. George's Parish, Bermuda

Chris watched the checkered navy blue and white Opel with the jaunty yellow stripe disappear down Nea's Alley. Rooted in place, he couldn't move. Terror crowded his senses, drowning out reason. What could he do? What was going to happen to David? He had to do something to help, but what? Panic danced in the back of his mind.

He knew he had to stay calm. He couldn't help David if he panicked. If he were back home he'd know what to do: call Martinez, call Des. But they couldn't help him now. What he really needed was to call a lawyer, but who?

He thought of asking the hotel manager, but the last thing he wanted was to alarm her with the prospect of harboring a criminal. Then it hit him; call Imani.

He scrambled back inside their suite and scooped up the phone. Imani. What was her number? He'd written it down someplace, hadn't he?

It only occurred to him when he was in the middle of dialing, that Imani had just lost her father, and David, her half-brother, was somehow being linked to that death by the local police. Before he could hang up and rethink his plan the phone was picked up. A female voice breaking with grief said, "Hello?"

"Imani? Don't hang up, it's Chris."

"C-Chris? What? How—?"

Chris rushed in, before he could chicken out and keep silent, or she could hang up. "I'm so sorry about your dad. It's horrible…" His voice almost cracked. "But the police have taken David away. I think they believe he had something to do with this." His words were rushed now, as though he had to spill them before she could stop him. "But he couldn't have. David is too good to do such a terrible thing. He never would have done anything to hurt your dad—his dad. Never in a million years. You gotta believe me."

"How could you call here like this," Imani's voice took on a hard edge Chris had never heard before. "You destroyed my family. How dare you—"

"No! God, no it wasn't—we didn't. David wouldn't hurt anyone. Joel was his *father*."

"The father who wasn't there for him," Imani was shouting now. "The father who left him with his nasty mother. Oh, I can see how it went. David resented Dad for leaving him. Then he met him and realized this man had a whole life that had never involved David. He hated it—"

"Oh God, Imani. You can't believe that. Please—" Chris was grasping at straws now. If Imani wouldn't help what the hell could Chris do to help David. "Listen, David did meet Joel last night. He told me when he got back from seeing him. Joel… Joel was already making plans to work things out. He wasn't giving up on his family. He told David he'd never told your mother about him and how ashamed that made him. He was a good man, Imani, and David would never have hurt him. He wanted David and me to join you for a barbecue, some big cricket match between St. George's and Somerset. He said it was like the American Super Bowl. He even admitted he asked David here to talk to Jay. That Jay was in some kind of trouble…"

"D-Dad said that?"

"Yes, he did." Chris was desperate now. "There wasn't any animosity between them. Yes, David was confused and maybe even a little scared and hurt, but he could never hate anyone, certainly not his own father. He doesn't even hate his mother, though I think he should."

Imani gulped, swallowing a rush of tears. "Dad was at his wit's end about Jay. He couldn't get through to him, and it ate him up." She took a deep breath. "I don't know what he hoped David could do, but I know he wanted to try something. He was so impressed when he found out his first born was a police officer—"

Suddenly the phone was snatched from her, despite her weak protests.

A male voice, thick with scorn, came on the line. "What are

you doing calling here, faggot? You have the balls to disturb us after what you did to my father?"

It had to be Jay. Chris knew the man wasn't going to listen to reason, but he had to try, for David's sake.

"Neither of us did anything to your father. David was happy to find out he was still alive. The last thing he would have done is hurt him—"

"Don't call here again. Or you'll be sorry," Jay screamed. Chris could almost hear the spittle hitting the phone. He recoiled from the onslaught.

"Jay, please—"

The phone slammed in his ear. He sagged into the easy chair beside the bed. For a moment he sat like that, his head in his hands, fighting the urge to cry. He had to help David. Nothing else mattered.

With nerves jittering he got up and paced through the bedroom, then back out onto the veranda. He gripped the railing with white-knuckled ferocity and stared blindly toward the harbor where lights were starting to come up as the sun dipped west.

Behind him the phone rang. He raced inside and snatched it up.

It was Imani.

"I'm sorry, I can't talk long. They're all on a rampage, swearing up and down that David must have done it. But I'm not so sure… The police arrested David?"

"I don't know, they didn't say he was under arrest, but they took him away. I'm scared, Imani. What are they going to do to him?"

Imani's voice was still hoarse; she'd clearly been crying. "I can't believe it."

Chris wasn't sure she meant she didn't want to believe her father was dead or that David was involved. He wasn't about to ask her.

"Thank you," he whispered, feeling something in his chest

loosen. "I still don't know what's going on, but I desperately need a lawyer to talk to and prepare for the… worst. Do you know anyone?"

Imani was silent for several heartbeats. Chris began to wonder if she had changed her mind. Or Jay was back. Then she said, "I don't, but I know who I can ask. Let me get back to you."

"Oh thank you, Imani. I am so sorry about your dad, and we'll do our best to help out any way we can."

"It's better if you don't call my place again. I'll call you later today, or early tomorrow, if I find anything. And please, let me know what's happening with David. I was just getting used to having another big brother…" Her voice broke. "I don't want to lose him and my father."

Chris listened to her cry, wishing he could say something to comfort her, knowing there were no words in the world that would offer her solace at this point.

"I'll be here," he whispered. "Please call"

He hung up on the dial tone, feeling more bereft than ever. He wandered into the kitchen and stared into the fridge for an age, knowing he wouldn't be able to eat, but knowing he had to. Finally he took out the bottle of wine he had bought the day before, when all he and David had to look forward to was a fun-in-the-sun vacation. Now all that had crumbled to bitter dust and Chris was at a loss as to what he could do to help. He drifted back to the veranda, carrying the bottle, a glass and the portable phone. Almost immediately he went back inside to grab his laptop.

Daylight began to fade. The monotonous song of the local tree frogs intensified as the sun slipped behind a bank of clouds. The cruise ship lit up, a beacon in the dark. Chris thought of the passengers, tourists without a worry in the world, pleasure seekers whose greatest concern was what shirt to wear for a night on the town.

He waited, half an ear cocked for the phone beside him on the glass table, wondering if he should call anyone back home. But what could they do except offer sympathy, and Chris didn't think he could stand any of that. Des was a great friend, but he'd be as helpless as Chris. He'd be outraged, and he might feel obligated to fly down and offer a shoulder to cry on, but really, what could he do? Ditto for Becky. Martinez would just bluster and curse over the stupidity of it all, but in the end he could do nothing. Chris was totally on his own this time.

He bent over his laptop and did some random Google searches. He found the report of Joel's death, but no details that would help him in his search. He didn't even know the name of the cop who had taken David away. The police had no other leads, or they weren't interested in looking anywhere else.

Until he could learn more, he was at a dead end. With a curse, he shut the laptop and picked up his wine.

He knew he was feeling sorry for himself. Not good. They'd been through worse in their seven years together. David's outing had nearly derailed not only their budding relationship, but his position with the LAPD. It had cost Chris a steady job with decent benefits. Okay, he had hated the job, but it had been a damn good paycheck. Then the mess with Jairo that even now his mind shied away from.

But that too had passed. Just as this would. He had to believe that.

It was after ten. He knew he should get some sleep, but the thought of going to bed alone made the idea impossible. He kept starting at every sound, wanting the phone to ring. When it finally did he nearly jumped out of his skin.

He snatched up the hand set and turned it on.

It was David.

Chris sagged into the lounge chair, every bone turning to jelly. "David! Where are you? What's happening?"

"I still don't know." Chris could hear the weariness in David's normally strong voice. He heard what could only be the rasp of unshaven cheeks as David rubbed his face. "They haven't formally charged me, but I think it's only a matter of time…"

"What do they think you did?"

David sighed and didn't speak for several heartbeats. Finally he said, "They seem to think I murdered Joel."

"That's insane."

"Unfortunately the circumstantial evidence supports their belief."

"Oh, God," Chris moaned. "This can't be happening."

"Listen to me, Chris. I need you to find a lawyer. Ask around, someone must know a good one."

"I already asked Imani. She says she may know someone who can help."

"How is she taking it?"

"Rough." He didn't tell David that Imani had thought he was involved somehow. David didn't need that tidbit of information.

David's voice dropped. "What about Joel's sons?"

Chris mulled over his answer. Did David really need to know? "They blame you," he blurted. "I'm sorry, hon."

"I kind of expected it. I'm just grateful Imani believes us. But I have to get out of here. I don't think the local cops are going to work very hard proving I wasn't involved. It's easier to lay it all on me. I'm not local. I'm American and I'm gay. None of which are good qualities right now," David added.

"So what can we do?"

"Look into who might have had it in for Joel. Someone must have, to do that to him."

"Are you really going to investigate this?"

"If I can get out of here, I will."

Chris wasn't sure he liked the sound of that. But the more he thought about it, the more he knew David was right. Who else would look out for him? Chris heard a muffled voice. David came back on.

"I have to go," he said. "Do what you can about getting me a lawyer. With any luck I can get out of here soon. I'll let you know if there's a hearing."

Before Chris could respond David hung up.

Chris scrambled out of his chair and pulled his laptop onto the table. He logged in and began Googling. He plugged in Joel's name again. This time he knew enough to narrow the Cameron family down. He found one site that someone in the family must have put up. A family bio. He read the piece completely. In an odd twist, it looked like Daryl's side of the family was cousins through marriage and blood on Joel's side. They had worked alongside the Camerons, fishing their own fleet of deep-water boats.

In sixty-eight Joel had enrolled at Columbia in New York City. The rest, as they would say, was history.

A new search on the two sons produced next to nothing. He'd have to get more creative there. He switched over to his Linux partition and his more powerful tools to probe government portals. With practiced skill he began delving into the murky depths of the Internet, finally finding and dipping into the Bermuda government Intranet. He poked around judiciously, not wanting to alert any nosy sysadmins to his back door activity.

It yielded results. Jay, it turned out, was often on the police radar, mostly petty stuff, like shoplifting, public drunk and disorderly, but once for a more serious drug charge. His younger brother, Baker, looked clean. At least Chris couldn't find any records for him. Neither did Imani, to his immense relief. He even checked out Cedarbridge, the high school both Baker and Jay had gone to. He found a web portal, which didn't contain anything. He did find an alumni site. He dug into it and found all three of Joel's children had graduated.

Chris delved deeper into the criminal angle. Jay really had quite a record. No wonder Joel had been concerned. Concerned enough to engage a total stranger to help him? Even if David was the man's son, he was still a stranger, an unknown entity. Chris studied what his probing had uncovered. A felony bust on someplace called Court Street that resulted in an eighteen-month stay at the Westgate prison facility. Joel must have been real impressed with that. In the short time he had known him,

Chris could see that Joel was a man on the straight and narrow. A second narcotics bust had come not long after Jay was released from prison. This one was tossed on a technicality, no jail time.

It hadn't taught him anything. In fact it looked like David's younger half-brother was currently waiting for yet another sentencing on more drug charges. He was out on a bond, pending a court date. This time he'd not only been caught with a nice stash of meth, but he had also assaulted the officer who apprehended him. Even Chris, who knew nothing about the Bermuda legal system, had the feeling Jay might have run out of luck. He might be facing hard time on this beef, whatever constituted hard time in Bermuda.

Wednesday 1:15am Hamilton Police Station, Parliament Street, Hamilton, Bermuda

After his phone call to Chris, MacClellan led David back to the interrogation room. They put a cup of tepid coffee on the table in front of him, and for the first time produced a tape recorder. David glanced at the recorder, then across at MacClellan.

After recording the time, date and interview site, along with his name and full rank, MacClellan said, "Please state your full name and current address for the record."

They went through it all again. Exhaustion rode David hard; it was a struggle to maintain his composure. The coffee, bad as it was, didn't help. He knew that's exactly what they wanted. Make him sweat and hope for a slip up. The interview took nearly two hours. David was blinking away sleep before it ended, and he could feel MacClellan's energy increasing, its focus sharp and riveted on him, like a cadaver dog pawing through garbage for a corpse. He knew David was losing it, and it only made him press harder, hoping to widen the crack until the whole dam burst.

There was a knock at the door; MacClellan answered and returned to the table with a sheaf of papers. He skimmed through them, his lips pursed, not making eye contact with David.

Finally he put the papers aside. Constable Lindstrom returned and David watched in dismay as he removed a pair of handcuffs from his belt.

"Please stand, Detective Laine," MacClellan said. "You are under arrest for the murder of Joel Astwood Cameron. You are not obliged to say anything unless you wish to do so. Anything you do say will be taken down in writing and may be used in evidence."

"Do you wish to say anything?" MacClellan asked.

David stood up. "Where are you taking me?"

"Westgate," MacClellan said. "Where you'll be held pending trial."

"What's your proof? I demand to see a lawyer—"

Lindstrom snicked the cuffs around David's wrists, the metal cold against his bare skin.

"You'll get your chance," MacClellan said.

David resisted the instinctive desire to jerk away ashe fought to keep his voice steady. A rush of adrenaline swamped his exhaustion, leaving him lightheaded, but more alert. He would pay for that alertness later.

He tried again. "What about bail?"

"No bail," MacClellan said. "Once you secure a lawyer you can proceed with a bond, if the courts let you." His tone said he very much doubted that would happen.

"And when can I do that?"

They were jerking his chain. They'd run him around in circles until he gave something away they could use against him. Or maybe in his exhaustion he had already said something they took as guilt. Now they'd make him sweat in jail. It was an old cop trick. He'd played it too many times to count.

It was only midday when they exited the police station. Lindstrom put David into the back of a squad car and slid into the front seat. MacClellan had gone back inside. The lights of the station stared balefully down into the vehicle, only vanishing when Lindstrom turned onto Front Street and headed east, following the harbor around to Middle Road. From there they headed west, passing the road that would have taken him back to Aunt Nea's and Chris, then turning onto Middle Road, past the Gibbs Hill lighthouse and its beacon of light sweeping the ocean, finally crossing tiny Somerset Bridge.

David recognized where they were—very near the Dockyard where the four of them had eaten a carefree lunch just the previous day. They turned off just before the Dockyard.

The prison was a modern, low slung structure beside an ancient building that looked like a medieval fortress.

"Casemates," Lindstrom said. "The old prison. Be thankful you're not going there."

David caught a glimpse of ocean before they turned into the prison yard. In alarm, David saw a TV camera and several reporters who instantly surrounded the squad car, pressing against the still moving vehicle. It was eerily reminiscent of the horrible time when he and Chris had been hounded by reporters eager for blood during his outing and near death at the hands of the Carpet Killer. He wondered who had alerted the media. No doubt the murder of a local man by an American tourist was rich fodder for the local rags. Flash bulbs flared, and he instinctively ducked his head away from the light. Lindstrom guided him out of the vehicle and David kept his face averted as they passed the gauntlet of reporters who hurled questions at Lindstrom and himself.

"What is he being charged with, Constable?"

"Did you kill your father, David?"

They already knew his name. What else had they uncovered? Their next question gave him the answer.

"Is it true you're an LAPD homicide detective? Why would you kill your father? Did he find out you were gay? Did the local authorities know you were gay? Is it true you married your lover? What did your father think about that?"

David silently urged Lindstrom to get him out of the inquisitive eye of the reporters and out of sight, but the constable seemed to take a perverse pleasure in playing to the media.

He jerked on David's arm, sending sharp pains down to his shackled wrists. "Come on, these are your fans. You don't want to disappoint them, do you?"

Tension rippled across David's back. His shoulders, held at an awkward angle by the cuffs, began to ache under the strain. He was glad to enter the prison compound. Lindstrom left him with a blue-shirted prison official, who signed him in and processed the paperwork that would see him a ward of Bermuda. Inside he was patted down, then divested of all his personal items: his watch, his wallet, his belt, the St. Michael's medal Chris had given him last year, his LAPD class ring as well as the plain gold band Chris had put on his finger last year at their wedding. They also took his silk tie as though they were afraid he would despair and take his own life. His clothes were replaced with drab prison garb, which barely fit his large frame, and he was given a pair of scuffed slippers. Finally, they handed him a thin pillow and even thinner blanket, and took him down a dimly lit hallway that smelled of bleach, human sweat and boiled noodles.

He was led down the dank hall to a small cell that barely had room for the concrete slab and lidless toilet it contained. At least he was getting a single cell and wouldn't have to face another inmate. That was SOP for any incarcerated law enforcement officer, whether or not it was necessary.

He didn't turn when the guard shut the door behind him. Footsteps echoed down the hall, until finally they faded away and David was left alone. He spread the blanket over the stone slab and dropped the pillow at the head of the "bed." Then he sank down and stared up at the ceiling, stained with things he didn't want to identify.

A distant voice rose in fury, shouting incomprehensible curses. Somewhere a heavy door banged shut. Then a silence more deafening than any noise fell.

CHAPTER FIFTEEN

Wednesday 5:40am Aunt Nea's, Nea's Alley, St. George's Parish, Bermuda

Chris climbed out of bed and stared balefully around the room. He glanced at the bedside clock, then at the phone. He remembered all too clearly Imani's warning not to telephone. He had to wait until she called him, praying she wouldn't regret her decision to help and leave him alone, without hope.

He got up and paced. He passed through the kitchen, but knew he couldn't possibly eat. He pulled out the coffee pot and got out the coffee they had bought at the market their first day. He drank two mugs before the phone rang.

He snatched it up. It was Imani.

"How are you holding up?" he asked her.

"I'm okay," she said. "Wishing this was all a bad dream."

"Trust me, I know what you mean. Thank you for believing me, for believing in David, Imani. You gotta believe this is a nightmare for both of us."

"I know," she said. "At least I think I do. Maybe I'm just a dumb, naive kid, but I can't see David doing those horrible things. Did you hear from him?"

Chris rubbed his forehead, pinching the bridge of his nose, trying to ease a growing headache. "Yes," he whispered. "He called last night."

"How's he holding up?"

"About as well as can be expected. He really needs a lawyer…"

"I think I can help. I talked to a friend of mine and she recommended a litigation attorney, Aidan Pitt." She lowered her voice. "She didn't think I should help you. They all think David k-killed my father… Oh, God Chris, what am I going to do?"

"Help me, Imani. If they think David did it, what must the police think? It means they won't look for the real killer. Everyone loses, and the killer gets off… Please, please, give me his number."

She rattled off a phone number. "He should be in the office in about an hour if you want to call then. He's supposed to be one of the best."

"Thank you."

"I miss my dad." Imani's voice broke. "I want him back, but that's not going to happen. I don't want anyone else's life to be ruined too."

She was weeping softly now. Chris felt his own throat close up and he felt like joining her.

"I'm so sorry, Imani. Maybe if we hadn't come none of this would have happened and—"

"Don't say that! My dad wanted to meet his first born more than anything. He lived with so much regret when he found out David was alive; regret that he couldn't have been there for him. He loved the family he had, but he wanted his family whole again. He would not have passed up this chance for anything."

"Thank you, then. I'll let you know what the lawyer says."

"I'm going with you," she said.

He stared at the phone. "Why?" was all he could ask.

"I'll drive. I've got a scooter, too." Her voice grew harder. "Besides, if you are trying to pull one over on me, I want to be there when it falls in your face."

He couldn't blame her for distrusting him, but still her words hurt. He didn't respond. What could he say?

"Besides," she went on. "It'll be quicker than trying to get a cab from your place. Call and make an appointment first thing. Tell him it's an emergency. I'll get ready and leave right now."

Chris stammered he would, then hung up. He rushed through a hot shower, trying to clear his head so he could make sense of the last twenty-four hours. The he made a fresh pot of coffee and waited until he could call the attorney.

He got Pitt's secretary. Chris didn't give her time to stonewall him. He blurted out, "I have to speak to Mr. Pitt. It's very urgent."

"And what is the nature of your business?"

"We're tourists from Los Angeles. My partner is an LAPD homicide detective and he's being accused of murder."

Maybe it was the word murder that got her attention. Chris doubted Bermuda was exactly a hot bed for homicides.

A deep, mellifluous voice came on the phone. He had a British accent that made Chris think of smoking jackets and packs of English foxhounds baying on the moor.

"Yes? Whom am I speaking to?"

"Mr. Pitt? My name is Christopher Bellamere. My partner is Detective David Eric Laine of the LAPD. I think he's about to be charged with the murder of his father."

"You'd better start at the beginning," Pitt said.

"I'd like to come down and see you. I can pay, whatever you want."

"You aren't much of a bargainer are you, Mr. Bellamere? You tell most men you'll pay anything and that's what you'll be charged."

"I don't care," Chris said. He'd put himself in the poorhouse if it would help David. "Please, will you see me?"

"Is ten early enough?"

"I'll be there."

Wednesday 9:15am Aunt Nea's, Nea's Alley, St. George's Parish, Bermuda

Imani's scooter trundled up the driveway over a half hour before Chris's appointment. He was dressed in the most conservative suit he had packed, a gray pinstripe Brooks Brothers.

He met her at the head of the drive. She looked spiffy in a jade blouse and figure hugging culottes. She waved a greeting but didn't get off the bike. Gingerly he straddled the pillion seat behind her. He'd only ridden a bike once before, during a brief, but incandescent fling he'd had with a guy who owned a Softail. He'd known exactly what to hang onto on that ride. He never heard any complaints either. But this wasn't Gord.

He clamped his hands over the vinyl-covered seat and grimaced when she opened the throttle and spun out of the drive onto Nea's Alley. He was white-knuckled by the time they reached Hamilton. Imani found parking in a bike's only area near the bus depot. It took him a minute to unclench his muscles and stand straight again.

Aidan's office was less than half a block away, across from the Bermuda National Gallery. They climbed a set of plush carpeted stairs to the second story office. The receptionist, a cool-looking black woman, looked up at their entrance.

Chris gave his name and the receptionist nodded. "I'll let Mr. Pitt know you're here." She picked up the phone.

Chris looked around the reception area. It was tastefully decorated with Bermuda memorabilia, including prints from famous Bermudian artists of early settlements and sea-going sailing ships. There was a single photograph of an ornate stone edifice labeled Gates of Oxford. Aidan's alma mater? Chris's mental picture of an English country gentleman returned. He envisioned pipes and leather-patched jackets and snorting horses readied for the hunt.

Imani and Chris sat on an uncomfortable horsehair Victorian sofa, perched uneasily on the edge of their seat. The inner door opened and a tall, impeccably dressed black man stepped into the room. He held out his hand.

"Christopher Bellamere?"

Chris stood up. Aidan's grip was strong. He smelled faintly of something citrusy. Chris was startled by his brilliant green eyes and again he found himself mesmerized by the man's subtle British accent.

Aidan indicated his office. "Please, come in Chris. Would you like coffee?"

"Yes, please." Chris glanced back at Imani, who smiled and said, "I guess I'll just wait here. But I'd love a coffee, too."

Aidan returned to his office, emerging moments later with a delicate china cup. He indicated to his receptionist. "Mrs. Cooper will show you where we keep the cream and sugar."

Chris followed him into the office. Aidan shut the door. The office was an extension of the reception area. More images of what he assumed were Oxford, plus several signed certificates from various law institutions filled the ecru walls. On Aidan's desk there was a framed picture of a beautiful black woman and two young children, both in school uniforms. There was also an IBM laptop opened on a web page.

"Please sit," Aidan said, gesturing toward a black leather chair facing his desk. "Now, perhaps you could start by filling me in on what's going on."

So Chris recounted everything David had told him, including what he had related to the police. Aidan frowned.

"David told the police that he had met Mr. Cameron just before the police claim he died?"

"Yes. Was that wrong?" Chris said even though he knew from his own experience that it was never smart to tell the police more than you absolutely had to.

"He would have been wiser to wait until he could get counsel with a lawyer. The police are too eager to use such information out of context. It is in their best interests to find a perpetrator quickly. It's good for their bottom line, as you say in America."

Chris knew all too well how overzealous cops could work hard to pin a murder on an innocent person. He'd nearly been railroaded into taking the fall for the notorious Carpet Killer; the case that had brought David into his life. It was only David's dogged belief that the man he had fallen in love with couldn't have been the killer that saved him. But it had been close.

"Will you take our case?"

Aidan seemed to consider the request. Finally his green eyes met Chris's. "It would be prudent if you told me everything. Just exactly what is your relationship to Mr. Laine?"

The moment of truth. Chris raised his chin. "We're married."

"Ah," said Aidan, not looking at all surprised. "And did Mr. Cameron know this?"

"Yes, he did. Neither David nor I hide the fact. Though we have been ah, discreet since we arrived in Bermuda."

"Probably a wise choice. Though Bermudians have never been noted for violence in that regard."

"There's always a first time," Chris muttered.

Aidan tapped his desk. "I will take your case. My normal practice is to ask for a seventy-five thousand dollar retainer, billing at six-fifty an hour."

Chris tried to swallow, his mouth suddenly dry. He hadn't expected it to be so much. "I'll have to make arrangements to have the money wired. Are US funds acceptable?"

"US dollars are accepted at par."

He called his bank on his BlackBerry. It took some finagling, but within half an hour, the money was on its way. "I'm staying at Aunt Nea's, a guest house in St. George's. You can reach me there pretty well anytime." He also gave Aidan his card, which listed his BlackBerry and email address. "I check it regularly. What will you do first?"

"I need to secure a meeting with David if I can. But access to individuals in police detention is at the discretion of the officer investigating the alleged offense—lawyers cannot insist on seeing a client while he's in custody. I have some friends in the department, I'll involve them. It might also be in your best interest to contact the American Consulate. I'll get you a name and number. They can advocate for David."

"If they let you see him what do you do then?"

"First I let the police know I am on the case and to see what, if anything, they have charged David with."

"Will you be able to get him out on bail?" Chris had visions of the courts refusing to release David since he'd be a flight risk.

"I don't know," Aidan admitted. "It will be difficult. The Consulate may help sway them, which is why you need to involve them as early as possible. That may be a moot point," Aidan said. "I warn you it will not be cheap. The police will also wish to confiscate his passport."

"We're not going to run, if that's what you think."

"The courts will only be satisfied with the strongest possible deterrent. I suggest you extend your stay at this guest house, since you may be here a while. I'm afraid you'll only be able to stay twenty-seven days. After that only a government intersession will allow you to stay longer." Aidan scribbled some things in a yellow legal pad. He swiveled around to access his laptop. He typed in some commands and wrote something else on his pad. He tore it off and handed it to Chris. "This is the American consulate's number. Talk to this man." He tapped a name. "He can help you."

Chris scanned the pad. "Randall Harding."

"I'll warn you now, if the case drags on you may need to return overseas, then return at the trial date."

Chris felt lightheaded. "Do you really think it will come to a trial?"

"It may. I won't try to sugarcoat it. It largely depends on what the police have in the way of evidence, or whether they find a more viable suspect."

"I'll find one for them."

Aidan looked alarmed. "Please, Christopher, don't interfere with this investigation. The police won't take kindly to a foreigner butting in. You might only make it harder for David."

"I'm not going to let them railroad David, either."

"Leave the legalities to me. I assure you I won't let David be 'railroaded' either."

As good as the man's intentions were Chris had no desire to leave it entirely in his hands, but rather than get into an argument neither of them could win, he nodded.

Aidan seemed relieved. He stood up and extended his hand to Chris, who took it. "It was a pleasure meeting you, Mr. Bellamere. I will keep you advised of my progress."

"Do you think I'll be allowed to visit David?"

"I'll try to arrange it. Let me call you once I make the preliminary inquiries."

Chris found Imani still sitting in the reception area. She stood when he emerged from the office. He took her arm and led her toward the door.

"How did it go?"

"He's going to take the case," Chris said. "I have to call the American consulate. After that, we wait."

Imani made a face. "Let's get you home then."

"Thanks, Imani." He wanted to kiss her for her show of support, especially after she had so much trouble believing him. "I don't know what I'd have done without you."

"I don't think you would have let David down no matter what."

No, he wouldn't have, but it was still nice to know there were others in his corner.

CHAPTER SIXTEEN

Wednesday, 6:50am Westgate Correctional Facility, Pender Road, Ireland Island, Sandys Parish, Bermuda

David lay down, but sleep eluded him. The concrete slab was too small for his six-four frame and his feet dangled over the edge. The blanket smelled musty and started a tickle in his throat. Every sound was magnified; even his own heartbeat was like thunder in his head. His breathing was hoarse and his throat felt like sandpaper when he swallowed. He heard the guard's footsteps echoing down the corridor as he made his rounds. David turned on his side, averting his face.

Silence fell again, except for the snores and muffled grunts of nearby prisoners. David was surprised at how quiet the place was. In any American prison he'd ever been in, no one was silent. Being silent meant you were a pussy, all they knew how to be was violent. This was almost eerie.

He lay on his back with his eyes closed. Even so he grew aware of the sky lightening beyond the cool walls.

He wondered if Chris had any luck finding a lawyer. Would anyone even want to take the case? He was a foreigner, an American cop in a land where the local police didn't even wear guns. He never left the house without his. They were in the same profession, but they were miles apart in sharing common ground.

He slung his arm over his eyes, blocking out the dawn. After a while they slid a breakfast tray into his cell. He forced himself to eat the unpalatable food, knowing it was the best he was going to get for a while. Later, he must have dozed because he woke to new footsteps, which stopped in front of his cell.

"Mr. Laine," said a guard he hadn't seen before. He released the door lock and slid the cell door open. "You have a visitor."

David sat up. "Chris?"

"Who? It's your lawyer."

"My lawyer?"

"That's what he said."

Chris had worked fast. Relief flooded David. Maybe that really was a light at the end of a tunnel.

He was led into a small room that was only slightly better than his original interrogation room. An urbane looking black man stood at his entry.

"Mr. David Laine? I'm Aidan Pitt. Christopher has retained me as your lawyer."

David sank into the chair opposite Aidan.

"How are they treating you?"

"Fine. As well as I'd expect."

"I'm working on getting you out of here," Aidan said, music to David's ears. "It may take a few hours, possibly even a day. I'll warn you they may very well request you surrender your passport before they will issue your bond."

"Just get me out of here."

"You'll be out soon. But I must insist that any further conversations with the police be held in my presence. You have said far too much already."

David didn't really need a lawyer to tell him that, but it was the cop in him that made him talk. His honor demanded he had nothing to hide. Unfortunately, the local cops didn't share his zeal and they clearly didn't think he was innocent. Not when it was the choice between an easy case and one they'd have to work hard to solve.

"Agreed," he said.

"Good," Aidan said. He slid a briefcase up on the table between them. "Now I want you to tell me everything that has happened since you arrived in Bermuda."

David went even further. He told Aiden about learning that his father wasn't dead and about their visit with his family in

New Hampshire. He didn't mince words, but laid out the entire fight and the stony silence that had followed. Then he talked of meeting his real father for the first time. "I'm not going to pretend it was all roses, hell, I resented him for disappearing like that, but I never hated him. He was my father. I thought for sure we'd work it out, but we never had the chance."

"How did your mother talk about your father, besides telling you he was dead? She must have said something."

David shook his head. "You don't know my mother. She made it very clear she wouldn't talk about him. I knew I'd been born in San Francisco, but I always had the impression he left before I was born. Turns out he stayed with us for over a year. He wanted to be part of my life. She refused to allow him to get involved. She lied and told him I had died, just to get him out of her hair. Her and my grandmother." David grimaced and shook his head. Heat flooded his face. "I'm afraid they didn't like the fact he was black."

Aidan looked thoughtful. "All this will be food for the prosecution's fodder. They will contend you resented your father and his neglect and thus had motive to murder him. They might even argue you hated the fact that you were half black. That I'm afraid will let them play the race card. Bermuda has seen too much of that lately." He held up his hand when David began to protest. "It's not fair, but it is what they will argue."

David knew it was true. In similar circumstances back home he would have thought the same thing. Most homicides were committed by family members. That was a cold, hard fact every cop knew.

"If your parents were asked to testify, would they?"

"For you or for the prosecution?"

"I suppose it would depend on what they might say."

David grimaced. He could just imagine what his mother and grandmother would say. His stepfather was another story. He couldn't imagine Graham bad-mouthing him.

"I think my stepfather would be pretty supportive. My

mother… well I wouldn't count on her, not with my grandmother behind her."

"So if the prosecution calls on one to testify, we must ensure the other one speaks for us."

"Great, pit the family against each other. I ought to be real popular then."

"If it will mean the difference between freedom and imprisonment it would be worth it." Aidan was sardonic.

"Yeah, I guess so."

"I believe Christopher wants to visit you. I'll talk to the sergeant in charge of the case and facilitate his meeting if you like."

"Yes, please." David knew he gave away his feelings for Chris, but Aidan didn't seem surprised. Knowing Chris, he'd already told the man. "Just so you know," he said. "My parents also hate the fact that I'm gay. Again, not my stepfather, he's fine with it, but my mother and her mother…"

"Understood."

"Are they likely to bring that up at the trial?"

Aidan sighed. "I wouldn't be surprised. They'll use it to color your interaction with the deceased. They expect the jurors to assume Mr. Cameron shared the usual distaste for the lifestyle." He looked shrewd. "Did he?"

"No, I don't think so. At least he never gave any indication— he defended us pretty vigorously to his sons."

"What about the daughter?"

David smiled at his memory of Imani. "She's a sweet kid. It definitely didn't bother her."

"Perhaps we can use her to refute the prosecution's arguments. She hardly has any reason to speak against her own brothers unless she's telling the truth."

It made sense. "Just get me out of here."

"Consider it done."

"You're that good?"

"I'm that good."

Wednesday, 3:50pm Aunt Nea's, Nea's Alley, St. George's Parish, Bermuda

"I've got some things to take care of so I'll be going then." Imani brushed his cheek with her lips and trotted down the steps. Chris followed. "I'll be back in a bit."

He waited until she climbed on her bike and flew down the drive, disappearing toward Devonshire Parish.

Then he went back upstairs and called Randall Harding, the American consul.

Harding was a gravel-voiced man who Chris pegged as mid-fifties and a heavy smoker. "Tell me the whole story," he said.

Chris did. Harding stopped him a few times to clarify or expand on certain points. When Chris told him about hiring Aidan, Harding made a low sound.

"Something wrong?"

"No, no. I'm familiar with Mr. Pitt."

"Is he as good as he thinks?"

If Harding had a sense of humor the next sound might have been a snort. "He might be better. What can I do to help you, Mr. Bellamere?"

"David's an American citizen. He's being railroaded by the Bermudian police. Isn't that reason enough to get involved?"

"Our normal policy is not to interfere with local law enforcement. Do you have any proof of David's innocence?"

"He's a homicide detective, for God's sake. There's nothing on his record to say he's ever done anything illegal before. He's clean. He's the most honest man I know."

"The absence of wrong doing doesn't mean there isn't wrong

doing."

Chris closed his eyes and rubbed the bridge of his nose. "Please, Mr. Harding. I swear David didn't do this. You have to help us."

He heard the rustle of paper. Harding came back on the line.

"I'll do what I can, Mr. Bellamere. Give me your contact information."

Chris gave him his BlackBerry number. Then he grabbed his board shorts and went for a swim, punishing himself through the light surf until his arms and legs ached. Back in the apartment, he showered and dressed, then thought about food and decided he'd eat later. Instead he poured himself another coffee and sat on the veranda.

Before he finished the second coffee, Imani rode back up on her scooter and climbed the stairs, where he met her at the door and let her in. She dropped her bag on the veranda and settled into a chair opposite him. She handed him a carry-out bag from some place called Swizzle Inn. It was a burger and fries.

"I figured you probably didn't have the sense to eat, so I grabbed this."

The burger was good, not as good as the Frog and Onion, but still tasty. Suddenly finding himself ravenous, he scarfed it down in several bites, sipping the ice tea she had included.

"You hear anything?" she asked.

"I called the American consul. He's going to, quote 'Look into it,' unquote."

"Well that's good, isn't it?"

His BlackBerry vibrated against his leg. He stood up and unclipped the device. It was Aidan. Chris held up a finger to forestall Imani's next words.

"Good news." Aidan didn't waste time on niceties. "David will be out soon."

"Thank God," Chris whispered, sinking back into the padded

lawn chair. Imani stepped forward in alarm. Chris signaled her to keep waiting. Then, "It's okay. It's the lawyer."

She sat beside him, her expression torn between somberness and delight. "David?"

He nodded.

Aidan was still talking. Chris tamped down his elation and focused on the lawyer's words.

"You may want to start thinking about how you're going to secure the necessary bond. I wouldn't be surprised if they request a million on David's own bond, plus an independent surety in the same amount. Is that likely to be a problem?"

Chris sagged into the chair. He felt the blood leave his face. The hamburger he had recently consumed threatened to come back up. "Do you mean cash?"

"No, it's just an irrevocable promise to pay if the accused doesn't show up for court."

Chris's mind raced. He had money, but even he couldn't come up with two million on short notice. He had to find that second million. Des immediately came to mind.

"Let me make a phone call," he said, all too aware of how hollow his voice sounded. "I'll get back to you as soon as I learn anything."

He hung up and pressed his face into his hands. Beside him Imani grew alarmed. She pressed her nails into his arm.

"What is it? What's wrong?"

He told her and she gaped at him.

"Two million? How can you come up with that?"

"I guess I don't really need to produce the cash, just a guarantee that I can pay it. I need to make a call."

He slipped into the room and dialed Des's number. Trevor answered. This time there was no bantering. "I need to talk to Des. It's important."

Des's voice was subdued when he came on. "What's wrong,

baby? Is it David—?"

"Yes and no," Chris said. He explained what had happened to date and what the lawyer had just told him.

"I can't believe you didn't tell me," Des said. "How could you not call and tell me? You knew I'd be pissed, didn't you? Well I am. This isn't like you, Chris."

Actually, it was exactly like Chris. He couldn't count the number of times he'd tried to protect Des from his actions. Des had a bad habit of overreacting to the littlest thing. And Chris had the equally bad habit of doing things to make Des overreact. Everyone protected Des.

"Believe me," Chris said. "I had other things on my mind. Up till now there wasn't anything you or anyone else could do. I had to concentrate on David."

Barely mollified Des said, "I can understand, but you still could give a guy a head's up. Poor David. Poor Chris!"

That was exactly why he hadn't called. Des's pity-fest dug at his gut, bringing a fresh round of tears. He avoided looking at Imani. "Please, don't." He rubbed his eyes and swore he wouldn't cry. Not yet, not until David was safe. "I can come up with some of it—I can put the house up as collateral, but the other million is just a bit beyond me."

"Don't you worry about a thing. I'll take care of it. I can call my accountant right now and set it up. I'll get back to you."

Chris couldn't help it; he felt tears well up. He dabbed at his eyes with the sleeve of his T-shirt and took a deep, ragged breath. "Thank you. You have no idea what this means, hon."

"Hey," Des sounded teary-eyed too. "What else are friends for? Even friends who forget to let me know what's going on."

Chris waited for Des's call that things were in the works. Then he called Aidan back.

"You'll need to come down to the courthouse to sign some papers," Aidan said. "But once that's done, David can be released. When can you get down here?"

Chris glanced at Imani standing in the doorway. She met his gaze, her eyes full of sympathy and glazed over with her own tears. "I need to get into Hamilton," he said to her.

"And bring David's passport," Aidan said. "They'll want to hold onto that until this matter is cleared up."

"Tell him we'll be there in fifty minutes," Imani said.

Chris relayed the news. They broke the connection. "Give me a minute to get changed."

He emerged five minutes later in his Brooks Brothers suit. They climbed back onto Imani's bike and headed into Hamilton, where they met Aidan and the police, and signed the necessary papers to secure David's release. In return, Chris handed over David's passport and the officer wrote up a receipt for the document.

Once they were outside again, Aidan shook his hand. "I'll see that David's processed as quickly as possible, probably within four or five hours. It's best if you get a cab to pick him up. The local cabbies will deny it, but many of them won't pick up fares from the prison."

Four hours. That would give him time to hit the nearest grocery store and grab at least enough for dinner. He thanked Aidan again before they said goodbye, then turned to Imani. "One more stop. I need to pick up some grub."

Her scooter had a wire basket on the back. It would hold all the groceries he needed for the next few days. He climbed onto the bike behind her and she shot out onto Front Street, heading east to the SuperMart. There he grabbed a cross-section of food and scooped up a *Royal Gazette*, the island's daily paper, when he saw the headline in bold words: AMERICAN CHARGED WITH FOURTH MURDER OF THE YEAR.

Once he'd loaded all the groceries into the apartment, he turned to Imani. "You have no idea how much I owe you. I think you literally saved my life. We'll find who did this to your father, I promise—"

"Don't." Imani put her finger to his mouth. "If you start

talking about Dad I'll cry, and I swore I wouldn't cry anymore. Just promise you won't leave the island without saying goodbye." She rubbed her bare arms. "There's one good thing that came out of this. Daryl finally asked me out. He feels so bad about Dad he wants to help me get over it. Isn't that sweet?"

"Yeah." Chris was too distracted to really hear Imani's words. He nodded, knowing he had to say something. "I'm happy for you. He seems like a good guy."

Chris watched her roar away and, before the emotions could overtake him, he slipped back into the room and set about arranging the groceries, deciding what they would eat tonight. He prepped a marinade for some chicken and stuck it in the fridge to work its miracle. Then he grabbed a shower and threw on more casual clothes. He glanced at the queen-sized bed in the middle of the room and shivered in anticipation.

David was coming home.

He knew just how to welcome back his big bear. He smoothed his hand over the flowered comforter. They were going to rock tonight.

He sat outside on the veranda and skimmed the paper. It was light on international news. The local stuff was pretty smalltime. None of the gory headlines that marked a major US paper. Bermudians were big on local sports teams. Cricket and soccer seemed to get the most coverage. The cricket cup match Joel had mentioned to David was big news. But it was David who had made the front page. He stared at the horrible picture of David captured by some insensitive photographer whose only interest was in generating fear and loathing. The article read like David had already been tried and found guilty, but Chris was inured to the press's hackneyed recipe for instant readership. Forget fact-checking in favor of the lurid and shocking. Another front page report seemed to bear that out, giving a skimpy report of a vicious rape that had occurred the same day Chris and David had arrived in Bermuda. A woman had been accosted in a Hamilton park at night, beaten and raped. Police had no suspects, but the paper hinted it might have been carried out by a tourist. The woman had described the man as "good looking. He didn't look like he would rape anyone," which Chris knew was so bogus. Rapists never *looked* like rapists, whatever that look was. He'd learned that one the hard way.

In L.A. rape was rarely even covered unless it was particularly gruesome or happened to someone from ritzy Bel Aire or Hancock Park, and then it was always blamed on outside elements. Most rapes were just too common to titillate jaded and tragedy-weary Angelenos.

A quick Google search online yielded the local crime stats—four homicides for the entire previous year. L.A. would have more than that in a day. Chris wondered what it would be like to live in a place like that. Would he really feel a lot safer or was it a matter of perception? He clicked on a link on world crime stats and Bermuda came up as having more murders per capita than even New York. Whoa, now that changed *his* perception. Maybe it was a lot more dangerous here than he thought.

He turned his attention to Aidan Pitt. Several hits came up, including a Bermudian *Who's Who* web site of local hotshots. He'd been right; David's lawyer had graduated from Oxford, with honors no less. He had taken the British bar ten years ago, then moved to Bermuda, when he married a Bermudian woman. He'd established his private practice two years ago. Since then, he'd handled some high profile cases. Maybe he was worth the money he charged.

Better yet, the site listed Aidan's home address and phone number. Chris jotted it down in his BlackBerry.

Before putting the laptop away he did one more search and came up with the official Bermuda police site. As he'd expected, it was essentially a puff piece. The tag said it all: "To ensure a safe, secure and peaceful Bermuda for all, because we care."

Along with the official site were several less than official ones that Google also unearthed, including a few with very unflattering things to say about the local cops. Some wit had corrupted the LAPD logo on one site into Subvert and Betray, and had very little good to say. Botched narcotics investigations, brutality and sexual assault. What a mess. It sounded more like the LAPD of the Ramparts years than a police force on a tiny, bucolic island. He wondered how much was trash talk to get attention and how much was based on facts.

He browsed through a few sites, knowing a lot of anti-cop rhetoric came from those who were on the wrong side of the law, so their truthfulness was suspect. Still, it was disquieting in the face of what they were doing to David.

He closed the laptop down, left the paper on the table inside and changed into his board shorts. He jogged down to Tobacco Bay beach park, and plunged into the deliciously warm water. He swam the equivalent of a dozen laps, then draped himself on a beach blanket and tried to add some color to his skin. Time crawled towards the end of day while he waited for David to call.

CHAPTER SEVENTEEN

Wednesday, 7:30pm Westgate Correctional Facility, Pender Road, Ireland Island, Sandys Parish, Bermuda

David stepped into the nearly empty parking lot of the Westgate prison. He shaded his eyes against the glare of the setting sun. It danced off the rolling surf he could see through a stand of casuarinas and glittered off car hoods. They had dragged him all the way into Hamilton to have his bond hearing, and then insisted on sending him back to Westgate for release. He still fumed over the bond they had set. It was outrageous in light of what the same thing would cost back home, although he had to admit he probably wouldn't have gotten bail at all in L.A. Not for first degree homicide. But two million dollars? It made Chris's extravagant spending habits modest by comparison.

Aidan had told him Chris would be picking him up in a cab. He trudged toward Pender Road, one eye open for a taxi. Thankfully, no one had alerted the media to his release. The last thing he needed was to have to run a gauntlet of reporters. Traffic was sparse, mostly moving east toward the Dockyards. Car lights began to come on as dusk settled over the verdant landscape. Once on the road, he turned west, knowing Chris would come from that direction. His nerves were too frazzled to stand still and wait. He was eager to leave this experience as far behind as he could.

A late model Honda slowed as it approached him. The high beams flared, blinding him, and he thought he heard a voice shout, "There he is."

It wasn't Chris's voice. The cabbie?

Then darkness cloaked him again when the high beams were suddenly extinguished. Behind him, he heard car doors open on loud, strident music, and slam shut to merciful silence. He blinked to clear his sight, but before he could regain his vision, something slammed into his head. He grunted and tried to step back but someone pinned his arms and a fist drove into his stomach. The air exploded from his lungs and he went to his knees. No one spoke again. They didn't have to; he realized he recognized the voice all too well.

It was Jay, Joel's son.

The next blow was a booted foot connecting with his kidneys.

Pain flared. This time the darkness that settled was deeper.

Wednesday, 7:50pm Westgate Correctional Facility, Pender Road, Ireland Island, Sandys Parish, Bermuda

Chris could tell the cabbie hadn't wanted to take him to the prison, but he couldn't turn down the currency Chris flashed. Chris sat back on the bench seat, staring straight ahead at the winding road, first flanked by rolling surf, then hemmed in on either side by heavy brush or low stone walls. They crossed the low Causeway, passed through Black Watch Pass, then skirted Hamilton and got out onto Middle Road. They passed the big pink hotel that Joel had said was the Southampton Princess, as night swallowed everything up. The hotel was a glowing pink giant squatting in the perfumed darkness.

Traffic built up as they crossed the bridge to Ireland Island where the prison was located, probably because it was also the way to the Dockyard. Chris hadn't realized the prison was so close. He wondered if David might want to eat there, instead of going all the way back to their new place, then he rejected the idea. He wanted to be alone with David and not worry about revealing his feelings in a public place. Besides, he had some serious plans for David later tonight.

Immersed in his private fantasy, Chris nearly missed the cabbie's curse and the sudden swerving of the van. The cabbie stood on the brakes and nearly sent Chris toppling off the seat.

"Hey!"

The cabbie ignored him, and throwing open the door, jumped down onto the road. Confused, Chris watched him through the window and saw what looked like a bundle of clothes, lying half on, half off the south side of the road. He stared at the figure, thinking incongruously that it looked like an L.A. skid row wino lying on the trash strewn road. Wearing Dockers? Just like David's—

His heart nearly stopped when he realized who it was. He scrambled out of the cab.

"David!" He pushed the cabbie aside and threw himself onto his knees, cradling David's bloody head in his lap. David's eyes fluttered open and he groaned. "Oh, Jesus, what happened?" Chris asked.

The cabbie crouched down, then abruptly jumped to his feet when David groaned again. "I'm calling an ambulance," he said and disappeared into the cab. Less than a minute later he was back. "It's on its way. Do you know this man? What happened to him?"

"I don't know. Why would anyone beat him up? We're just a couple of tourists—"

"Why do any of these vultures attack?" The cabbie nodded shrewdly. "For your money."

Chris searched David's pockets, finding his wallet, which still contained forty US dollars and several colorful Bermudian bills. Not robbery then. Something more sinister?

"Maybe we scared them away," the cabbie offered, but Chris didn't think so. What were the odds a run-of-the-mill mugger would stumble on David just at the moment he was released from prison? Hell of a coincidence.

It was nearly fifteen minutes before they heard approaching sirens. A green and white ambulance pulled up in front of the cab and two men in scrubs got out. They quickly checked David's vitals and looked from the cabbie to Chris.

"Who found him?"

"I was taking this young man to the prison to pick someone up," the cabbie said, his voice thick with distaste. "I saw this man lying on the road."

"We're traveling together," Chris said. "His name is David Eric Laine. We're from Los Angeles."

The EMTs seemed to agree with the cabbie that it was probably a mugging until Chris pointed out that David's wallet was intact. The lead EMT shrugged.

"Tell it to the police," he said. "We'll transport him to the King Edward. Direct the police there."

"King Edward?"

"King Edward Memorial Hospital. Finger Road, in Paget."

The last thing Chris wanted was more contact with the local police, but he knew he had to call them. He needed to call Aidan too and inform him of the attack, not that he expected the lawyer to do anything, but it might shed some new light on what was going on with Joel's murder. Chris didn't believe for an instant that this was a coincidence.

The cabbie agreed to take Chris to the hospital. Chris pulled out his BlackBerry and dialed 9-1-1 first, explaining the situation to the responding operator, telling her the ambulance had taken David to the hospital. Then he called Aidan and left a voice mail. He didn't expect to hear from him until the next day.

The cabbie dropped him off at the hospital. He hurried up to the receptionist, a heavy white woman with coarse gray hair piled atop her head. She peered at him over the top of her bifocals.

"David Laine," he said.

She looked the name up in her online records. "He's being moved out of emergency to the ward."

"Can I see him—"

"Are you family, sir?"

"What, yes—no, not blood family, but—"

"I'm sorry, sir. Only family is allowed."

"You don't understand—" Only Chris did understand. In Bermuda he'd never be considered David's family, no matter how many years they were a couple. He simply didn't exist. "Can I talk to his doctor then?"

He thought she was going to refuse even that, but finally she picked up the phone and told whoever answered that she wanted to talk to Dr. Zelmer. After a short conversation she hung up and met Chris's eyes. "The doctor will be out soon."

Soon turned out to be forty-five minutes later. A balding, fifty-year-old man in surgical scrubs came through a door marked 'No Admittance.' Chris immediately stood up.

"Dr. Zelmer?"

In a thick Polish accent he said, "Yes, are you a friend of Mr. Laine?"

A friend, yes. "How is he?"

"His injuries were moderate. His left kidney has suffered some mild bruising and he has some trauma to his face and head. There are no signs of concussion, but as a precaution we will observe him for the next twelve hours."

"When will I be able to see him?"

"He is being moved into a semi-private room as we speak. But I'm afraid visiting hours ended at eight."

Chris swore. Zelmer must have sympathized with him. "Come with me. I think I can allow you a few minutes."

"Thank you, Doctor."

Zelmer led him onto the hospital ward. He left Chris in the room where an older man was asleep in the first bed. David was propped up in the second, sipping an orange juice. His face lit up when he saw Chris.

"You're here fast," he said.

Chris perched on the edge of the bed, resting against David's legs. His voice was shaky when he said, "Hey, I found you. How else do you think you got here so quick? I was coming out to pick you up."

"I wondered about that."

"So, what happened? Did you see who attacked you?"

"It was Jay," David said quietly.

"J-Jay? But— Did you tell the cops?"

David grimaced. "I did. I'm not sure they believed me. They said they'd, quote 'look into it.' I want you to call Aidan. He might be willing to take it more seriously. He may be able to force the police to act."

"I've already left Aidan a message, but I'll call him again." Chris glanced toward the open door when a nurse walked by. "I can't stay long. The doctor said they wanted to keep you in for observation. They say anything to you?"

"I should be released early tomorrow. I can call a cab."

"I can come get you."

"Waste of cab money. I'll be there as soon as I can. Just don't forget to call the lawyer."

Chris knew from his tone that David couldn't be argued with. And David would be home quicker if he didn't have to wait for Chris to show up.

He risked a quick look toward the door and seeing no one he stooped down and kissed David. Then he stood and forced a smile.

"Okay, I gotta go. I'll call Aidan right away. I don't care if I do wake him up. You take care of yourself and get home as soon as you can."

"I will."

Chris grabbed a cab outside the hospital. Once in the cab, he looked up Aidan's home number and punched it into his phone. A woman answered.

"I need to speak to Aidan Pitt, please," Chris said.

Aidan came on less than a minute later. Chris could hear a TV's muted voice in the background.

"Yes? Chris? What is it?"

Chris told him about the assault outside the prison. "David recognized Jay's voice. The cops seem to think he's making it up."

"I will look into it tomorrow. Now go home, Chris. And go to bed. There's nothing more you can do for David tonight."

St. George's harbor was empty of cruise ships. Lights abounded in King's Square, and he could hear the sound of distant revelry from one of the numerous pubs. He leaped up the steps two at a time, where he took a quick shower then threw on a robe. In the kitchen he made himself a pastrami sandwich, which he ate outside on the veranda, along with a glass of wine. The song of the tree frogs was loud enough to drown out traffic noises from the nearby Duke of York Road.

Around eleven he checked out the local news and caught the tail end of a report on Joel Cameron's death. David was named as a suspect currently being held by police. There was a short, spastic video clip of David being led into the prison where Chris had found him after his attack. Well at least the part about him being held by the police was no longer true, but Chris didn't kid himself that the threat was over. He couldn't even begin to understand what Jay's involvement meant.

He glanced at the bedside clock. It was only seven-fifty in L.A. Des would probably be at home. Chris broke down. He needed to talk to a friend.

Trevor answered. "Hey babe," he said in his smoky voice that still sent shivers down Chris's spine. "How's Bermuda treating you?"

"Not good." His voice broke and he gulped back a sob. Now that he was talking to a friend Chris started losing it.

"Whoa, hon, you want to talk to Des?"

"Yes, please."

When Des came on the line Chris broke down completely. He lay back on the bed and hugged a pillow to his chest. Tears streaked his face, soaking into the cotton pillowcase.

"Oh my God, what is it, hon? Please, tell me. Didn't you get the money? I told my accountant to process it immediately—"

"They attacked David."

"What?"

Chris told him everything this time. He ended with David's assault and his subsequent trip to the hospital. "He's coming home tomorrow," Chris sniffed. "But I'm scared, Des. What are the cops going to do to him? They think he's guilty, that he killed that poor man. They aren't even going to investigate his attack. They want him in jail."

"We know that's crazy. David wouldn't hurt a fly. Do you want me to come out there? I'll give those damn bobbies a piece of my mind, you wait and see."

Chris almost smiled at the image conjured up by those words. Diminutive Des standing toe to toe with a Bermuda-shorted constable, taking a pound of flesh with his biting tongue.

"Thanks, Des, I don't think you need to do that. I found a great lawyer, so I think we're good. I just needed to vent."

Des wasn't mollified by Chris's words. "I should just ignore that and come anyway. You've never been able to take care of yourself. You're such a pudding head."

"Pudding head?"

Trevor came on the phone. "Don't worry, Chris, I'll take away his passport. But if you want to keep him down on the farm you better call every day with updates, or I won't be responsible for what he does."

"Thanks, Trev. Do me a favor, keep him occupied so he doesn't fret all the time."

"Oh, I think I can keep his mind on other things."

Same old Trevor.

"Tell him I'll call tomorrow after David gets home and we've had a chance to talk to his lawyer."

"I'll hold you to that."

Chris went to bed soon after. Sleep was a long time coming though, and when it did he was plagued by bad dreams that woke him often, drenched in sweat and shaking. Just before dawn he finally slipped into a deeper, dreamless sleep.

The next morning he lingered in a hot, leisurely shower, and took extra care to primp and pamper himself in anticipation of David's return.

He toweled himself dry and carefully selected a tight fitting pair of Bruno Pieters jeans that showed off his basket, and a butter yellow shirt that made his newly tanned skin glow.

Then he brewed a pot of coffee and sat on the veranda, waiting.

CHAPTER EIGHTEEN

Thursday, 10:40am, King Edward Memorial Hospital, Point Finger Road, Paget Parish, Bermuda

David pulled on his jeans and the torn shirt, damaged by the assault. Blood had splattered the front of it and one sleeve was ripped. He doubted it was fixable, but it would get him home. The tie he hadn't even wanted to take with him was missing. Why take that, but not the money from his wallet? It reminded him more of a trophy-seeking psychopath than a regular mugger. Could that have been Jay's work? Was that why Joel had been so concerned about his second oldest son? Did he suspect something sinister like a twisted psyche? He stopped at the front desk and took care of the bill, then filled the script the doctor had given him. He went in search of a cab.

The cab dropped him off in the courtyard of Aunt Nea's. He could see Chris on the veranda and he hurried up the stairs, but before he reached the top Chris flung the door open.

David took in his husband's figure, reacting instinctively to his beauty. Suddenly he smiled and before Chris could make a scene, slipped past him into the apartment. The bed hadn't been made and the room smelled of coffee and Chris. David inhaled, revitalized by the familiar and bewitching scent.

"You got more of that?"

Chris grabbed a mug and poured him a coffee. He topped up his own and sat at the table beside his laptop, which had been turned on and had gone into screen saver mode. Beside it was a crumpled *Royal Gazette*. Even from where he stood David could see the headline about Joel's murder and his subsequent arrest. Also visible was the memorable image of him being led into the prison by the all too accommodating Lindstrom.

Chris was staring at his face. He knew he looked rough, he

could feel how tight his skin was and his jaw felt hot and achy. "Hey," he said softly. "Deja vu all over again."

Chris looked confused at first; David knew he didn't get the reference. Then his face cleared and he offered a humorless smile. "Right," he said. "You forgot to duck again."

"Yeah."

"You hungry?"

"After a day of hospital and jail grub? What do you think?"

"I got some chicken we could barbecue."

"Barbecue?"

"Down by that Mexican courtyard. I've got potato salad, too."

"Isn't it a little early for barbecue?"

"Never. How can Wheaties compete with grilled chicken?"

"You got me there. You do know the way to a man's stomach."

"I know the way to yours." Chris's smile was sultry.

David responded. "Let's eat first," he said, watching Chris's eyes darken.

"I'll hold you to that."

"Yes, you will."

The chicken wasn't hurt by its extended stay in the marinade. David performed his usual magic on the barbecue and Chris presented his potato salad in a plastic tub with a flourish that had them both laughing. Dinner done, Chris cleaned up the dishes and made sure David took his meds, including a pain pill. He had put the last plate in the rack and was cleaning the utensils when David came up behind him.

"I locked the door." He nuzzled Chris's neck, inhaling the achingly familiar scent. Chris bowed his head to allow him to get at the skin below his hair. David took advantage. He could feel Chris's pulse leap.

"What about the windows?" Chris stammered.

"Curtains closed." His lips continued their foray down Chris's satiny skin. "Anything else I can do for you?"

"Yeah," Chris whispered, turning around. He tugged at David's belt. "You can take that off."

Friday, 9:20am, Aunt Nea's, Nea's Alley, St. George's Parish, Bermuda

Chris was frying bacon and whistling *Somewhere* from West Side Story when David surprised him in the kitchen the next morning.

"Umm, I can feel my arteries clogging as we speak."

"I haven't even started the eggs yet. Omelet with Emmental and onions?"

"What, no chicken?"

"Well, there's always me," Chris said. "Or eggs. Your choice."

David took him in his arms. "To hell with cholesterol."

After breakfast David called Aidan. Chris puttered around the kitchen cleaning up the last remnants of breakfast and their interrupted supper.

David talked to his lawyer for nearly forty minutes. He had already spoken to the police about it. They still seemed to think it was a random act of violence.

"Muggers who take souvenir ties as trophies," David muttered. "That's a new one on me."

"What do you mean?"

David told him about how a lot of psychopaths took trophies from their victims. "It lets them relive the glory."

He could almost see Aidan frown. "I think I've heard of that. But what kind of trophy hunter would target you—or would even know how to find you? Are you sure it was Jay you heard? Could you have been mistaken in your identification? After all, you were under stress—"

"It was Jay."

"Was he alone?"

"No, there was at least one other person present. Not all serial criminals are solitary actors. We had the Hillside Strangler in L.A. years ago. That was two cousins. There was definitely at least two guys who jumped me last night. And one of them took my tie."

"I'll take this back to the police. I'll make sure they take it as seriously as I do," Aidan said. "Now, I'm pushing for an early hearing. The prosecution's stalling, which tells me they don't have the evidence they need to convict. They want to wait until they can find more."

"Or manufacture it."

"Well, I dare say that won't happen now."

"Why not?"

"The case is too much in the public eye. The police must tread cautiously, lest they be observed doing something improper."

In David's experience, cops didn't stop because the public was on to them. But maybe they operated differently in Bermuda. From what he'd seen so far, he didn't hold out a lot of hope.

"Don't worry, David. I'll see that the police behave themselves, even if they're not so inclined."

David felt a rush of relief, even as he realized it wasn't over yet, not by a long shot. "So what's our next move?"

"I'll move to quash the results of their search. Their efforts are notoriously sloppy. It won't take much to suggest their crime scene processing wasn't up to acceptable standards. This is well documented in past cases."

David hated it when lawyers turned their dogs loose on the science of crime scenes. It was sometimes the strongest weapon the police had in their arsenal and all the lawyers could do was seek to undermine it by casting doubt on both the science and the ones how collected it. He opened his mouth to protest, but quickly shut it again. If playing clean was going to get him a criminal sentence and a lifetime in a foreign prison, and he knew the truth was being ignored, didn't he have the right to defend himself?

"Do you think it will work?"

"If I was a betting man—and I'm not—I'd say it's a sure thing."

"Couldn't happen soon enough."

"Patience, David, patience." David thought he heard Aidan ruffling through papers. "I should give you my cell phone number. Just in case the police get overzealous and my office is closed. Chris, I believe, has my home number."

"Right."

David found Chris down in the pool spa, in his flowered board shorts. He changed into his own suit and grabbed a towel. He paused on the step to watch Chris, his golden body stretched out, his face relaxed in the soothing movement of warm water. David felt himself harden just watching the man he loved. It never ceased to amaze him how strong his desire remained after so many years. When Chris opened his eyes, David was beside him in the water.

"You know we're about five minutes from the beach," Chris said, lazily swirling his fingers through the water, lightly brushing David's thigh.

David shook his head. "Yeah, but look at the crowds."

Chris looked around. "What crowds?"

"My point exactly. Come on." David slapped his butt under the water. "Let's go get some of that pink sand in our crevices."

"Ewww."

They returned to their room long enough to grab T-shirts and shorts and Chris's digital camera. Five minutes later they trotted across Church Folly Road, past the Ruined Church and up Government Hill Road to make their way down into Tobacco Bay beach. The parking lot was empty except for a couple of scooters and a Volvo. In the jagged limestone separating the beach from a swath of green park, a man and his young son were flying a large, circular rainbow-hued kite. Chris paused to take a couple of pictures. After climbing down a stone path they found themselves in a cozy inlet surrounded by limestone. A longtail drifted in on the sea breeze. Aside from a couple frolicking at the far end with their young children, the beach was almost empty. Over the rolling surf David could hear their laughter and high voices. They had an accent, Australian, he thought. Chris caught the quiet beauty with his camera; David was the target of several surreptitious clicks.

They lay their towels down on the sand and shed their outer wear. Chris handed David the camera and with a rebel yell he made a run for the waves, throwing himself into the shallow surf. David followed more sedately. He was up to his knees when Chris swam up to him. Dolphin-like he erupted from the water, laughing and splashing David.

"So what did Aidan say?"

David sat cross-legged on the pink sand, water lapping at his chest. Idly he pointed the waterproof camera at Chris and captured a couple of images. Small fish darted around his calves, nibbling at his leg hair. "He thinks he can quash the search on grounds of incompetency." He scooped up a handful of pink sand and let it wash through his fingers, rinsing it off before he touched the camera again. "Or at least throw a reasonable doubt into the jury."

"That's good, isn't it?"

David wouldn't meet his gaze. "It's good. Aidan seems to think they have a history of incompetence."

"Jesus, David." Chris dropped onto his knees. "He's not the only one. I found a few online accounts of their tactics. They make the LAPD at its worse seem positively progressive. Good to know Aidan's on top of it."

"I know, and I want this gone as much as you do. But I don't want to sell my soul to do it."

"They fight dirty, so should you."

Only David didn't see it that way. If he didn't have his self-respect what the hell did he have? If he could only win through dirty tricks, was that really winning?

"I called Des last night," Chris said.

David didn't ask why. He knew Chris and Des were close, in some ways closer than he and David were. In the beginning David had been unsure about their friendship. To be honest, he felt threatened by it, until he realized that Chris loved him, not Des. What he felt for Des was a once in a lifetime friendship, but it wasn't love.

"And?" he asked.

"He was all ready to fly out and beat some Bermudian ass. I've got Trevor keeping a leash on him."

"Isn't that a little bit like putting the fox in charge of the hen house?"

"Don't ever let Des hear you call him a hen."

"God forbid."

Chris floated on his back, his hand brushing David's legs. He used David's knee to pull himself upright. David thought he was going to do something foolish like kiss him, but abruptly Chris flung himself backward, falling into the water with a grunt.

"What the hell are they doing here?"

David swiveled around to find two police officers at the head of the limestone path, staring over at them. They stood, hands on hips, both wearing Bermuda shorts and sunglasses, making it impossible to read the expression on their faces.

David scrambled to his feet and marched out of the water. Chris stalked after him as he scooped up his own shorts and pulled them on, followed by his T-shirt. He shook the sand out of his towel, while Chris got dressed. Chris was about to head back to the road that would take them to Aunt Nea's, when David put his hand on Chris's arm.

"Wait," he said.

Before Chris could speak, he snapped several images in a row of the staring cops. Finally, he guided Chris toward the roadway.

"Go on," he said. "Let's see what our buddies in blue want."

"As if you don't know."

The two of them stepped onto the road to find the cops still there, watching. Two patrol cars sat side by side in the nearly empty parking lot. Through their open windows David could hear the chatter of staccato voices over the police radio.

Chris made to pass them, but David wasn't backing down this time. He stopped and took two more pictures, making sure he captured each constable. He could tell it pissed them off. He strode up to the nearest cop and planted himself in front of the older black man he assumed was the senior constable.

"Help you, Officer?"

The few people in the park, including the kite fliers, had been drawn to the scene. David pretended to ignore them, but he knew the cops were all too aware of their audience. It might not have gone as well for him and Chris if there'd been no witnesses. Chris came up behind him; he remained silent, but David could feel his growing anger.

"Can I ask what you are doing here?" the older officer asked. His partner stared through his shades. He eyed the digital camera dangling from David's hand. "You got pornography on that thing?"

David knew he didn't have to answer, but he also knew better than to antagonize the local law any more than he had to. "No," he said, making to hand the camera over. "Unless you call a couple of mutts harassing innocent tourists porno." He withdrew his hand, pulling the camera out of reach. "You want to look? Come back with a warrant."

"Where are you staying?"

David inclined his head toward town. "Aunt Nea's."

The younger cop smirked. "The fag hotel."

David hadn't heard it called that before. More enlightenment. "Want me to prove it?"

The cop's smirk became a leer. He took his sunglasses off. His irises were a startling blue-gray. His gaze slid over Chris, then back to David. His eyes were cold, like the stormy Atlantic off the coast of Provincetown. "No, that won't be necessary. Have a good day, gentlemen."

The pair sauntered back to their patrol cars. The younger constable with the storm-colored eyes was a burly guy with a shock of red hair. He leaned against the hood of his car and watched Chris and David. His partner was speaking through his two-way. Looking for outstanding warrants?

David jerked away from the probing gaze and, touching Chris's back, indicated it was time to go. They walked stiffly up the road to Aunt Nea's. Both patrol cars passed them on Government Hill Road, driving slowly, their windows open.

David ignored them. They waited for the cars to vanish west, before crossing the street. "No sense letting them give us jaywalking tickets," David muttered.

They were in a much more somber mood when they finally climbed the steps to their room.

"I can't believe you did that," Chris shut and locked the door behind him. "Aren't you afraid of pissing them off?"

"What more can they do to us?"

Chris threw his wet T-shirt on the bathroom floor in a fit of pique. "Is that what we have to face until this is over? Constant intimidation?"

"They're slick, not doing enough to raise harassment charges, but enough to let us know they're watching. They must have seen us go into the park, so they decided to check us out."

"Don't they have better things to do?"

"They don't think so."

David scooped up Chris's dirty clothes and added his own to the laundry basket. Chris had bought some laundry soap in his last shopping foray. David added it to the pile now and trudged down the stairs to the laundry room. Chris trailed after him.

"Why aren't you mad?"

David looked up from filling the washing machine. "What makes you think I'm not?"

"I'm spitting—"

"I can tell," David said. "That working for you?"

"Working how?"

"Is it making you feel any better?"

"Well, no, of course not…"

"So the only one you're hurting is you. You'll make yourself sick, letting them get to you. Trust me; they'd like that just fine."

Chris made a face at him. "You're so bloody smart."

Back upstairs Chris transferred his images to the laptop, clearing the camera's memory. Then his BlackBerry vibrated on the bedside table. He answered it. After listening for a minute, Chris said, "Trust me, hon, no one could ever forget you." Chris rolled his eyes and mouthed the word "Des." David grinned and sighed. It was way too early to have to deal with Des and his Beverly Hills hysterics.

Chris handed David the BlackBerry. "He wants to talk to you."

"Hey, Des," David said.

Des sounded breathless. "I've been waiting for you to call. You're such a beast, forgetting all about me."

"I never forgot you, Des."

Des sniffed. "So have you put those island bumpkins in their place?"

David switched the BlackBerry from one ear to the other. "We're working on it. Consider it a work in progress."

"I hope Chris got you a good lawyer."

"Oh, I think he got me a good one." David shared a warm glance with Chris. "Don't worry about us, we'll be okay."

"You better be. I want you both back here soon. I told Chris you shouldn't have gone. I told him it wasn't a nice place."

"We'll be okay. I promise. Have I ever broken a promise to you, Des?"

"Well, no…"

"Have a little faith," David said. "I'm not going anywhere except home. Count on it."

"Well, I know where to find you if you're wrong."

David laughed and handed the BlackBerry back to Chris, who talked a few more minutes, then rejoined David.

"What else did you pick up for us to eat?" David asked.

"I got some pasta. I can put together an Alfredo sauce if you're interested. Or I got some salmon steaks."

"Pasta." David picked through some grapes Chris had set out on the counter. "Can I help?"

"Grab the pasta, I'll get the sauce going."

Over dinner David was thoughtful. Finally he put his fork down and asked, "Have you had any chance to think about what I said? On the plane ride over?"

Chris seemed to know immediately what he meant. "About leaving the LAPD? Yeah, I've thought about it, a lot."

"And?"

Chris sipped his wine, twirling the Sauvignon Blanc around in the glass. "I think you should do what you want," he finally said. "You're a damn good cop and if that's what you want to be, I support you one hundred percent."

David was skeptical. "Yeah? I thought you hated it."

"I don't hate it. I'm scared for you. I don't want to get a phone call from Martinez some night that you've been shot, maybe dead." Chris shivered. "But I also know that could happen anywhere, anytime. Hell, look where we live. There's no guarantees even if you became an accountant that some act of random violence wouldn't hit you."

"An accountant?" David made a face. "I'd die all right. Of boredom."

"I'm sure even accountants can be hot and sexy."

"You haven't met many accountants, have you?"

Chris laughed. He reached across the table and took David's hand. His eyes darkened when he said, "No, but I do know one very hot and very sexy homicide detective. Maybe you know him? I found him and brought him home and I plan on keeping him, for forever and ever." Chris raised his hand and kissed it, then sighed, growing serious again. "The bottom line is, you love being a cop, and if becoming a private investigator is only on account of me, then don't do it. I want you to do what makes you happy. Honest. Don't compromise that just for me. I don't want you resenting me." He let his fingers dance up David's muscular chest. "I can think of a dozen other ways you can make me happy."

David squeezed his hand and raised it to his mouth.

After supper Chris wanted to go swimming one more time. David sat on the beach reading his book. He glanced occasionally at Chris, noting how brown he had become from a few days of lazing in the sun. If anything it made him even more beautiful. Too beautiful for mere words, and David still didn't understand what Chris saw in an aging, beat-up cop like himself. Finally, as the sun slipped behind the screen of ice plants and casuarina trees, they returned to their room. David flipped on the TV and found a local news broadcast. Chris brought in a Bud for David and a glass of Sauvignon Blanc for himself.

They were still talking about the tropical storm Fay heading toward Bermuda. The prediction now was that it might make landfall by Saturday.

"And we can't leave even if we wanted to," Chris said. He sprawled out on top of the flowered comforter, his wine on the table beside him.

"We're fine if we stay inside," David said. "This place is pretty solid. Remember what the cabbie said, these homes don't blow down."

"It would be a lot safer if we were watching it from Los Angeles. Makes me miss the earthquakes."

"Are you forgetting the floods the fires? And let's not overlook the mudslides? The bumper-to-bumper gridlock every morning and every night?"

"Yeah, but those are disasters I'm used to."

When the news ended they got undressed and climbed under the blankets. David spooned Chris's body and stroked his still sun-warmed topaz skin with his lips. He rolled Chris over and began to kiss his hairless chest, moving lower, while Chris held his head in shaking hands.

Chris groaned. "David…"

"You want hot and sexy," David growled, pressing his mouth against Chris's navel. "I'll give you—"

There was a furious pounding on the door. They broke apart, fumbling to throw the sheets off and grab their robes. The knocking didn't let up. Whoever it was wasn't going away any time soon.

"We're coming, we're coming," David roared as he threw open the door.

Two uniformed constables and Detective Sergeant MacClellan stood in the doorway.

CHAPTER NINETEEN

Friday, 11:40am Aunt Nea's, Nea's Alley, St. George's Parish, Bermuda

It was the two constables from the Tobacco Bay beach park. They'd taken off their sunglasses and they watched the two Americans in front of them with open contempt.

Chris steadied himself on David's arm, his fingers dimpling his skin. His husband froze, his face blank, only the whiteness at the corners of his mouth giving away his tension.

"I guess maybe they came back to give us that jaywalking ticket," Chris said. God was that lame. He bit his lip when all three cops studied him with disdain.

"This isn't good, is it?" he whispered to David.

The cops pushed passed them into the suddenly too small room. They took in Chris and David's bare legs, the rumpled bed and crushed pillows; their fading erections under their dressing gowns.

David addressed one of the men. "What is it now, Sergeant MacClellan?"

Chris shivered, wishing he could step out from under their contemptuous eyes. Wishing he could shield himself with some real clothes.

"Did we disturb you?" MacClellan's voice held a wealth of sarcasm. One of his constables snickered. MacClellan looked around the small room. "What, no camera to record your diddling each other for future entertainment? And I thought all you people were perverts."

"Do I need to call my lawyer?" David's voice dripped ice. He grabbed his jeans off the floor and searched for the pocket. Before he could find whatever he was looking for, the two constables secured his arms and hauled him toward the bed, brushing past Chris.

"Hands over your head. Lace your fingers together. On the floor, Laine, now," MacClellan barked. David hesitated. "Now."

Chris lunged forward, but one of the constables, the barrel-chested redhead, stepped in front of him, arms folded over his chest. Chris froze. For the first time he felt fear.

The other constable, the older Black man, picked up the digital camera and Chris's laptop from the table.

"What the hell is going on? What are you doing with that?" Chris asked. His hands itched to wipe that smirk off the constable's face. "You can't just barge in here and harass us—"

"Your precious little pansy friend is going back to jail where he belongs," MacClellan said. There was a dark glee on his face.

"B-but I don't understand," Chris stammered as they shoved David flat on the floor and secured his wrists with handcuffs. "You're hurting him!"

"Call Aidan, Chris," David growled, his jaws clenched tight, his face averted from the cops. "Tell him…" He looked at each cop in turn. "Tell him MacClellan and his goons have arrested me again."

"What's the charge? You have to tell him what he's being charged with—what are you, barbarians?"

"No, Mr. Pansy," MacClellan said. "We're not barbarians, though I'm beginning to think your sweetheart is. First he kills an old man, now he's trying to take out the rest of the family. And God knows what kind of filth is on this," he indicated to the laptop and camera, which one of his constables now held. "Enough to nail *your* ass to the wall, I'm sure."

Chris felt the blood drain from his face. "What? Who was hurt?" His mind flashed on Imani. Oh God, no—

"The oldest son, Mr. Jayvyn Daniel Cameron was strangled to death outside a bar on Court Street."

"What time?" Chris asked.

"Around nine, according to witnesses."

"Nine?" Chris brightened. "David was here all evening. With me."

"You got anyone who can vouch for that?" MacClellan's voice was a self-satisfied purr. "I hardly think your word will carry much weight. You all lie for each other."

They hauled David to his feet. His robe fell open, revealing dark, muscular thighs.

MacClellan bent down and loud enough for Chris to hear said, "And this time we got the DNA to prove it."

Ice filled Chris's veins. "At least let him get dressed!"

They ignored Chris's protest and dragged David to the door. Chris darted after them, but a quelling look from MacClellan stopped him from doing anything foolish.

"Call Aidan," David said as he was hauled out the door, nearly losing his balance on the door jamb. The brawny redhead yanked him back to his feet. David grunted in pain. "Call him, Chris."

Chris scrambled to retrieve his BlackBerry. He dialed the number and hopped up and down nervously until it was picked up.

"Aidan! It's Chris. The police just rearrested David. They said there was another murder. Jay, Joel's oldest son. Well, besides David. They say he killed Jay. But he couldn't have, he was here all night. And they said something about proving it with DNA. How can they do that, since he was with me?"

"Calm down, Chris. What time did they leave with David?"

Chris glanced at the bedside clock. "Maybe five minutes ago. I called as soon as they were out the door."

"Good. You did the right thing. Now let me take care of it. I'll call you back as soon as I find out anything."

"Yes, please. God, this is a nightmare. Why do they think David is such a monster? They even took my laptop, claiming it had pornography on it. It doesn't, I swear. Why are they doing this?"

"I don't know," Aidan said. "But this has definitely gone beyond anything I've ever seen before. They have clearly overstepped their bounds. I don't think I'll have any trouble convincing a judge this is excessive. Not finding anything on your laptop will go a long way to helping our cause. Unless… there's no way they could download any is there? If they could plant some evidence…"

"No, I've got some pretty heavy password protection on it. They'd need a password just to get on the Internet. Most of my client files are encrypted." He swore. "Will they find that suspicious?"

"I'm sure that will arouse their suspicions, but it shouldn't be any problem proving their claims are invalid. Don't worry about it."

"Well excuse me if I can't relax over this. Just help him, Aidan—Mr. Pitt."

"I will, Chris."

Chris couldn't sleep. He paced the small room, but that did nothing to lessen his nervous energy. He glanced at his watch and realized so little time had passed since this nightmare began. It wasn't even midnight. He threw on a pair of jeans, a T-shirt and a denim jacket. He grabbed his wallet and his BlackBerry along with the apartment keys and trotted down the steps and up the driveway. There was no sign of the police. Of course not, they were in a real hurry to get David back into a cell and scour his laptop for lascivious images.

Before he could cross the Duke of York Street, he spotted a cab and waved it down. He climbed in behind the driver. "Court Street, Hamilton."

The cabbie did a double take and turned to look at Chris. His eyebrows almost met his hair line. "Are you sure that's where you want to go?"

"Yeah, I'm sure."

The reluctant cabbie dropped him off about two blocks from the harbor. The area looked more rundown than any place Chris had seen yet in Bermuda.

Pulling his thin denim jacket tight around him, he walked north. There were no large signs, billboards or fast food outlets in Bermuda, but Court Street still managed to look cheap and vulgar. Rough-looking men crowded the sidewalks and raucous reggae and hip-hop music fought for dominance. He saw a few women, some dressed like the men, others he was sure were men, though he wasn't positive. How likely could that be here? And there were hookers, looking exactly like what they were. Like the ones back on Sunset Boulevard. He heard jeers and cursing, but didn't stop to see if it was directed at him. Now he understood why the cabbie had been loath to bring him here.

A buxom woman in six-inch fuchsia heels, fishnet stockings and hair extensions, stepped in front of him. "Have some fun, cutie?" she said in a deep, gravelly voice.

"I don't do fun," Chris said, sidestepping her. Then he stopped. "You know the guy who was killed here tonight? I think his name was Jay?"

"Sure I do, sugar." She caressed his denim-clad arm with four inch nails that matched her shoes. "He a friend of yours?"

"Yeah," Chris said. "A good friend. It was tragic. So, what happened?"

"He down here looking to score, sugar, what else. Someone didn't like him being here and—" She made a hanging gesture, fat tongue between her blood red lips, her eyes bugging out. Chris grimaced. "Bloody mess if you ask me." The incongruity of her faint British accent seemed surreal.

"Did you see who did it?" Chris leaned forward, trying to ignore her rancid breath. She had a tweaker mouth, broken teeth weakened by acid and continual grinding, just like so many meth heads did.

"Yah, I seen him." She smirked, showing even more decaying teeth, some no more than rotten stumps. This girl was long gone.

"I was kinda busy, you know what I mean? But I seen him before down here. Both of them." She smirked. "That one you looking for like it rough, but he pays real good. He real kinky with a silk tie."

Chris tried not to think about it. The images were disturbing.

"Know anyone else who might have seen it?"

"Why you looking for this guy? He's bad news. Mess your pretty face up good. I know, I seen him do it. He's a mean fucker, when he goes off."

"I need to find him. You got a name for him?"

Out of the corner of his eye Chris saw a cop car cruise by, slowing to a crawl to take a closer look at them. The woman ignored the vehicle and Chris tried to disappear. The cop moved on.

Chris sighed in relief and turned to find the woman watching him.

"Maybe you need to talk to Josie," she said. "He was there. He be around here earlier tonight. Ask him about Mosby."

"Mosby? That the killer? Where can I find this Josie?"

"Try the bar Outer Bank, backatawn near Dundonald."

Chris slipped her a twenty and kept heading north. Dundonald was about two blocks up; the Outer Bank was on the east side. A half a dozen men stood outside smoking and taking surreptitious sips from brown bag bottles. Loud calypso music drowned out their equally loud voices. An alcohol fueled argument broke out and fists flew.

Taking a deep breath, he slid his sunglasses out and put them on. They made him feel less conspicuous. He lowered his head and ducked past the growing melee, hoping no one would drag him into it. Music assaulted his ears. He paused inside the door to let his shaded eyes adjust to the darkness. A scarred bar lay along one side, and opposite it a few rickety tables and chairs that had seen better days were scattered. The bar was crowded and most of the tables were occupied. It stank of beer, rotgut whiskey, and sweat. Chris approached an open space at the bar and waited for the bartender to notice him.

Finally a pot-bellied man in his fifties, with heavily tattooed arms and a face that looked like it had met the wrong end of a knife, stepped up to him. His eyes were a startling blue, oddly alive in a face that looked half-dead. His gaze brushed Chris, taking in the shades and a face that was too white despite his newly acquired tan. Chris was all too aware he was one of few Anglos in the bar. The bartender wasn't the only one staring.

He ordered a beer, figuring if it came out of a bottle it would be safe. He knew better than to order a glass. The brew was tepid and tasted like bitter water. He handed over a twenty.

"Josie around?"

"Who wants to know?"

"What about Mosby?"

"You a friend of his?"

"Nah, he's just someone I want to talk to. Know anything about the guy who got hit tonight?"

The bartender eyed him up and down and clearly found him wanting. "You a cop?"

"Shit, no." Chris tried to sound tough, though he knew it didn't come off well with his looks. He knew what he looked like, an American faggot trying to be hip in the wrong part of town. He just hoped no one was feeling the need to test their *cojones* this early in the night. He knew he was way out of his league here, but what choice did he have? David's freedom, if not his life, was at stake. "I'm no cop. I just want some information, is all."

"You a Yankee?"

"Yeah," Chris said, hoping it would win him some brownie points. "L.A."

The bartender brightened. "No kidding. I crossed de pawn to L.A. when I was nineteen. Got a couple of bit parts in some movies." He leaned over as though confiding something secret. His breath smelled of tobacco and beer. Chris resisted the urge to wave his hand in front of his face. "Cool stuff."

Another tinsel town wannabe. Chris nodded as though the ins-and-outs of making movies were second nature to him. "Yeah, I can see it. You'd be a natural alongside Vin Diesel or Eastwood. So," he said. "This guy, you see what went down?"

"I didn't see it, but my ace boy did. Mosby was mad-dog rabid. Took a knife to my boy and cut him good."

"He see who got Jay?"

"Yeah. Terrible thing, what with his father being jonesed by some crazy ex-pat."

At least they didn't know David's name. "Who's your ace boy?" Chris asked. "He here tonight?"

"Why you want to know? Why you asking after Josie?"

"Josie's your ace boy? I need to talk to him."

"Ain't here. He split home. Mother fucker scared shitless," The bartender laughed. "Can't say I blame him. No one wants to see that kind of shit go down."

"What about the police? Why aren't they down here trying to find this mad dog?"

"Cops don't come in this part of town much," the bartender scoffed. "Too pansy-assed for that. They let a couple of drive-bys scare them off. We need some of your bad ass L.A. cops. SWAT'd take care of them real good."

Chris didn't tell the guy David was LAPD. Instead he asked, "Where can I find your ace boy? This Josie? I really need to talk to him."

"He live out on de pint."

"The what?"

"The pint, Spanish Point."

"He got a full name?" Chris went back to his wallet and held up another bill to sweeten the pot.

The bartender eyed the money before he scooped it up

and made it disappear. He kept glancing at the other twenty, pretending to wipe a glass down. "Josie," he said. "Josie Curson."

The hooker had mentioned Josie, too. Chris thanked the guy and hurried out of the bar. He walked as fast as he could toward Front Street hoping someone in the bar hadn't spotted the exchange of cash. Finally, he spotted a cab and flagged it down. Once inside the safety of the cab, he called Aidan, who answered so fast Chris thought he might be sitting by the phone. Chris pocketed his shades.

Chris told him what he'd found out. Aidan was not amused.

"You went down to Court Street? Do you have any idea what that area's like?"

"Yeah, I kind of found out." He tried to make a joke of it. "Reminds me of home."

"You could have been seriously hurt, or worse. Jay isn't the only one who's been killed on that street. And your bartender friend's right, the cops don't like the area. A lot of turf wars down there. There have even been drive-bys. Would you walk in a gang area in Los Angeles?"

"No," he muttered. "But you weren't listening. I found out two names you should check up on. One is Mosby, no idea if that's his real name. I think he's the one who strangled Jay. Met a…" he was going to say hooker, then said, "prostitute, who said he was a customer and he liked his sex rough. Used a silk tie to play asphyxiation games with her. The other one is a Josie Curson. He lives in a place called—"

"What did you say?"

"He liked rough sex—"

"No, no, about the tie. You said it was silk?"

"That's what she said. Why?"

"David said the muggers only took his silk tie, they didn't touch his money. He said it felt like they were collecting trophies."

All too familiar with the trophy seeking habits of psychopaths, Chris felt the blood leave his face. "You think this has something to do with Joel and Jay?"

Aidan seemed unwilling to commit himself. Instead he asked, "You mentioned a Josie Curson. Where does he live?"

"Place called Spanish Point. If you can find either one of them, then maybe you'll find the witness the cops seem to think doesn't exist."

"I'll get on it, but you have to promise me, Chris. No more stunts like this one. I don't want to have to be the one who tells David you got hurt."

"I'll stay out of it," Chris lied. He wasn't going to leave David's safety in anyone's hands, not when he saw how easy it was to snatch it away. "I'll keep my nose clean."

"See you do that."

Back at Aunt Nea's, Chris tossed his funky clothes in the hamper. He reached for his laptop, only to remember the police had confiscated it. Swearing, he flipped on the TV and settled down to watch the news. He was in luck, as another crime on Court Street had drawn the press and camera crew down there. Another rape, the media making much of the fact that a serial rapist was on the loose. A white-haired, perfectly coifed cop Chris didn't recognize smoothly denounced the serial label. "There's no reason at this point to believe this is the actions of the same man. Our lab will analyze the DNA and make a determination."

Following the rape report the reporter gave a brief rundown on the history of Court Street. She raptly told her audience that everything was worse on Court, muggings were higher, car and bike thefts and even a couple of home invasions had occurred in the poor area of town. Gang violence had exploded in the last few years and the police seemed unable to handle it. A stern faced woman introduced as a member of the opposition party decried the root cause of the new crime wave.

"Drugs have flooded Bermuda, imported from other countries by foreigners who do not belong here. They bring their violence and their weapons and the drugs that are ruining our youth."

It sounded so much like home. Were the gangs everywhere

these days? He knew there was some racial tension on the islands. Was that what the woman meant? Chris was all too familiar with what racial tension could lead to, he'd lived through the '92 riots. He'd seen what hate could do. Scars from the destruction still remained.

Chris couldn't help but wonder why the rioters were always so dumb as to loot and burn their own neighborhoods, but he knew logic wasn't their long suit. Mobs don't think, they just act.

He turned the TV off and crawled into bed. He had no energy to do anything tonight.

He was asleep almost as soon as his head hit the pillow, which smelled achingly of David.

CHAPTER TWENTY

Friday, 3:45am, Westgate Correctional Facility, Pender Road, Ireland Island, Sandys Parish, Bermuda

David warily eyed his cellmate, a surly hulk who hadn't said word one since David had been dumped into his cell by a smirking guard. So much for protective custody. MacClellan had taken the gloves off and instead of putting him in solitary, had dropped him into the general population. Now David had to watch his back every second or this joker was going to try to make his street creds by taking out the L.A. cop.

It didn't help that he was beyond exhausted. MacClellan had kept him in interrogation for nearly three hours, drilling him again and again on his movements during the day and why did he kill Joel and Jay. "Your own kin," MacClellan had said, hard eyes watching every movement, waiting to pounce on any perceived break in David's facade.

David sat on the edge of his cot, knowing he was an eye blink away from passing out. He kept one eye on the hulk in the other cot, who appeared to be sleeping. David didn't know whether to buy his act or not. Eventually it wouldn't matter. He had to sleep… had to grab some shut-eye.

He closed his eyes and sagged back on his cot, trying to sleep like a cat, always aware of what was going on around him. In the end, his body betrayed him.

Violent visions played themselves out behind his eyelids, making his nap restless and uneasy. Twice he snapped awake, sure his cell mate was awake and ready to start bouncing his head off the concrete floor. Both times he found the mutt sleeping like the baby he wasn't. In the end David drifted into a deeper sleep.

He struggled to sit up, but the weight on his chest held him down. The hands that closed over his throat blocked the air from his starving lungs. Hot, sour breath washed his face as a guttural voice rasped, "God damn fucking cop. Think you're such a goodie-two-shoes."

Spittle sprayed David's cheek and through red eyes he saw the twisted face of his cellmate. He bore a prison tat on his neck with the incongruous name Timmy. Using his last bit of strength David kneed Timmy in the groin and swept his arms out, knocking the other man's grip lose. Not expecting the move, Timmy lost his balance and David flipped him onto the floor, rolling after him. He ripped Timmy's hands from around his throat again and head butted him. Timmy's head banged against the concrete floor, blood flew out of his nose, but he still managed to snake out from under him, giving David a fist in his already sore kidneys.

Timmy's fist connected with his chin, driving one of his teeth into his lip. He grunted. He avoided a follow-up punch and tried to kick Timmy in the balls again, knowing it might be the only thing that would slow the gorilla down. He was dismayed to realize Timmy wasn't wearing standard prison issue soft-soled slippers, but had on a pair of leather shoes.

Somebody had definitely set him up to do some major damage.

MacClellan.

Knowing he was now fighting for his life, David renewed his assault. He slammed his elbow into Timmy's gut, driving the air out of Timmy's lungs. Before the man could recover, David head butted him again. This time his skull connected with a solid thud square into Timmy's throat. He heard a sharp gurgling and Timmy went limp.

David shoved the now slack body off him and rolled onto his back, taking deep lung-searing breathes. Warily he watched Timmy out of the corner of his eye, but the other man didn't move. His chest rose and fell in a steady rhythm, so David knew he was alive. Not that he cared, but the last thing he needed was a prison beef for homicide, no matter how justified.

David thought for sure this time a guard would show up.

Someone had to have heard the commotion. But the corridor remained empty. He kept watching Timmy, until finally the would-be hit man grunted, rolled over and tried to sit up. David was on his feet, hands held ready at his side.

"Don't do that again," David rasped, swallowing with a throat that felt raw and packed with glass. He coughed and the glass tore his wind pipe. He hawked up blood.

Again he glanced toward the corridor. No sign of the guards, of course. He knew it would be a waste of time to call for one. Instead he stood up and, sidestepping Timmy's cot, went up to the bars. The place might as well have been a morgue, like they were the last two people on the island.

Timmy had obviously decided he wasn't worth the extra effort. He crawled back to his bunk, choking and spitting up blood. He hawked a bloody loogie on the floor near David's feet. He glared at David one last time before rolling over and facing the wall.

David sat back down on his cot, nursing his newly split lip. He stared out of his left eye through a film of blood where Timmy had landed a lucky blow.

David wasn't sure if MacClellan had thought he'd be spooked into a confession, or driven to kill someone for real. Maybe the guy was that crazy, or maybe he just didn't care if someone took David out for good. It would be one less headache for the sergeant. And it was a lot easier to stick a murder rap or two on a dead man.

The mutt now lay on his cot, his arm thrown over his face, snoring and drooling.

David knew the assault wouldn't end there. The guy would pick up once he woke up and got his bones back. He just had to hope Aidan would come through again.

The goon snorted and rolled over. David tensed. He had to stay alert since the minute his defenses went down the guy would be on him like white on rice. He'd got in a few good licks himself, but he was already weakened by his previous assault outside the prison gates. If he couldn't hold on, what then?

Had Timmy gotten the word that this particular cop was better off dead? Prisons usually had a finely tuned underground communication network. Hits were pretty easy to arrange if the right price was paid.

He glanced down the corridor, but it was still dark out. He had to wait for sunup to expect Aidan to show up.

It might be too late by then. Already exhaustion was dragging his eyelids shut. He wasn't sure how much longer he could evade sleep. Did he dare risk closing his eyes for five minutes or was the goon waiting for that, feigning sleep to catch him unawares again. David had never felt more vulnerable in his life.

He shifted on the cot to try and relieve the ache in his damaged kidney.

He closed his eyes and leaned back against the wall.

Saturday, 8:30am Aunt Nea's, Nea's Alley, St. George's Parish, Bermuda

His BlackBerry woke him at dawn. Chris rolled over and scooped up the PDA. It was Aidan.

"I'm on my way to visit David," he said. "I've booked a meeting with Judge de Icaza. We'll meet in chambers with the prosecution team and I can seek some answers as to the reason behind David's treatment."

It was Chris's experience that the authorities only dug in their heels when they were challenged. He didn't see what good that would do David. He said as much.

"Ah, but whether they like it or not, we must all appear to be impartial handmaidens to the law. We may not have laws especially written to protect gays, but there is still protection under the law for unjust accusations no matter who is being accused."

"I hope you're right," Chris muttered. "Will I be able to see him today?" Not that he looked forward to seeing David in jail. He just knew it would break his heart and that would only upset David more.

"I doubt it. I'll do what I can. I'll get back to you once I've talked to David and the judge, but don't expect miracles."

Chris didn't hold out much hope, he didn't need Aidan to tell him that. But he kept his doubt to himself, figuring a vote of no confidence wouldn't help Aidan's case. He had to trust that Aidan knew what he was doing. For David's sake he had to believe that.

He took a brisk thirty-minute swim to clear his head of cobwebs, then grabbed a quick shower and did the laundry. The idea of breakfast tugged at him but he couldn't decide what he wanted. He was saved making the decision by a call from Imani.

"And I believed you," her voice was low and full of venom. Chris had never heard such malice in anyone's voice. He tried to interrupt, but she shut him down. "I fell for your sob story about Dad only wanting to be a family, and you were so happy to go along. How could you? How could you destroy my family like that?"

"Imani, please. It wasn't like that. You have to believe me."

"I don't have to believe anything you say. I don't know what my father ever did to deserve this, but I hope the law nails you both. I hate you." She broke down and wept.

"Imani, oh God, please, listen to me. I wouldn't... David wouldn't. You gotta believe me—"

The phone slammed down in his ear. When he tried to call back he only got a busy signal. He slumped down on the bed. Grabbing a pillow he hugged it to his chest and buried his face in it.

It was a nightmare, pure and simple.

He wished he dared call her back; to try and make her see that David could never have done any of the things the police were accusing him of. But he knew she'd never listen. He had to do something. But what?

He changed into a pair of jeans and called a cab to take him into Hamilton. The first thing he needed to do was re-arm himself. He needed access to the Internet and his cracking tools.

CHAPTER TWENTY-ONE

Friday, 9:25am, Westgate Correctional Facility, Pender Road, Ireland Island, Sandys Parish, Bermuda

David wondered what Chris was doing right now. Fretting over him? Frantic with worry? Chris was such a worry-wart and he had so little faith in things working out.

David scratched his face, now heavy with morning beard growth. He knew he probably looked like a skid row bum in his prison garb with his face bruised up and his lips puffy from the damage Timmy's fist had done on it. Chris would be horrified if he could see him.

He returned to his cot, unwilling to stand with his back to Timmy, and gingerly sat down on the rumpled, bloody mattress. Timmy lay on his back staring at the stained ceiling, one arm flung over his forehead.

Footsteps approached. The same guard who had released him before stopped in front of the cell.

"You must like it here, you keep coming back."

David grunted, refusing to rise to his barb.

"Come on, your lawyer's here. Guess money buys it all, don't it?"

David wiped the blood off his mouth and winced at the pain when he pulled a scab open. "Not everything."

The guard shackled him this time under Timmy's grinning gaze, and led him shuffling down the corridor to the same room where he'd met with Aidan the first time.

Aidan took one look at him and snapped, "Take those things off."

The guard complied. But he took his time.

David took a seat without meeting Aidan's eyes and waited for the smirking guard to leave. When he looked up Aidan was staring at his face.

"Who did this, David? The police? Who—"

"Not the cops, though I'm sure they were behind it," David said. "They put me in gen pop."

"They have to know better than that. A police officer in general population is a sitting target."

"You think?"

Aidan picked up the desktop phone and hit an extension. "I'll see about this."

He barked some angry words into the phone, then hung up. He was agitated and kept looking at David's face. Finally a knock came at the door and a man entered. He glanced at David then at Aidan.

"Is this the one?" he asked.

"Yes, Warden Francolini, and it should be as plain as the nose on your face that he's been assaulted. What do you plan to do about it?"

"How do I know he wasn't involved in a brawl? The intake report from the arresting officers claimed he was belligerent and hostile."

"Wouldn't you be if you were wrongly accused?"

"Now, that hasn't been proven," the warden protested.

"No it hasn't," Aidan said icily. "Nor has his guilt been established. He's entitled to fair treatment either way. Why was he put in general population? As an officer of the law he should be in segregation."

"Agreed." Francolini frowned. "I'll look into why that wasn't done. I'm sure it was just a misunderstanding." He glanced at David. "I'm sorry for this problem, Mr. Laine," he said stiffly. "I'll see it doesn't happen again."

"You do that," Aidan said.

Friday, 5:45am, Westgate Correctional Facility, Pender Road, Ireland Island, Sandys Parish, Bermuda

They put him back in solitary. David lay down on his cot, breathing a sigh of relief as his pain lessened. Trouble still loomed, but at least he didn't have to watch his back every second. Aidan had made sure he saw the prison doctor, who cleaned up his cuts and prescribed an antibiotic and Tylenol. He verified that there was nothing broken, that there was no internal damage and that it was all surface injuries, mostly minor hematomas. The doctor also arranged for David to come back in a couple of days if he was still incarcerated. If not, he was to go to his own doctor.

David wished he could see Abrahms, his L.A. doctor. He rubbed his lip where the doctor had put in a couple of stitches. He still ached, even when he was lying down, but he was too enervated to ask for more pain meds. Exhaustion overcame him and he drifted into a deep, dreamless sleep.

He woke up late in the morning when Aidan returned. This time he wasn't shackled when he was led to the meeting. He sat across from Aidan.

"Well, you look a whole lot better," Aidan said.

"Yeah, thanks to you. Now if you can only get me out of here things would be perfect."

"I spoke to the judge and the prosecution and both claim not to know anything about your treatment. They professed great horror, but the bottom line is you are being released on another bond. I'll speak to Chris about this. But this time I can assure you the police will not be taking matters into their own hands."

Saturday, 12:35pm Aunt Nea's, Nea's Alley, St. George's Parish, Bermuda

Chris returned from Hamilton with his new IBM laptop and the information he needed to get his Internet connection up and running. Within twenty minutes he was online and connected to his home server where, as part of his work arsenal, he kept a software library of every tool available to test and crack most online systems.

At first he just checked out the recent headlines and police bulletins about David's arrest and subsequent legal fights. Aidan had successfully argued for his release and Chris was surprised. Given the so-called *evidence* they had he would have thought the cops would be more successful keeping David in jail. But it looked like he had finagled another stay for David. He'd be out soon.

Chris had to be ready for him.

This time he delved deeper into the police Intranet. He pulled up Jay's records, even finding a couple of charges that had eventually been dropped for lack of evidence. A name he hadn't expected to see came up in one report.

"Daryl," he whispered. What the hell was he doing getting mixed up with Jay's criminal activities? It didn't make any sense.

Then he remembered Joel's antipathy for the young man. At the time they had all thought it was just an overprotective father not wanting his little girl to grow up.

Maybe there was more to it.

This time he dove back into the depths of the police servers, sifting through bytes of data on a furtive hunt for Daryl's name. To his dismay he found it.

Daryl made himself out to be quite the ladies man. And there was enough scandal attached to him to besmirch a lesser man's reputation. One high school classmate accused him of rape. The charge was dropped, a case of "she said, he said" with no clear cut crime beyond bad judgment. Then another accusation, but by now Daryl had left the country and was presumably in Florida, pursuing an education.

When had Daryl returned?

Things got tricky then. He found and teased access to the

inner workings of the Bermuda government's portals. There he found a database of Bermudian personal data. A treasure trove of knowledge: birth dates, school records, including off shore travel. Daryl had left Bermuda fourteen months ago to attend the University of Florida at Miami. He had enrolled in the bachelor's program.

But he didn't even complete the first semester. His grades, as far as Chris could see, were exemplary. So what had made a young man, apparently on his way up, give it all up and run home?

Saturday, 12:10pm Aunt Nea's, Nea's Alley, St. George's Parish, Bermuda

Aidan was as good as his word. David was back on the street shortly after noon. This time Chris picked him up and they headed home, where he was able to get out of his dirty, torn clothes. Dinner was the salmon steaks Chris had picked up earlier in the week. David relaxed on the veranda with his feet up, a Bud in his hands.

"I hope your lawyer saw you before you were released," Chris said. "Otherwise they're going to say you got it outside."

"Oh, he saw it. It's not all bad. It was instrumental in getting me out. And he swears there won't be any more harassment from MacClellan or his goons."

"That's good, but are they going to be punished or is it just one of those good old boy things? A slip of judgment?"

"Don't count on anything but a wrist slap. But personally I'm happy they're out of the picture, at least until my court date."

"That's a fucking farce. What about Mosby and Josie? Have the cops done anything about even looking for them?"

"What do you mean "What about Mosby and Josie?" Where did you get those names?"

Chris realized he'd blundered mentioning those two. But one look at David's face and he knew he couldn't lie. "I knew the police weren't going to do anything so I had to."

"Had to what? What did you do, Chris?"

"I went down to Court Street."

"You did what?"

"I talked to some people down there and they gave me those names. I think they either know something, or they're directly involved."

"Chris..." David stopped and took a deep breath. "I really wish you hadn't done that. Do you have any idea how dangerous that was?"

"I know. If it makes you any happier, I already got reamed a new one by Aidan. He does a much better job than you do."

"How so?"

"He's not sleeping with me."

"Not funny. Promise you will not do anything that stupid again."

"Can I do something more stupid?"

David shook his head and stared up at the brilliant blue sky. "Des is right. You do need a keeper. And a cage with locks."

"But I got some names. That has to be worth something. Doesn't it?"

"Nothing is worth your life."

Desperate to change the subject Chris said, "You really think the cops will do anything."

David shrugged, sipping his beer. "Aidan says he'll insist on it. If they refuse he can use it as proof of their sloppy police work. They're damned if they do and damned if they don't. Assuming they're more interested in nailing me than finding the truth."

Chris suddenly got up and went back inside. When he came out he was carrying his laptop.

David did a double take. "I thought the police confiscated that thing. Aidan must have worked fast to get it back to you—"

"It's a new one," Chris popped it open and fired it up. "I want you to see this."

After a few minutes he swung the laptop around so David could see the screen. David had no idea how the Bermuda police handled their data, but this looked suspiciously like an official Bermudian police document. He even caught sight of the name MacClellan before he raised stormy eyes to Chris.

"What are you doing with that?"

"Saving your ass."

"Chris—"

"So sue me," Chris snapped, without an ounce of regret. "Just check it out first. Then tell me you don't want to know."

David started to object again. Chris could get into some serious trouble hacking a police force database, but then again if he'd found something…

He bent over and read the small print of the report. He squinted, wishing Chris had brought his reading glasses out with him. Then a name caught his eye.

"What the hell?"

"That was my reaction. Think it means anything?"

David rubbed his thick hair with stiff fingers. "I don't know. Daryl? I thought he was some kind of golden boy."

"Remember Joel's reaction when he showed so much interest in Imani?"

"Sure, but I figured it was just Daddy protecting his daughter. That's how Imani took it."

"Well, what if it was more?"

"Damn," David said. "You tell anyone about this?"

"Not yet. I wanted to run it by you," Chris said. "Besides, how do I explain how I got it?"

"Oh, right. Have you talked to Imani yet?"

"She won't talk to me," Chris's voice was full of pain. "When Jay ended up dead, she fell off the deep end. I can hardly blame her."

"Doesn't help us much right now. We have to talk to her," David said with more calmness than he was feeling. One of the repercussions of being a cop was that he had learned to compartmentalize his feelings a long time ago. Sometimes it was necessary to do a distasteful job no matter who it hurt. He knew it was the one side of his job Chris hated the most.

Chris snorted. "Good luck with that."

Chris took his empty bottle and brought back another Bud. He sat down, stretched his legs out and crossed his ankles. He raised his eyes to meet David's.

"I want you to come with me to Court Street. Then we can go talk to Imani and you can use your not inconsiderable cop charm to make her talk to us."

David's feet came down. "Didn't Aidan tell you to stay away from there?"

"Well, you might have faith in Aidan, but I'm not counting on that. We know we can't trust the cops. You're a boil on their collective butt and they aren't likely to forget the humiliation anytime soon."

"You have a charming way with words."

Chris flashed his teeth in a massive grin that held little real humor. "If the metaphor fits…"

The sun was veiled by the thickening clouds. A blue heron flew overhead, the fading light glinting off its broad wings. The loud voices of the party-goers in King's Square were muted.

They finished their drinks and Chris went in to get changed. David trailed after him reluctantly. He followed Chris's suit and chose his oldest jeans and an ancient leather jacket that he'd brought in case it rained or got cool, even if he hadn't expected much bad weather.

Chris called a cab while David finished dressing. They had the cabbie drop them on Front Street near the docks. The harbor was still empty, though the streets were as busy as always.

CHAPTER TWENTY-TWO

Saturday 6:50pm, Court Street, Hamilton, Pembroke Parish, Bermuda

Chris led the way toward the Outer Bank. He saw the buxom hooker he had spotted the twenty to for information. She saw him and tottered over on her six-inch heels. She'd changed her fishnets for something shimmery, which only seemed to emphasize the thinness of her skeletal legs.

"Sugar, you back? Still looking for your killer?" Her eyes skated over David. "Who are you, sugar?"

David opened his mouth, but Chris didn't give him time to answer. "He's with me." He guided David north, leaving the all too friendly hooker behind.

"Friend of yours?"

"Funny."

The Outer Bank was more crowded than it had been the previous night. Chris was glad to see the same tattooed bartender manning the taps. David looked around in bemusement.

"Not exactly your typical hangout," he whispered in Chris's ear. His breath was warm on Chris's skin. David grinned. "I like it."

Chris shot him a poisonous look, but David's grin never faltered. "Oh, you are in so much trouble," he said.

Chris strode up to the bar and signaled the tatted bartender. He extended his hand. "We met the other night. I'm Chris. This is my friend, David."

The bartender nodded. "Moe," he said. "You were looking for Mosby."

"And Josie."

Moe grunted. He raised a glass. "Beer?"

"Two," Chris said.

Moe delivered two Buds. David ignored the glass and tipped the bottle to his mouth. Moe studied David and his eyes narrowed. "You a cop? I know your buddy here isn't, but don't try to tell me you ain't."

"Don't worry," David said. "I've got no jurisdiction here. I'm an American."

"But you guys all work together, right?"

"Not hardly," Chris snipped. He ignored David's look. Knowing he was lying, he said, "Whatever you tell us stays here. We've got no reason to tell anyone, especially not the cops."

"So why you looking for these guys?" he asked shrewdly.

Chris leaned forward, resting his elbows on the gummy bar. He ignored the sensation of his denim jacket sleeve sticking. "Mosby owes us money."

Moe threw his head back and laughed. Chris didn't let his confusion show.

"You are fucking crazy," Moe said. "You're insane if you think you can collect anything but pain from that one."

Chris traded looks with David. "Why? Is he violent?"

"He's damn near as crazy as you." Moe looked David up and down. "You're a real bruiser, ain't you? Bet you know how to take care of yourself, too."

"He can," Chris said. Again he pulled out a wad of cash.

"Well, I still think you're both crazy." Moe looked around the bar as though making sure no one was listening. He palmed the first twenty Chris slid his way. "I'll give you this—you won't find either of them around here tonight, but I practically guarantee they will be here tomorrow—less this storm shuts us down."

"What's Mosby's real name?" Chris asked. A second twenty appeared in his hand, half extended toward Moe.

"You don't know?"

"He never said." David caught on quick.

"I'm sure." Moe grinned, showing a gap between his teeth. "Daryl."

Chris felt goose bumps crowd his arms. His scalp prickled. He traded an alarmed look with David. "We were right. Imani," he whispered. Chris threw the twenty back on the bar. "And Baker. He might be in danger, too."

They were both on their feet. They flew outside and began searching for a cab. David spotted one turning down Victoria Street. He ran after it, waving his arms frantically. They piled into the van so fast the cabbie stared at them askance.

"What you want?"

"The Rose Grotto, College Hill Road," Chris snapped. The cabbie opened his mouth to argue then thought better of it and took off down Court Street. Chris and David couldn't look at each other. A silence lay between them in the stuffy interior.

"College Hill Road, Devonshire. It's important."

"Sure, sure." The cabbie studied them in the rear view. "Whatever you say."

"Shit," Chris said. "I should have known. All this time the guy snowed us. Do you think Joel knew? Is that why…" He pulled out his BlackBerry and feverishly punched in Imani's number. For his trouble all he got was the blat of a busy signal.

"Busy."

Traffic out of Hamilton was heavy. The cabbie glanced at a cop directing traffic onto Crow Lane.

"Running from the storm," he said, picking his teeth with a well-chewed toothpick. "It's gonna be a mean one."

Already the winds had picked up, blasting dust and debris across the busy streets. No rain yet, but the sullen sky hung low over the island, promising a deluge to come.

David looked grim. "Try again," he said.

Chris did. Still busy.

The cab inched slowly through increasingly heavy traffic. The winds had picked up ominously. Chris saw more cops patrolling the streets, and fewer bikes than normal.

Another call. Busy. He was aware of David watching him. His mind raced now. "Maybe she's just on the phone. It doesn't mean anything."

David took his hand and squeezed his fingers. Chris squeezed back. Wind lashed the palms lining the roadway. In the harbor boat masts dipped and bobbed in the growing swells.

David snapped at the cabbie. "Can't you go any faster?"

"In this?"

"Just get us there as soon as you can."

The traffic eased as they split away from the more westward moving vehicles. The cabbie swerved around a fallen cluster of palm fronds that lay across the right side of the road.

"You think he had something to do with Joel's death?" Chris asked. He stared ahead for his first glimpse of the Rose Grotto.

"I'd bet on it," David said. "And I'd bet he was the second person who assaulted me at the prison. He and Jay must have had a falling out. The question now is, do we call the cops or what?"

"You really think they'll believe us?"

"I don't know."

"Maybe she's not at home. Maybe she's out. Maybe she got cold feet and called the date off."

"You really want to take that chance?" Chris muttered. "You know she was crazy about him. You didn't hear her talk about him the last time."

Chris stared blindly out the window, thinking of David's beautiful half-sister and wondering what a monster like Daryl could do. "No. We're almost there."

They passed Lindo's market, the parking lot crowded with people stocking up on supplies for the coming storm.

The cab pulled up in front of the Rose Grotto. The house

looked ominously empty, though the pickup truck was under the makeshift garage.

David paid the cabbie and they climbed out. Around them wind snatched at their jackets and lifted a thatch of hair off Chris's forehead. Chris followed David up the stone steps to the front door. He pounded on the painted wood. No response. They traded looks.

Chris went to peer in the nearest window. The living room was gloomy, what little light there was didn't penetrate far. Continuing silence greeted a second knock. The living room looked much as it had during their first visit; the anthuriums had been replaced by fresh roses. Two glasses of half-empty beer sat on the end table by the sofa. Chris strained to hear a sound, any sound that would tell him there was somebody in the house. Nothing.

David tried the front door. It opened with a click.

Then from inside: a muffled scream. Chris nodded toward the back of the house. David took the lead. Chris followed. They passed through a modernized kitchen and down a short hall. A half-opened door led into a darkened room.

David tried the door. It popped ajar; he eased it open and they listened. Now they could hear harsh breathing and another muffled whimper that raised the hairs on the back of Chris's neck.

"You like it, don't you bitch?" Daryl's almost unrecognizable voice said. "You bitches are all alike; think you're better than us. Lead us on, make us hard then say no, like you got that right. Now how do you like this—"

Before Chris could react, David slammed his weight into the door, sending it crashing open, rebounding hard enough to catch his shoulder when he followed. Chris had a brief glimpse of a partially unclothed Daryl pinning Imani to a rumpled bed. One hand held her struggling limbs down and another covered her mouth. Her hair was askew and one side of her face bore an ugly bruise. Her nose was bloody. Daryl reached down to wrench her skirt up and tried to untangle her underwear. Before he could enter her, David had him by the scruff of his neck and threw him onto the floor.

Daryl rolled away from the impact, flying to his feet and kicking David in the knee caps. David fell back, catching Chris by surprise, limbs tangling. They both went down. Daryl lunged at the bed and grabbed Imani's arm. Before either Chris or David could react he had shoved the curved blade of a knife against her bare throat. He dragged her off the bed. "You're coming with me, bitch." He waved the knife almost languidly at David. "Back off, big brother, or you'll have another one to bury."

Imani only had time to throw one more terrified look at Chris and David before she was hauled out of the room.

Seconds later they heard the roar of the pickup truck's engine as it was red-lined. They caught a glimpse of Daryl racing onto College Hill Road, nearly sideswiping a Jeep Liberty exiting the driveway next door.

Chris jerked his BlackBerry out of its case and hit 911. David watched him, eyes glittering.

"What good is that going to do? You really think anyone's going to believe you enough to go chasing after someone in this storm?"

It was true. The storm had picked up in the little time they'd been inside. Tree tops whipped from side to side, spraying the ground with leaves and limb-sized branches.

He had to shout to be heard over the growing roar. "Well, what are we gonna do? We can't just let him take her and do nothing."

David ducked into the makeshift garage. At the back of the structure, Imani's bike was propped up on its kickstand. A helmet sat strapped to the vinyl seat.

"We take that," David said.

"Are you serious?"

"You got a better idea?"

Chris didn't. "Where's the key?"

David checked the bike. Nothing. He stomped into the house and scoured the kitchen, still nothing. Chris followed helplessly, until he remembered the jacket Imani had worn the last time he'd seen her. It was hanging up in a front closet along with jackets presumably belonging to Baker, the unfortunate Joel, and Jay. No sign of Baker. They would have to hope the man was simply elsewhere. And safe.

The bike keys were in the side pocket of the denim jacket.

Without a word, Chris and David hurried back outside. David straddled the bike that looked minuscule under his greater bulk. Chris gingerly swung his leg over the pillion seat. He clutched David's leather clad arms. "You ever drive one of these before?"

David glanced back over his should as he fired the engine up. "No. It can't be that hard. Kids do it all the time."

Before Chris could say maybe they should rethink this thing, David had spun out of the garage and skidded onto College Hill. Chris screamed, the sound swept away by the wind that threatened to tear him from his perch. He molded himself to David's body, for once not thinking of anything but getting out of this in one piece.

He was sure they had lost Daryl, but on the way to Middle Road they spotted the pickup truck ahead of them, the way blocked by a fallen palm. The driver's door was open. They could see Daryl standing outside it with Imani, his hand clutching at the hair at the back of her head to keep her from fleeing, staring at the natural barricade. Then he spotted them and jumped toward the open door, shoving Imani inside before leaping back in the truck cab. A heartbeat later the truck spun onto a sloping lawn, tearing up great clods of sod and mud as he fishtailed around the fallen palm.

Chris thought for sure the truck was going to get stuck and he braced for the inevitable fight, knowing Daryl had a knife. However the truck caught purchase and lurched around until it was back on solid ground and roared north.

David barely slowed as he followed his path through the rutted yard. Chris felt the viscous mud splattering his legs and soaking through his thin socks. He hugged David even tighter as the bike skidded and wobbled around the blockage until finally, it was back on the road.

At Middle Road Daryl turned east and in less than five minutes on the empty road, spun out onto North Shore Road. Without hesitation, David turned east.

Chris remembered Imani saying Daryl's family lived in St. David's, the town across the bay from St. George's. They owned a deep-water fishing fleet. Shit.

"He's going to St. David's," Chris shouted into David's ear. David barely nodded to let him know he'd heard and understood. He gunned the 100cc engine and demanded more power out of the tiny bike.

The wind picked up even more. The sky was now a roiling mass of dark clouds and when they got to the North Shore, ocean surf pounded the shoreline, sometimes scarcely a foot from the roadway. Water swamped the narrow concrete ribbon of road from all directions, as they fought to stay upright. Chris pressed his face against David's sodden jacket. Both of them were hunched forward in an attempt to minimize the impact of the wind and pounding rain.

He struggled to keep his balance neutral, neither hindering nor trying to help David as he slipped and slalomed around curves and obstacles blown into the road. Thank God there was no other traffic.

Each time Chris was able to look up, it was obvious Daryl was pulling away from them. He was only slowed by the odd tree limb crashing in front of them, or the violent gusts of wind that sent the small tuck rocking. One violent gust sent their bike slewing left, nearly plowing them into a jagged pile of limestone and throwing them into the roiling surf. David righted the bike, and without pause continued their pursuit of Daryl and Imani, Chris clinging on even tighter. His arms and legs were beginning to cramp as the muscles were chilled and locked in their death hold. He didn't dare loosen his grip to try and get the circulation back in to them. He clenched his jaws against the growing pain. Every bump was agonizing; every jerk sent jolts of agony along his nerve endings, as the bike responded to the erratic road conditions.

And still Daryl widened the gap between them. They passed the Bermuda Aquarium, heading toward the market where they had bought wine for Joel.

The only consolation was that Daryl wasn't going to be able to further harm Imani. It had to have taken two hands to travel at the speeds he was going and maintain control. So as long as she had started out okay, she would remain that way for now. Small comfort.

Saturday 7:10pm, Shelly Bay Beach Park, Hamilton Parish, Bermuda

Palm fronds cart-wheeled across North Shore Road, clattering against the undercarriage of the bike as David slalomed around wind-blown obstacles on the road. Thankfully there was no other traffic, though Chris could understand why. They had to shout now to be heard above the roar of the storm. Even then it was hit or miss, and half the time the words were snatched out of his mouth.

Trees were bent in supplication at nearly 90 degree angles. Some had lost the battle and lay like broken soldiers on their sides. The rain was coming down in sheets now. Even with his head bent down till his chin hit his chest, Chris could barely breathe without inhaling water. He couldn't imagine what it was like for David, who couldn't avoid the rain.

Chris thought he recognized the Grotto Bay Resort on their left. This time there were no tourists and no pink and blue buses carrying them in and out of town.

Around the curve was the causeway. A police car blocked the

entrance to the long narrow bridge. Chris's heart sank. Behind the car, probably what he was guarding, were two cement barriers. To punctuate the message, a palm tree had been blown across the road.

Chris could see no sign of the pickup, not that it meant much. He could barely see the beginning of the Causeway. But he knew there'd be no way Daryl could drive out onto it, not with this barricade in place. What would he do with Imani then?

Just before they reached the stone barrier Chris saw something down a narrow dirt road, half concealed by hibiscus bushes and palmettos.

"What's that?" he screamed, pounding David's back.

David glanced where he pointed, then threw the bike into a fishtail as he braked. David scrambled off the bike and bulled his way through the battering wind and underbrush. Chris hurried after him.

"What—?"

It was the pickup. Empty. Both doors ajar. Chris stared at the water-logged seats. They were devoid of any sign of struggle. No blood. Chris sucked in his breath and released it in a tremulous sigh of relief.

David must have felt some of his tension fade. He turned to meet his gaze, then grabbed Chris's arm and hauled him away from the abandoned pickup, toward the Causeway, still unseen behind a screen of horrendous rain. Winds howled around them, whipping their hair off their face one minute, covering their eyes the next. Their open jackets flapped madly in the gust, acting like mini sails that the wind tried to grab and send racing headlong into the storm. Ahead, the blue and white vehicle loomed out of the growing gloom.

The Bermudian police car had been parked where the Causeway ended and the road began. Behind it lay the concrete barriers that had been put up to stop traffic from crossing the Causeway.

David gestured broadly that he meant to approach. Chris

tugged his hand and shook his head, his hair splattering across his forehead. Angrily he dashed it back.

"No," he shouted. "What if they arrest you?"

"We have to let him know what's going on. Maybe he can call for help."

Chris and David moved, bent over at the waist against the force of the wind and the slashing rain, toward the checkered Opel with the yellow stripe. There was no motion inside the vehicle and Chris began to feel goose bumps crowding his skin under his sopping wet jacket.

"What are you going to say to him?" Chris asked.

"I don't know," David said. "The truth, maybe."

"Hasn't done you much good before this."

"This is different."

Chris hoped he knew what he was doing. "Something's not right—"

David tapped on the window. Nothing. They could vaguely make out a man-shaped figure in the driver's seat. David rapped again.

Chris wasn't surprised the cop was loath to leave the dry warmth of his patrol car.

"He's not about to come out of there," Chris said. "Not as long as he can stay warm and dry inside."

The car was facing away from them, looking out over Castle Harbor. There was no way to tell what the driver was doing. Dozing in his cozy haven? Listening to radio chatter? David had often told him how in his early days on patrol in the streets of L.A., that boredom was a cop's worst enemy. And out here there wouldn't be that sense of danger that an LAPD cop grew inured to. He could only imagine the excruciating boredom that the constable would face under these conditions.

David yanked the door open.

Chris screamed when the uniformed constable toppled out

onto the sodden pavement with a meaty thud. One arm flopped over his head, his wrist watch clinking against the road.

Chris stared at the open, glazed eyes and the gaping wound across the man's throat. Daryl's attack had been so savage he had nearly severed the constable's spine. The car seat was saturated with viscous blood that still looked fresh. He watched, appalled, as David approached the open door. Before he could object, David crouched by the body and felt for a pulse, though even Chris could see the guy was beyond help.

David stood up. Chris could see his fingers were smeared with blood, which quickly washed away in the relentless rain.

"He hasn't been dead long," David said. "Less than thirty minutes."

Chris hugged himself as he looked out across Castle Harbour. The water was rough now, pounding against the Causeway, sending salt spray over Chris's face. He couldn't tell if he was crying or if it was just seawater.

"Don't look," David said. "Get back, Chris. We can't help him now."

Chris obeyed, blindly staggering toward the nearest concrete abutment.

David followed and took him in his arms, pulling him tightly into his embrace as Chris buried his face against David's chest.

"D-David?"

"I'm sorry, hon."

"God, what's he done to Imani?"

David stiffened. "Wait here," David said. Without waiting for him to comply, David spun around and headed back toward the patrol car.

"Where are you going?" Chris demanded.

"I have to go see if I can call for help. They need to know what's going on." He slapped the abutment. "Stay here."

Chris made no move to follow. He turned so his rump was

pressed against the concrete, sagging against the solid support. Chris wasn't surprised to realize his shoulders were shaking. Tears poured down his cheeks.

Then David was back, enfolding him into his embrace. "Oh, hon." He reached for Chris, awkwardly patting his denim-clad back. Chris's fists closed over his jacket and nearly strangled him with the ferocity of his grip. "It's going to be okay. I promise, hon. It'll be okay."

Something in him snapped. Chris jerked away from him, pounding his fists against David's chest. "No, you're a liar. It's never going to be okay again. Never!"

David grabbed his wrists and held him tight until finally his rage was spent and he had dissolved into tears in his embrace. He murmured against his hair, wordless soft sounds that finally penetrated his fury.

Chris hiccupped softly. "Did you get through to anyone?" he asked.

David nodded. Wearily he tilted his head back. "I don't know how fast they'll be getting out here. Things are pretty hairy back in town."

"In other words we're on our own," Chris said.

"Yeah."

They both turned to look out toward St. David's, where Daryl had fled. If anything, the wind had picked up and the rain was heavier, pounding the ground and abutment with machine-gun intensity.

"Wait here for the police," David shouted. "You can let them know where I've gone."

"No," Chris said so low David had to stoop down to hear it. Chris dug his fingers into the lapel of David's jacket. "I'm not staying here."

"Chris—"

"I'm going with you."

David stared at him for several heartbeats before nodding. "Okay, but stick close."

"You seriously think he walked out on that?" Chris asked, staring out at the small stretch of causeway he could see through the blur of rain and sea foam.

"You don't think he was desperate enough?"

Chris stuffed his hands into his pockets.

"I think he was," David answered his own question, peering at the water covering the cement like sheets of flawed crystal. "And I won't leave Imani to his madness."

A blast of salt water and grit slapped Chris in the face. He gasped and buried his head in his chest, rubbing his eyes. He leaned over and spit salt and sand into the storm. Laughter with an edge of hysteria burst out. Talk about spitting into the wind.

David hunched over and moved along the length of the abutment, with Chris following. Every so often a gust of wind would attempt to hurl them to the ground. Chris found it hard to keep his feet under him, the ground was slippery and the sodden debris made it even more treacherous. It was like trying to walk on marbles.

Chris's feet skidded out from under him. He went to his knees, feeling a muscle wrench in his thigh. He swore and climbed back up, biting his lip as hot shards of pain lanced down his leg. Strong hands clamped under his armpits and hauled him upright. He hugged David, pressing his sodden face into David's equally soggy chest.

"Why don't you go back and wait?" David murmured against his hair. Chris shivered and clung to him. "You can hole up in the pickup, out of this. I can do this quicker alone."

Chris savagely shook his head. "No."

"Come on, Chris. It doesn't take two of us to do this."

"N-no?" His voice was shaky. "But it does take both of us to protect each other's back. I'm not letting you stay out here alone. Don't ask me to."

He could feel David sigh. "Okay, champ. Let's do this."

Together they inched their way onto the Causeway, sidestepping fallen branches and slick piles of sandy mud.

David peered out at the growing storm. "Unless he took refuge at Grotto Bay, he's out there."

"Maybe if we wait a bit," Chris said. "The storm will let up…"

"Nice idea," David said. "But when? And how far does he get? We know if he reaches the other side we'll never find him. Or Imani."

At least not alive, were the unspoken words between them. Chris took a deep breath. "Then let's do it."

David squeezed his sodden shoulder.

CHAPTER TWENTY-THREE

Saturday 7:30pm, The Causeway, Hamilton Parish, Bermuda

They waded through a litter of blood red petals that stuck to their pant legs and slipped under their feet. Sheer instinct kept them on the smoother surface of the roadway and out of the sand and rubble that littered the edge of the stone wall.

In between blasts of rain laden wind Chris could see further. When he caught his first glimpse of Longbird Bridge at the north end of the Causeway, he touched David's arm. They huddled close, as much for warmth as to hear each other.

"Can you see any sign of him?" David asked.

Chris strained to see through the rain but couldn't make out anything even vaguely human.

"Nothing," he shouted.

David pointed right, toward the open ocean, and shouted, "Let's go around that way."

Bowed under the force of the storm, they struggled to cross the last section of road. As they made their way toward the bridge, they tried to keep the fallen palm fronds from tripping them. For the first time since his release he almost envied the inmates at Westgate. No doubt they were on lock down, warm and dry in their cells, away from the storm surge. No worries except whether their next meal would be edible.

They reached the bridge. They were almost on the other side, in St. George's Parish. David grabbed a steel frame that allowed the drawbridge to be raised or lowered for ships moving through the harbor. Wind roared and whined around them and now he could hear the boom of the all too near ocean. Waves crashed over the Causeway, at least a foot of water lay over the roadbed, washing back into the harbor, sucking everything with them. Winds screamed overhead and tried to pry their fingers loose and knock their feet out from under them. It was as though the sea wanted to claim them for itself.

Finally, they were beside the bridge abutment. Chris's fingers slipped off the wall he was clinging to. He cartwheeled his arms as he lost his balance and nearly toppled over the short stone wall that separated the road from the bay. David grabbed his saturated jacket and hauled him back. Chris yelped and fell into David's arms.

"Are you sure you can do this?" David shouted. "Or should we go back?"

"No!" Chris pushed away from him. He struggled back to the wall and didn't even look to see if David followed.

Chris felt like he was blind. He forced his head down to prevent his eyes from filling with salt water. He could taste salt in the back of his throat and up his nose, his lips were caked with sand and salt. Chris and David clung to each other as much to protect each other as to stay upright.

Chris knew they had made a terrible mistake. What were they going to do if they found Daryl? David had no weapons, nothing more than his size to intimidate Daryl. Any physical fight out here could lead to them all being swept over the side into the unforgiving sea. If they turned back now, they might have a chance. On the other hand, if they turned back now David would lose everything. His job, his self-respect; it would all be gone. And then he thought of Imani and what abandoning her would mean. More than even David faced. Even if they could convince the police of Daryl's guilt, it would be too late to save Imani. Their only chance was to catch Daryl here, on the Causeway.

He forced himself upright and tried to see through the veil of rain and pounding surf, but there was still no sign of their quarry.

Wouldn't it be ironic if after all this, Daryl was killed by this storm?

He put his head down and kept walking.

Saturday 7:50pm, The Causeway, St. George's Parish, Bermuda

David wrapped Chris in his embrace and could feel the younger man's strength ebbing. It matched his own exhaustion. Both of them had been through so much since they had arrived in Bermuda. Was it worth it? Or had he already sacrificed too much? For what? To discover a father who had abandoned him years before? To finally realize that his mother was an award-winning bitch who had never really been any kind of mother at all? But was that fair? She had faced her own demons and had dealt with them as best as she could. The fact that she did such a lousy job was probably as much a result of her upbringing and her own unbending mother.

Beside him Chris stumbled and nearly took them both down. David sat him down and crouched next to him on the pavement, his back against the stone wall. When Chris looked up at him in alarm, he bent over him.

"Just sit here for a minute." David rubbed Chris's legs through the soaking wet denim. His own were cramping up from the cold and damp so he could only imagine what Chris's were like. It was only recently that Chris had been bed ridden. Normally a fanatic about his fitness, he hadn't been to the gym in weeks. He'd gotten over the flu, sure, but no way had he regained his strength. Now he was out here doing this and risking it all, for what?

David stretched his legs out, doing his best to ignore the water that soaked everything. After he'd worked the kinks out of his legs, he went to work on his husband's.. Chris groaned when David's fingers dug into tight muscles, forcing them to yield.

A hitch developed in David's side and he tried to take in several diaphragm relaxing breaths. Chris did the same and David felt him wince from the pain.

"Breathe slowly. Try not to inhale any water."

Chris's eyes were bleary. "Easy for you to say."

David forced a breathy chuckle as he continued to try to imbue Chris's legs with warmth. "So, was it the vacation you imagined it would be?"

"Oh yeah, Disneyland for the criminally insane," Chris muttered. When he struggled to his feet, David reluctantly helped him up. They both stood swaying in the gusting wind. "Let's do San Quentin next year."

David smoothed Chris's spiky hair back from his forehead. Even wet it remained golden, like spun sunshine. David's own shaggy mass lay plastered to his skull, feeling abnormally heavy. Water poured down his back.

Chris leaned into his shoulder. His eyes had a dreamy, faraway look. David suspected he was going into shock.

"Come on," he said as gently as he could, given he had to shout just to be heard. "Let's finish this once and for all."

Swaying and stumbling under the barrage of wind, rain and pounding surf, they pressed forward. If it wasn't for the presence of the stone wall, they couldn't have kept their course. Even with it, they staggered back and forth, banging already skinned knees and hands on the hard limestone rocks.

Chris shied away from the wall, bumping into David's chest. David grabbed him to steady him. He was startled to see a dead gull lying against the stone abutment. Had it lost its way and smashed into the Causeway as it tried to find its own shelter? It looked pathetic, a sodden mass of feathers and dull, lifeless eyes. The gull's broken wings twisted in the wind, making it look like the bird was trying to take flight again.

They skirted the hapless gull and pressed on, both of them ignoring their failing strength, neither willing to surrender.

Ahead of them, two dark figures appeared through the gray shroud of rain.

David gripped Chris's arm so hard he stumbled against him again. Before Chris could cry out, David pointed ahead of them.

"There," he said. "That's gotta be them."

CHAPTER TWENTY-FOUR

Saturday 8:15pm, The Causeway, St. George's Parish, Bermuda

Chris crept along the rock wall after David, trying not to do anything that might attract attention. A figure leaned against the bulwark. No longer stylish hair hung down over his face. At his feet Imani had collapsed on the sodden pavement. From his gesticulations, it was plain Daryl was shouting at her. Nothing could be heard above the storm. That was probably why they caught up to the fleeing pair; Imani had put up a fight all the way, slowing Daryl down.

David pulled Chris over into his embrace. David was shaking nearly as hard as Chris. He pulled Chris down against the wall. "We can't let him see us just yet."

"How do we reach him?" Chris asked through chattering teeth.

David considered their options for a minute or two. Finally he said, "We're going to have to split up." He pointed to his left, showing a sweeping arc that would take one of them around Daryl, going between Daryl and St. George's. "I'll go that way, you approach him more directly. If he spots you, chances are he'll spook and try to take off. If he does, or worse, tries to grab Imani, I'll be ready and I'll head him off."

"What if he's armed?" The cold Chris felt this time had nothing to do with hypothermia. "I mean besides his knife."

"None of his crimes seem to involve firearms. No reason to think he's got a gun at this date."

"You like to gamble, don't you," Chris muttered. But David was right. They had no proof Daryl had ever had any weapon beyond a knife and the silk tie that he had stolen from David. He hadn't needed one, had he?

"He's been out here even longer than us." David's speech

was growing slurred and Chris could hear his teeth chattering. "I doubt he's in any better shape than we are."

Chris hoped he was right. But then Daryl was unpredictable in the worst way, a man who may have graduated to murder, even if it wasn't intentional. Chris could imagine a dozen ways the whole mess had gone down. Daryl had left Florida abruptly, even though from all appearances he was doing well. Why? Had he raped someone there? Killed someone? And if he had, was that what Joel had figured out about the man who was so interested in his daughter? Had he known why Daryl left Florida? In retrospect, it seemed obvious that Joel had been suspicious, and if he confirmed that suspicion, or was about to, what would have happened to Daryl if the truth had come out? Is that why Daryl killed him? Desperate people did desperate things; things they were sorry for later. And if the hot-tempered Jay had let himself be talked into the assault on David and then later reconsidered his action… The way Chris saw it, Daryl had two options: accept the consequences, or eliminate the problem all together. He might even have regretted Jay's death. But a man facing a lifetime in prison might do unthinkable things to avert that fate.

"Including killing his best friend," Chris said.

David leaned closer. "What?"

"Nothing." Chris wiped the water out of his eyes. Not that it did much good, the rain and wind were unrelenting. He broke away from David's grip and began to beat his way toward the other side of the Causeway. He ignored everything but putting one foot in front of the other.

Wind slapped and howled around him, driving water that felt like a thousand spikes into every piece of exposed flesh.

He swore it took hours, but was probably only minutes, before he reached the far stone wall. He clung to it for several seconds, trying to still his racing heart. Taking deep, lung-clearing breaths, he tucked his chin into his chest to keep the water out of his nose. His mouth was agape in a vain attempt to suck air into his starved lungs. Moving parallel to the wall, he inched along it, using it as support. He could finally see Daryl again, but couldn't make out where David was. Imani remained huddled at Daryl's feet. Chris hoped his attention would be on Imani, that he wouldn't be paying attention to things around him.

But Daryl must have seen something. His head snapped back and he grew rigid. Then he whirled and darted toward the airport. David appeared out of the thundering rain and ran after him. Chris wondered where he got the energy from. He tried to head Daryl off. Daryl didn't see Chris right away, but when he did, he stumbled, trying to turn sideways. Chris wondered where he thought he could go. It was a good thing Daryl had no idea how weak Chris and David were.

Daryl either wasn't paying attention or he was really desperate. Maybe he figured the water this close to shore was shallow enough he could wade ashore in it. He slammed into the wall, and bent over at the waist. Chris shouted and bolted toward him, even though he knew there was no way Daryl would hear him.

David reached him first. He and Daryl went down as David jerked him off the wall. Their feet got tangled and neither of them could get up. Chris reached them as David threw Daryl off and tried to scramble away on his hands and knees. Chris hurled himself at Daryl, ignoring the snap of overworked muscles and joints. Together the two of them slammed onto the hard pavement. Daryl grunted as the breath was knocked out of him. He gasped, writhing helplessly under Chris, who wasn't doing much better. Daryl thrashed around as he caught his breath and tried to buck Chris off.

"Get off me, you fucking faggot!" he roared, wrapping his hands around Chris's throat. "Leave me alone."

Chris's vision grayed and he could feel his consciousness failing. He grabbed Daryl's wrists, but he was too weak to budge them. Then, in one last desperate bid he rammed his arms in between them and with a shout, dislodged Daryl's deadly embrace. He rolled free, feeling the bite of Daryl's boot in his side.

Chris ignored it. He crab-crawled over to where Imani lay unmoving. He pulled her into his arms and smoothed the tangled hair off her brow. Her eyes fluttered open.

"Hey, Imani. You're okay."

"C-Chris? Where? How—?"

"Shh, it's okay. You're safe now."

"Oh, God. Daryl… Daryl came over…" Chris leaned in closer to hear her tiny voice above the roar of the storm. "He wanted to tell me how s-sorry he was about Dad. H-he seemed so sweet. I thought—"

"Don't," Chris managed to say. "Don't talk about it. He can't hurt you anymore."

"I'm so sorry I didn't believe you. I should have known better, should have known David would never hurt anyone…" She struggled to sit up. "You have to tell him—"

"Hey, he knows. You're his sister. How could he ever think badly of you?"

Chris's vision was red-tinged and his throat felt like he'd swallowed rusty nails. He blinked when Daryl appeared in front of him and lunged for Imani. "Bitch," he roared, and ripped her from Chris's arms. "This is all your fault."

Something large and angry flew into Daryl, knocking him sideways. Chris clutched Imani and together they watched David pummel Daryl. Chris was mesmerized by David's fury. He blinked to clear his eyes of blood and water, and began to grow alarmed when David didn't back down, even when it became clear Daryl had no more fight in him.

Beside him Imani made a sound. She was staring at David, and Chris could feel her terror.

He crawled across the pavement and grabbed David's arm as he swung it to pound Daryl one more time. He was dragged between the two of them, knocking them apart. He shouted, "No, David. Stop. He's not worth it."

Finally Chris's words seemed to penetrate the enraged man. He shook his head and straddled Daryl's unconscious body.

"Please, David. You have to stop. Please."

David looked from Chris to Imani. He rolled off Daryl, who didn't move. David crouched on the roadway, his shaggy, sodden head in his hands. Chris was horrified to see his fists were covered in gore and blood. Gently he took one in his.

"Oh, David. You're hurt."

David took his hand away. He reached up to stroke Chris's face, brushing away his tears. "Don't, hon. Oh, don't do that. You know I can't stand it when you do that."

Chris snuffled and wiped the snot off his nose, giving David a weak grin. "Sorry, didn't mean to feel sorry for myself." He shot a glance at Daryl. "Is he…?"

David's face hardened. "No, he's okay, more's the pity."

"David."

"I know. Trust me, I'll refrain from killing him, though it's only what he deserves." David glanced over at Imani again. "How's she holding up?" he asked softly.

"Better than I am. Your sister's one tough lady."

"Hey, what did you expect?"

Daryl groaned and David was immediately on him again. He bent low, checking his pulse. When Daryl opened his eyes, David loomed over him.

"Don't even think about it," he said.

"Get off me," Daryl snarled. "You fucking fag—"

David leaned closer, pressing his knee into Daryl's chest. "I'd be real careful what you say, *Mosby*. Until the cops get here, I'm in charge. And if you piss me off I just might dump you in the damn bay and you can show me how well you do the Australian crawl."

Daryl's eyes shot over David's face then flashed to Chris, who tried to look as tough as David did. He didn't once look at Imani.

He wanted to say, "He means it," but knew his voice would be too squeaky to be menacing. Instead he put his hand on David's arm. David rose and turned away from Daryl. He took

Chris in his arms.

"God, I love you," he murmured, stroking Chris's back.

"We're almost there, aren't we?"

"Yeah, we're almost there. I'm going to be glad to go home. L.A.'s never seemed so sweet."

Chris leaned back and met David's eyes. He narrowed his own. "Don't think for one minute you're getting out of this holiday."

"Wouldn't dream of it."

Imani joined them. David hugged her and they bent their heads together. When they broke apart, Imani was crying. She dashed the tears and rain from her eyes.

"I'm so sorry, David—"

"Don't." David's voice was savage. "Don't you dare blame yourself for any of this. This is all his fault. He's the thief who stole everything from you. Put the blame on him." He nudged Daryl with his foot. "You need to keep on being strong."

The storm continued to lash them as they huddled against the wall. Daryl tried to raise his head, but the wind battered him down. He gave up and slumped into semi-unconsciousness. Chris looked at him, then looked away. He hoped Daryl would be okay, it wouldn't be good for David if he wasn't. But there was nothing they could do until the storm abated.

They huddled together, only moving when Daryl stirred, at which point David would crawl forward and inspect their prisoner. When he was satisfied Daryl was as good as he could be under the circumstances, he would crawl back to Chris and Imani. Chris was only half aware of David's actions. At some point he slipped into unconsciousness, only to wake up when David shook him, calling his name.

Chris stared up at him, bleary-eyed.

"Stay with me, hon. We're almost there," David's voice broke. "Don't you dare give up on me now."

Chris knew David was talking, but his words were a jumble of incomprehensible sounds, overridden by the roaring wind and surf that kept bathing his face in salt water. He shivered, knowing he shouldn't be cold. It was July on a tropical island. How could he be cold? But his denim jacket was too thin and too sodden to keep in body heat. He couldn't stop the shaking. His teeth chattered uncontrollably. David rubbed his arms, trying to work some warmth into his limbs. Chris wanted to tell him he was wasting his time. All he needed was a few minutes sleep. He'd be okay then. Just shut his eyes for a few minutes—

"No!" David stopped rubbing his arms and started shaking him. "Don't you dare."

Chris tried to answer, to tell him it was all right. But darkness descended on him and the last thing he saw was David's concerned face. His last thought: why does he look so worried? We're in the clear. Nothing can go wrong now.

CHAPTER TWENTY-FIVE

Saturday 9:45pm, The Causeway, St. George's Parish, Bermuda

Frantically David hauled Chris upright. He resisted the urge to shake him again. Instead he stroked Chris's head, smoothing back the hair on his brow. He stared down at Chris's face; he'd long ago memorized every line and mark of his beauty.

He heard a choking sound behind him. He'd forgotten about Daryl. He turned to find him pushing himself upright. He grinned at David, showing a broken tooth in his bloody mouth.

Imani gasped. Her hand went to her mouth.

"He's dead," Daryl said.

"Nooo—" David moaned. He buried his face against Chris's neck. A faint pulse beat there.

Daryl's smile became a ghastly grimace and blood dribbled from his mouth, washed away in pink streaks down his chin. He coughed, spitting out more blood. It only briefly stained the roadway before the rain slicked it away. "One less faggot. Bye, that stinky." His laughter turned to a choked gargle.

"Shut up," David's voice was low and deadly. Daryl ignored it.

"I killed your fudge packer. Fair's fair, right? If you kill me you'll be spending the rest of your life making new friends at Westgate. Bet you'll like that."

David straightened. "I said shut up."

"You could make it easy on everyone. Toss yourself over. There's no one to miss you now. You'd be doing the world a favor—"

"Animal." Imani lunged at him, taking Daryl by surprise, knocking him back toward David and Chris. She scratched his face, wringing a curse from him. He back-handed her, sending her sprawling to the ground at his feet. He reached for her, momentarily forgetting David now less than a foot away.

David hurled himself at Daryl, who dodged aside, throwing Imani back on the ground. He grabbed David's arms and the two cartwheeled backward across the flooded causeway. David's head slammed into the pavement, knocking Daryl's hands loose. He fell sideways, smearing his face with cold sea water. Before Daryl could recover David crab-crawled out of Daryl's reach, toward Chris.

"Only good faggot is a dead faggot, my poppa always said."

"I said shut up!" David yelled. Daryl only laughed harder.

David was poised to launch another attack when reason penetrated his rage-inflamed mind. Every cell in his body demanded he rid the world of this monster, but killing Daryl wouldn't save Chris. He reached out and caressed Chris's cheek.

Chris stirred under his touch. His eyes fluttered open.

"Chris, baby. You're going to be okay." He had to believe that.

Daryl wasn't giving up. He struggled back into a sitting position. "I'll fucking kill all of you."

David reached over Chris and smashed his fist into Daryl's chin. Daryl went down without another sound.

"I told you to shut up."

He pulled Chris into his lap. When Chris started shaking again, David looked around helplessly. His gaze fell on Daryl and the jacket he wore. It wasn't any better than the jacket Chris already had on. Then he glanced down at his leather one, which wasn't waterproof, but still afforded more insulation than denim did.

He stripped the jacket off and wrapped Chris in it as best he could, maneuvering his head back up into his lap where he hoped his own body heat would penetrate. Imani took up position on his other side.

"Is he going to be okay? God, he looks so pale…"

"He'll be fine. Won't you, hon," David whispered to the comatose man.

Chris moaned again. David hated the sound, but at least it proved Chris wasn't beyond help. There was still no abatement of the storm. It could drag on for hours. David didn't think either of them would last that long. Chris was too out of it to stand, let alone let David lead him back to the barrier and aid, or the other way, toward the airport. Would anybody even be there? Was it worth trying?

That was defeatist thinking. He wasn't going to give up on Chris without a fight. He wasn't going to let Chris give up, either.

"Is there likely to be anyone at the airport?" he shouted above the wind.

Imani shook her sodden head. "They'd send everyone home after they secured everything." She seemed to divine what he was thinking. "There will be people at Grotto Bay. They can't leave the tourists to fend for themselves. You want me to go there?"

"It's our only hope. I can't leave him. You can call the police again."

She nodded and stood up. Immediately the wind whipped around her, tossing her tangled hair around her face. Her jacket flapped in the tempest.

"Godspeed, Imani," David whispered. "Please hurry."

She couldn't possibly have heard him, but she squeezed his shoulder before bending into the wind and forging a path back toward Hamilton Parish.

David bent back over Chris. "Okay hon, this is it. Don't you damn well quit on me, you hear?"

He had no concept of time passing. Minutes crawled like hours. How long would it take for Imani to reach the hotel? How fast could she galvanize help? He grew stiff, hunched over Chris, trying to shield him from the worst of the storm.

He didn't hear it at first, the rain muffled all sounds. Then he grew aware of a sound he never thought he'd hear again. A car engine. A cop car rolled into view. A grim faced constable drove. Imani rode shotgun.

The squad car slid to a stop, bumping into the far wall. Before it stopped completely the constable, wearing a rain slicker and looking uneasy, had thrown the door open and scrambled out of the car. Imani beat him out.

David ignored the constable. Imani ran over, dropping to her knees beside them.

"I met Pete on the way out. They got your message and sent a patrol car out. Once they saw the body they got another unit." She looked down at Chris. "How is he?"

"Not good." He continued to hold Chris in his lap.

"Constable Pete?" Imani pointed at Daryl. "This is the man who killed my father and brother."

"And who are these other people?" Pete asked, eying both Chris and David uneasily. He paid particular attention to David's battered face.

David looked up. "I'm the one who radioed in when I found the constable's body.," he indicated the unconscious man. "Daryl killed the man before we got here."

A second vehicle appeared out of the rain. An ambulance. David muttered a prayer of thanks. He stood back as two EMTs hustled first Daryl, then Chris into the back of the ambulance. They ran some routine tests on David and Imani.

"You both need to check in to the hospital when you get back. We'll take these two."

"Chris has been ill lately. He just got over a bad flu. I think that's why he's so weak."

The nearest EMT nodded. "We'll take care of him, sir."

"Come with me," Pete said. "The two of you will ride in my vehicle."

David and Imani climbed into Pete's squad car. It was a far different ride than his last one. Pete accommodated them by cranking the heat up. Even with the welcome warmth flowing over him, David couldn't stop shivering. Beside him Imani wasn't doing any better.

They passed through the recently moved barrier and pulled to a stop in front of a second squad car. An older Black constable stood beside his vehicle, conferring with the EMTs.

"I need to go with you," David heard him say. "This man is under arrest for suspicion of murder."

The EMTs looked unimpressed. It was David's observation that emergency workers figured they had seen it all.

"He's probably hypothermic," one of the EMTs said. Both men looked at the battered Daryl, but made no comment.

David glanced at the lead car, where one of their own had been butchered. A pair of crime scene techs were already at work going over the car interior. A coroner's wagon waited on the sidelines. Their job never had to be rushed. Sirens screaming, the ambulance carrying Chris and Daryl raced down North Shore Road toward Hamilton.

"You want to explain yourself, sir?" Pete said. When he saw David's reluctance he added, "I'm going to find out what went on tonight. With your cooperation we can keep it short. Without it, I'll take you both back to the station."

David sighed, trading looks with Imani. He was done with the bullshit. He asked. "And who exactly are you?"

"Constable Peter deGraz."

"Okay, Constable deGraz. I'm David Eric Laine, LAPD homicide detective. What do you want to know?"

"You can start by telling me who that other man was. The one who looked like the storm did a real number on him, with fists. The one this young lady seems to think murdered her father and brother."

"And that other police officer," David said. "That's Daryl. I think he killed my brother, Jay. He also killed my father."

"Who was your father?"

"Joel Cameron."

"The man who was just murdered? You're Joel Cameron's son?"

"David Laine," David said. "Visiting from L.A."

"He's an LAPD homicide detective," Imani said proudly.

"Weren't you recently in custody for that murder?"

"Yes, and I didn't do it. The murderer was that man, Daryl Billings," he glanced at Imani. "This is my half-sister. I came to Bermuda to meet my family."

"How did it happen that you were arrested for the murder of Joel Cameron?"

The question didn't surprise David. He shrugged. "I'm still trying to figure that out," David muttered. "But I assure you, I didn't do it."

"I think it would be best if you come to the station with me, after all," Pete said. "We need to clear this up."

"I'm not going anywhere until I know Chris is all right."

Pete frowned. "What is your relationship to this Chris?"

David hesitated only a couple of heartbeats, then he drew himself upright and met Pete's eyes. "He's my husband."

David had to give the young constable credit. He didn't blink when David dropped his bombshell. He merely nodded and wrote it down in his notebook.

Then he flipped up his mike and radioed the ambulance. David could barely hear the disembodied voice at the other end, but Pete was nodding by the time he broke off the call.

"It appears your, ah, friend is going to be fine. The hypothermia isn't serious and he didn't lose any heart or brain function. They want to keep him at King George overnight for observation, but they assure me it's just a precaution."

"Fine. Let's get this over with then. Call my lawyer, Aidan Pitt. I won't talk until he gets there."

So David ended up back at the Hamilton Police Station. Imani was taken to a separate interview room to give her statement. This time David was served coffee. The constable even brought him a reasonably fresh muffin. By the time he finished it, Aidan had arrived.

Once again he went over what had happened since he and Chris had arrived on the island. This time though, he seemed to have found a more sympathetic listener. Pete recorded the entire interview, then had David sign a copy of the report—which he read over carefully.

"I hope you're a better cop than you are a client," Aidan said once Pete left with the report. He pulled up a chair and sat down. He must have been pulled out of bed, he looked more rumpled than David had ever seen him. "I don't think I've had anyone give me as much trouble as you and Chris."

David played with his empty coffee cup, twisting it around in his hands. "Yeah, well, let's just say I know how a homicide dick's mind works and they like things easy. And I wasn't about to make it easy for them."

"I guess I can understand that. But you really put yourself at risk with this stunt. You're just lucky it worked out."

David already knew that. He didn't need Aidan to remind him; all he had to do was think about Chris's slack face and what had nearly happened because of his "stunt." "What's going on with Daryl? Is he in the hospital too?"

"Yes, he is," Aidan said. "He has some serious injuries from his exposure. I gather he didn't cooperate."

"That's putting it mildly."

"Yes, well, it turns out Daryl Billings has quite a string of charges against him under a couple of assumed names. Mostly aggravated sexual assault, which is notoriously hard to prosecute in Bermuda. Most were dropped for lack of evidence, but he was finally put into mandatory counseling, which he failed to attend. Not that anyone did anything to follow up. But murder…" Aidan shook his head. "No one saw that coming. We don't have a lot of experience with these 'psychopaths,' I think you call them."

"I'll wager if you take a closer look at his stay in Florida you might find some unsolved rapes there. Maybe worse. These guys escalate; the thrills get harder and harder to reach, so they have to increase the savagery of their attacks just to achieve the same stimulation. I think that's why he came home early. I suspect it's what Joel found out about him."

"I'll let the police know that." Aidan actually smiled. "I know they've collected enough DNA evidence to convince even the dullest jury to hold Daryl accountable, once they run the proper tests. That, plus the trace evidence they collected from the site of Joel and Jay's murders, will no doubt point to Daryl."

"So, when do I get my passport back? And Chris's camera and laptop?"

"That should be returned within twenty-four hours. I'll need to settle up with Chris as well. I hope he'll be satisfied with my final bill. Will you be leaving right away?"

"Yes—no. Oh hell, I don't know. I have to talk to Chris first." David tore the rim of the coffee cup. "At the very least I need to go to my father's funeral. I can't very well leave without doing that. I owe it to the whole family, if nothing else." Especially Imani, but he didn't say that part out loud.

Finally he was allowed to leave. Back at Aunt Nea's he used Chris's BlackBerry to put in a call to Des. He got lucky, as Des hadn't gone to bed yet. Of course, he reminded himself, L.A. was five hours behind Bermuda. It was barely evening there.

"Des, hon, good news," he said, trying to sound cheery, knowing Des wasn't easily fooled. "We're in the clear. We'll be coming home soon."

"Great. Now where's Chris? Why didn't he call?"

"Ah, well Chris is in the hospital until the morning—"

"The hospital? I thought you just said everything was okay. You were supposed to look after him. What is it with you and him that you can't stay out of trouble for five minutes? What's he in the hospital for anyway?" Left unspoken was "this time."

"Hypothermia," David said, knowing that was going to trigger a new blast. Des didn't disappoint him.

"Hypothermia? How the devil do you get that in the fucking tropics? This is because he was sick last month?"

"I don't know, Des."

"It is. I knew he shouldn't have gone. I can't believe he would get sick again after all that. Tell me what happened!"

"It's a long story. I'll let Chris explain it all to you tomorrow. Suffice to say, he's fine. We should be back early next week."

"Why not sooner? How can you stay in that hell hole after what they've put you through?"

"I have to go to the funeral. After all, he was my father and Jay was my half brother. I can't just walk away from that."

"No, I guess not," Des said, though he didn't sound convinced "You know what your problem is?" Before David could formulate an answer to that one, Des told him, "You're too damn conscientious. It's the damn cop in you. You don't know how to look after number one—or yourself, either." He relented and said. "Chris is lucky, you know."

"So am I, Des. So am I."

The phone woke him the next morning. He glanced at the bedside clock as he reached for the portable phone.

It was Chris.

"They're discharging me as we speak. I'll grab a cab home. Anything you want while I'm out?"

David stretched out on the rumpled bed sheets. "Yeah." His voice was husky. "You."

Chris laughed. "I hope you haven't eaten yet. I'm starving and I hate eating alone."

It seemed an eternity, but it was less than an hour before a cab pulled into the alley.

Chris glowed with health when he kissed David, not caring who might see him. David drew him inside and returned the kiss. He nudged the door closed with his foot without releasing his grip on his husband.

Reluctantly, he set Chris aside. "You better call Des. If you don't, I won't be responsible for what he does."

Chris took his BlackBerry off the bedside table and punched in Des's speed dial.

Des sounded sleepy when he answered.

"Get up lazy-bones. Here I am, up for hours and you're still sleeping. That's no way to run a train."

"Chrissy," Des squealed. "You're out of the hospital."

"Yeah, I'm out."

"After all that trouble, too. You know what you are—you're a trouble magnet."

Chris heard a voice in the background. He recognized Trevor's voice.

Des came back on, giggling.

"Trevor says if you were here he'd turn you over his knee and give you a paddling."

Chris looked at David and raised one eyebrow. "You just might get a bit of an argument from David about that."

"You never know," Des said, his voice rich with laughter. "He might enjoy it. Teach an old dog new tricks."

"Tell him he's an old dog and he may teach you a thing or two." Chris reached over and tugged David's T-shirt out of his jeans. He admired the view while he let his hand roam over David's stomach, feeling the muscles clench and ripple under his touch. He undid the belt and slid the zipper down, reaching inside.

"Hey, Des," Chris said, mesmerized by the sight of David's rising cock. He stroked the glistening tip with his thumb, spreading a drop of cum around the barely exposed slit. "Listen, can I get back to you?"

"Sure. When are you coming home?"

"Don't know yet." Chris was beginning to lose his train of thought. Pushing the fleshy helmet back he exposed more of the purple, engorged head. "We have to talk about that. I'll, uh, let you know."

"We can have a little party when you're back home. I'll book a table at Soho House. How does that sound?"

Chris had only heard of the place. A members-only club in West Hollywood, open by invitation only. Trust Des to ferret out an invite. Or knowing Des, he was a member.

"You up for it?" Des asked. Chris barely heard him in his growing arousal.

David wasn't making things any easier. He stepped away from Chris's caress and wrenched his jeans off. Stroking his own cock, he sank to his knees in front of him. He pressed his lips against Chris's belly and Chris bit his lip to keep from groaning aloud.

"I really got to go, Des." Before Des could say anything else he disconnected and shut the BlackBerry off. He wound his fingers through David's thick hair.

"Don't you ever do that again," David whispered against the bare skin below Chris's T-shirt.

"What?" Chris was too dazed to think. "Do what? Call Des?"

"Risk yourself like that. I don't know what I'd do if I lost you. Don't make me find out."

"I won't." Chris gasped as David took him in his mouth. "I swear, I won't."

CHAPTER TWENTY-SIX

Thursday, 11:20am, St. George's Cricket Club, St. George's Parish, Bermuda

A burst of raucous cheering greeted the first run by St. George's. On the edge of the boundary Imani clung to David's arm as the team skipper made a dash for the far side of the grassy field.

Watching the two eleven-man teams race back and forth across the green field, swinging bats and hitting balls, Chris had no idea what was going on. He didn't care. He had a cold beer in one hand, and his other arm around both Imani and David. Even Baker stood nearby. While not completely thawed toward his big brother, he had at least reconciled enough to be polite. He too had been numbed by the tragedy that had struck his family and he hadn't let Imani out of his sight since then. The two siblings had only each other now.

From his own experience with tragedy, Chris knew they would need a lot of time and love to overcome this. He knew David had already suggested they seek professional help. He hoped they would do so. He also knew David would be keeping in touch with his newfound family.

Overhead, a flawless blue sky and brilliant sunlight made the greenery below their feet and the salmon clubhouse glow like gems. Tarps were spread over groups; umbrellas of every hue gave the whole day a circus air. Loud reggae and hip-hop blasted from speakers all over the assembly, competing with the roar of the crowd.

Earlier, at Imani's urging, Chris had tried his hand at the Crown and Anchor game where he won fifteen dollars, much to David's amusement. Now, with his winnings in his pocket and his arm around his husband, he finally thought that all was well in their world. The darkness was behind them.

The funeral for both Joel and Jay had been held three days ago. That had been a somber affair with more tears than Chris wanted to remember. Afterward, they had gone back to the Rose Grotto where family and friends had shared their grief and comfort with everyone, even Chris and David. It had been a wonderful, healing moment for all.

Now, the day before their departure, Chris and David were spending one last day with David's new family. Chris felt more rested than he had in years. Holidays could be a good thing, he finally discovered, once they actually happened.

"You aren't going to forget about me, are you?" Imani shouted over the roar of the crowd as Somerset attempted a run of its own, swinging the bat and missing the ball, scoring a leg bye instead. "I'll chase you down in L.A. if you do."

Chris grinned. He believed her. "You better tell her you won't forget. If she comes looking for you, you're on your own."

"Some husband you are." David smiled down at his little sister. "Not a chance in hell I'll forget you. Maybe we'll even come up to Canada for a visit."

"I'd like that," Imani said.

David leaned down and kissed the top of her head where it rested against his broad chest. His eyes met Chris's, and Chris didn't like the sadness he saw there. "So would I."

CHAPTER TWENTY-SEVEN

Sunday 10:45am, Mid-Atlantic, Delta Airlines bound for Los Angeles

Chris looked up from the travel magazine he'd picked up in the Bermuda Airport boarding lounge. David looked tired, his rugged face drawn. There was a defeated look about him, something Chris had never seen before.

He tried to lighten the mood. "Hey, let's take a cruise next year. I know just the place. The Mediterranean. See Italy and Greece. The Parthenon. Venice. The wine! The shopping! They feed you like princes on those ships."

David smiled, but there was no humor on his dour face. "Don't you read murder mysteries? Those cruise ships are deathtraps. We'd find ourselves up to our eyebrows in dead bodies as soon as we left shore. Let's go someplace safe, like San Quentin."

"Oh pish," Chris said, drawing the first real smile Chris had seen in days. "It wouldn't be like that at all."

David went back to staring moodily out the window at the ocean of clouds they seemed to float above.

After the flight attendant took their drink orders, Chris picked up David's hand, twining their fingers together. He grew serious. "So, have you given any more thought to retiring?"

David met his gaze. "What do you think?"

Chris played with David's captured hand. "I think it's up to you. I told you, I'll support you in whatever you want to do."

"You mean that?"

Chris played with the ring on David's finger, the gold one he had given him on their wedding day. Maybe the state of California would always waffle on whether they would recognize their marriage or not, but he was committed anyway. "Yes, I mean it. I don't love the fact you're a cop, but things can happen to you or me no matter what you do. I know you'll keep safe. You can't tell me you want to quit. Not really."

"Okay, you're right. I don't want to quit. Not right now, at least." He took the magazine out of Chris's hand. "I've only got a few more years till my thirty. When that comes we can take a look at it again. How does that sound?"

"I just want you to be safe."

David raised Chris's hand to his mouth. His lips tickled Chris's skin. "Yes," he whispered. "For you I'll always keep safe."

About the Author

PAT BROWN was born in Canada, which she is sure explains her intense dislike of all things cold and her constant striving to escape to someplace warm. Her first move took her to Los Angeles, and her fate was sealed. To this day she has a love/hate relationship with L.A, a city that was endlessly fascinating. L.A. Heat and the even darker L.A. Boneyard grew out of those dark, compelling days.

She wrote her first book at 17 – an angst ridden tome about a teenage girl hooked up with a drug user and went off the deep end. All this from a kid who hadn't done anything stronger than weed. She read her first positive gay book then too, The Lord Won't Mind, by Gordon Merrick and had her eyes open to a whole other world (which didn't exist in ultra conservative vanilla plain London, Ontario).

Visit Pat on the internet at: http://www.pabrown.com/

Trademarks Acknowledgment

The author acknowledges the trademark status and trademark owners of the following wordmarks mentioned in this work of fiction:

Banana Republic: Banana Republic (Apparel) LLC

BlackBerry: Research in Motion Limited

Brooks Brothers: Retail Brand Alliance

Bruno Pieters: bruno Pieters

Bud: Anheuser-Busch INBEV S.A.

BusinessElite: Delta Airlines, Inc.

Chevy coupe: General Motors

Crown Vic: Ford Motor Company

Death Race 2000: New World Pictures

Delta Airlines: Delta Airlines, Inc.

Disneyland: Disney Enterprises, Inc.

Dockers: Levi Strauss & Co

Ford: Ford Motor Company

Google: Google Inc.

Guinness: Guinness & Co.

Hermes: Hermes International

Honda: The Honda Motor Company

Hugo Boss: Hugo Boss UK Ltd.

IBM: International Business Machines Corporation

IChing: IChing Decor

Indy 500: Brickyard Trademarks, Inc.

Izod: Phillips-Van Heusen Corporation

Jeep Liberty: Chrysler Group LLC

Kistler Merlot: Kistler Vineyards

Los Angeles Times: The Los Angeles Times Media Group

Louis Vuitton: Louis Vuitton Company

Old Milwaukee: Jos. Schlitz Brewing Co

Opel: Opel International

Outerbridge's Sherry Peppers: Outerbridge Peppers, Ltd.
Peller Estates Merlot: Peller Estates Winery
Pig's Ear Brown Ale: Woodstock Inn Brewery
Rolex: Rolex Watch USA Inc.
Royal Gazette: The Bermuda Press (Holdings) Ltd
Saturn: General Motors
Smith & Wesson .40: Smith and Wesson Corporation
Softail: Harley Davidson USA
Somer's Amber Ale: North Rock Brewing Co.
Southampton Princess: Fairmont Hotels & Resorts
Sushi Tei: Sushi Tei
Toyota: Toyota Motor Company
Tylenol: The Tylenol Company
Versace: Gianni Versace S.P.A.
Webster's Dictionary: Thomas Nelson Inc.
Wedgwood: Wedgwood Public LLC
Wheaties: General Mills

9 781608 201600